B+T 7-15 $15.95

LI   S

b

Published by Akashic Books
©2015 Matthew McGevna

ISBN: 978-1-61775-347-3
Library of Congress Control Number: 2014955219

Kaylie Jones Books
www.kayliejonesbooks.com

Akashic Books
Twitter: @AkashicBooks
Facebook: AkashicBooks
E-mail: info@akashicbooks.com
Website: www.akashicbooks.com

ALSO AVAILABLE FROM KAYLIE JONES BOOKS

UNMENTIONABLES BY LAURIE LOEWENSTEIN
SING IN THE MORNING, CRY AT NIGHT BY BARBARA J. TAYLOR
THE LOVE BOOK BY NINA SOLOMON
STARVE THE VULTURE BY JASON CARNEY
FOAMERS BY JUSTIN KASSAB
WE ARE ALL CREW BY BILL LANDAUER

CHAPTER ONE

THIS IS THE TOWN OF TURNBULL. In the month of July, in the sweltering town, the heat reminds its people of their limits. There are the day's demands and not much else. The smell of salt from the ocean to the south is faint in the hot air. The people wipe their brows, try to sit still when they can. Damp rags draped over the back of necks. The *Pennysaver*, usually left rotting off the edge of the mailbox until replaced by the next one, is taken out of its plastic sleeve. Its glossy pages make for hand-held fans. Though hardly a square foot of paint exists not spotted with rust, the men go out to wash their cars anyway and spray their children with hoses as they run by screeching. They silently lament their move from the city, where hydrants were made to be opened. In Turnbull block parties are never spontaneous. They never evolve from a stream of water pouring from a spigot.

Turnbull, a stretch of land on the south shore of Long Island that juts out into the Great South Bay like a sore thumb, has one road in, one road out. Turnbull Road runs north and south, an artery of potholes. On the shoulder the workers huddle near the westside of their yellow truck to grab what little shade they can. Water from their lunch boxes is poured through their scalps rather than their lips as they watch the steam rise from the mound of blacktop and tacitly curse their lot. White tank tops, greased with tar, line up like dirty daisies along the runner of the truck.

The road moves north and south, while a narrow creek cuts the thumb in half by running east and west. And when the heavy rains come, the puddle where Turnbull Road dips into a small valley is knee deep. The barefoot children gather their towels, and frollick in their temporary swimming holes.

But the roadway has been dry all month. See how the blacktop shimmers near the fender of the sheriff's car as it cruises along on cool tires? Just pulled out from the gas station where the sheriff paid an extra three quarters to have them topped off with air. In the front seat is the street map of Turnbull and the page is open to where his red ink has drawn a circle around Meadowgate Road. Set your eyes upon Meadowgate, and how it rises up from the other side of the creek, just after Turnbull Road dips down into the small valley.

The sheriff almost always notices the sink in the road and sighs with relief that on this day, for this whole month even, he hasn't had to chase the children away as they splash and twist out of reach, cursing at him in the rain. Instead he makes his right turn onto Meadowgate Road and narrows his eyes when he sees the movers—three of them—sitting in front of the house, fat as frogs.

One of them is sprawled on his back across the hood of his truck with his shades on, sunning. Another is wiping sweat from his neck and rubbing it onto his pants. The third one has taken refuge from the sun by sitting on the ground in the slip of shade near the tires of their pickup. This one sees the sheriff's car approaching and squints. He says something. The one sunning on the hood sits up and moves his shades to the top of his head. That's all the movement the sheriff will get, until he pulls over, gets out, and points out that the sticker with the red seal from the county office is on the door, so what in the hell are they waiting for?

"Waiting to win the lottery," one says as the two resting on top of the truck slide and melt off like slugs.

The one squatting in the shade eventually rises to his feet. "And for a little rain," he adds to the sheriff, who has already retreated to the air-conditioning of his car.

In Turnbull the children, off for the summer and set loose throughout the day, make their plans early. Transportation is a rare thing, and where would they go? Staying inside means possibly getting taxed with chores. And yet there is plenty to do.

A construction site for a new home makes a treasure of dirt-bombs nestled in the mountains of earth created by the bulldozers. In the winter they have snowball fights, but in the summer dirt-bomb fights are a fine replacement. Better if the foundation has already been poured, for the walls and bump-outs from which the chimney will eventually rise are great corners for sneak attacks. Even better if some kids from another part of Turnbull wander into the neighborhood, for rather than bickering to make teams, they can unite and descend upon the outsiders with a hail of dirt and shouts about their territory.

For the boys who live nearer to the creek, a relief from dirt-bomb fights is to wrap muck into a skunk cabbage leaf and hurl it at an opponent.

A third option on a hot day like this is to go and secretly watch the evictions. Spy on the men who carry them out by hiding in the woods nearby. Each child, each wild group running with untied shoelaces, will make its own plan.

It takes straws, but on this day, as the muck seems to crust beneath the sun, James Illworth, Dallas Darwin, and Felix Cassidy crouch in the woods near the top of the hill on the other side of the creek, waiting for something to happen. Eventually they spy the sheriff's car pulling onto Meadowgate Road, and they know what it means.

See the sheriff searching the empty house for drugs and weapons? Observe the men standing in the heat waiting to be let inside. Look just behind the house where the woods from the creek abruptly stop and the tall grass of the overgrown backyard takes over the landscape. The three boys crawl on their stomachs inching ever closer to watch. When the sheriff, from inside the house, bangs open the back door, a dog bolts out and in only two bounds seems to make it across the backyard and into the dense woods. The boys, ears pressed into the grass, close their eyes as though it might render them invisible.

Dallas crawls ahead of them once the sheriff goes back inside, and makes it to a thicket of evergreen bushes at the front edge of the driveway. Once inside the bushes, he pulls his knees in like a fetus and looks past his toes to see if the others are following.

His father, Michael, drove him past two evictions this summer, slowing down as they approached the pile of belongings stacked at the edge of the property. His father pointed at the pile and said, "Lesson learned, Dallas. Take care of your responsibilities."

James Illworth's father hates when his son goes to the evictions, but he will never tell him why. All James ever gets from his father is a grunt, or a wave, or he'll mutter, "Gross," as he walks out the back door and retreats to his horse barn to read the newspaper. Dallas laughs whenever James tries to explain his father's strange reaction.

Felix never shares his parents' opinions on much of anything. They are an occasional ride to the movies. A hand waving out of a passing car window to James and Dallas as they play ball in the street in autumn. James and Dallas haven't yet made up their minds about this fact. They sense sometimes that Felix is shielding his parents from his friends, rather than the other way around.

In any case, it never stops Felix from watching the evictions. And perhaps Felix's behavior during the task provides all the answer Dallas and James need, for Felix almost always leads the charge, picks up his head in the tall grass, looks around for places to take cover, and inches closer to being caught than the other two would ever dare.

The movers have drifted over to the front lawn while they await permission to start. One of them lights up a cigarette. Just yards away, huddled in the bushes, the three boys catch the faint smell of menthol.

Abruptly the front door bursts open and the sheriff strides off the porch and stands there with his hands on his belt. He nods at the men. The one smoking drops his cigarette into the grass and steps on it as he makes his way to the front door.

This is what denial looks like. Piled beside the door in an unruly stack lies a bundle of unopened letters. The bank calling upon payment. LILCO demanding satisfaction of two month's negligence on electric. Jury duty. Your subscription is ending. Final notice. Like a team of wranglers hopelessly shouting at a doomed horse to rise up from the mud bank.

The movers ignore the envelopes and step inside the empty house. The scattered trail of human vacancy continues. Two holes punched into the wall opposite the front door. Imprints like white knuckles where the fist struck a stud on the wall. This is what anger looks like.

The men start with the couch that runs under the large front window, dragging it out of the house by its legs. They carry it to the overgrown bushes and turn it over to discourage a bevy of smart-aleck kids who no doubt will plop down on it and pretend to watch TV. The end tables go next—into the bushes—the lamps placed gently against them. Shades on the evergreens like paper cups tossed from a moving car.

Inside once again, the men look at bargaining. In the kitchen, written in pencil on the bare white wall—a list of phone numbers. *Connie—Dept. Social Services. Margaret—Loan Assistance (need proof unemployment). Tony—lawyer, bankrpcy. $850 (will take small payment). Tax returns for larger payment.* Bargaining.

Outside, the sheriff sits in his running car and pulls apart the *Newsday*. He chuckles as he glances at something Elly said in *For Better or For Worse*. Then he flips the paper over and sniffs. Dave Righetti's no-hitter against the Red Sox still dominates the coverage. A Mets fan, he turns it over once more. Every morning the real news makes his head shake. Gaddafi. Andropov. The Ayatollah. The rapidly dwindling column space devoted to April's embassy bombing in Beirut. In Reagan's greatest nightmares, how will they get off this island? Immersed in the few sentences updating the embassy bombing, he doesn't notice the bushes rattling, nor the three boys who shift their restless bodies.

All three men break new sweat when they carry out the kitchen table. It rolls over the couch and lands atop the lampshades in the bushes. One of the men plants his palms on his knees and stares down at the ground to catch his breath. He straightens when the sheriff honks his horn at him. The one next to him, whose boots are only feet from Dallas, stares up at the sky when he hears the familiar sound of seagulls. A flock has perched atop the phone lines, waiting for the refrigerator to come out.

The third man, whose shades are sliding off his head on beads of sweat, brings out the chairs.

The refrigerator follows, opening as it topples over to the other side of the pile. A rotten orange, three beers, and a near-empty bottle of cheap whiskey rattle out and roll into the street. This is what depression looks like.

Stripped of its sheets and pillows, the stained corpse of a mattress is added to the pile. Then the frame. A dresser with crooked drawers. A mirror. This the movers also turn over, along with the small TV—the invitation for kids to break too great. A bag of hangers. Another nightstand. The men let two abandoned hairpins slide off the stand and bounce onto the carpet.

The spare room gives up a bookshelf, which the men feed out the window rather than carry through the house. It crashes and falls into pieces when it hits the ground. A small couch. A stack of papers, a black tray filled with stationery. Two lamps. All go to the pile, which begins to rise above the evergreens like a pyramid. An empty dog's cage goes more easily through the back door.

A pantry full of detergents, dog food, three flashlights empty of batteries, a bicycle with a missing front wheel, a box of newspapers—the movers, cursing, drag them from around back and toss them against the bushes before heading inside again.

Paintings of wheat fields, the hillsides of Italy, a lake house overlooking its reflection in the water, lean against a rickety wooden chair at the front entrance. One of the men gathers the frames under his armpit and grabs the chair. On his way out he inspects a painting. Debates whether or not it would make a nice gift for his wife, then tosses it onto the pile.

The lights have already been turned off at the switch. As if the evictees glanced back for one last look and shut them off before closing the door behind them. This is acceptance.

The men drag the last of what they can carry and pull the door closed. From there the chains go on easy. With a lag bolt, one of the men mounts the chain from the doorjamb to the doorknob and slaps on the padlock. Then the sheriff gets out of his car and reaches into his top pocket. He tacks a white sheet of paper to the door as the men pick up the remains of what they've pulled from the house.

Buried beneath a graveyard of belongings the boys hold their breath as the sheriff approaches with the three men trailing behind. All four drift past them.

"Sorry, boys, no melodrama today," the boys hear the sheriff say. The men laugh and one of them says he'll always take an empty house over a full one. The men amble across the street and ease themselves into their truck. The sheriff stands inside his open door. The air-conditioning wafts across his midsection. It lightens his mood.

"Let me know if there's anything you can do for me," the sheriff yells to the men, as he squats down into his cruiser. He chuckles at his selfish twist on the phrase.

James peers through the branches to the front door. The silver padlock catches a ray of sun and flickers at him. The boys hear the sheriff's car door slam and the big vehicle rolls past the pile above their heads. The truck drives off in the other direction, but the boys still wait a full ten Mississippis before they finally crawl out of their hiding spots, laughing.

"I swear, the one who dropped his cigarette in the grass looked right at me," Dallas says.

"When that other guy leaned down to catch his breath,

all he had to do was look to his left and he would have nailed me," says Felix.

James pulls on the leg of an upturned end table and in so doing, sets off an avalanche of furniture that nearly spills out into the road. He rights the end table and sets it down properly on all four legs. Then he stares at the table and wonders why he did it. The other two seem to be wondering the same thing, and might have asked him but they all suddenly fix their attention on the sound of a clanking chain and immediately recognize Motor Murray. The old man is wheeling his bicycle over to the pile. The shopping cart he has affixed with chains to the back of the frame rattles like a can of pins.

Murray's nickname is simple enough. Drenched in all the sarcasm of his neighbors. His bicycle is his only vehicle. His pumping legs his only motor. The shopping cart, his trunk. The boys don't know if Motor Murray is aware of his moniker, but somehow they get the feeling that even if he does know it, he wouldn't mind.

In the coming nuclear apocalypse, we will all be stranded to our fate. Only Murray will escape on his bicycle and restart civilization. That's how it is in the movies the boys watch, after the TV screen flashes blood-red and the hillsides and treetops blush with light. A lone survivor pedaling westward. Weaving through the catastrophic debris and corpses strewn along the roadways.

Murray has a pride about his transportation that angers everybody.

Just about every morning during the school year the kids would watch Murray, racing along Turnbull Road on his bicycle as the school bus navigated the choking clogs of traffic and stop signs. Did he ever hear the tin echo of the children's laughter? He never looked over at them, otherwise he'd have seen the coach stuffed with little eyes and greasy hands pressed against the windows, giggling. And when he peeled away from the bus's trajectory by heading down a side street, the children would settle down and chant:

> *Motor Murray/in a hurry/for the bar was soon to close. When along came another/who'd been with his mother /and was wearing the same kind of clothes. I've got such a cramp/but I need a new lamp/said the one with the scraggly toes. So he saw Motor Murray/pedaled on with a fury/and stole one from under his nose.*

There were variations. New adventures. New vices to give Murray, though none of them knew if he'd ever had a drink in his life. The bus driver would curse at them and ask them how they were raised, which only added to the mirth. Dallas would remain quiet and grin while looking out the window beside James, but Felix always had an answer for the driver.

Now that the boys are not whipping past Murray in their school bus, chanting poems, they can get a better look at him.

Motor Murray is dressed in his usual reflector vest, which he got after being struck by a car two years ago. He was riding his normal route along Turnbull Road, only in the tricky shadows of dusk. When Murray was hit, he lay there for hours. Neighbors came out to the porch and raised their faces to the air as though some foul smell had wafted in, but they never went to him. Eventually, he pulled himself up to one foot and limped home. His right leg was shattered, and since the accident, he has walked with a considerable limp—his foot turned slightly inward. At some point he fished a cane out of a garbage pile and has grown dependent on it when he isn't on his bicycle.

Murray gingerly dismounts. Under his reflector vest he wears a greasy T-shirt that matches the streaks of gray in his dark hair. His pants are gray, and a hole where a wallet should be exposes the dirty lining of a pocket. James watches Dallas's face drop.

"Oh leave it alone, Murray, the cops just left a second ago," Dallas says.

It's the first time Motor Murray notices the young boys standing there, their shoelaces loose. A general look of uncombed humanity.

"You see the owners coming to claim it?" he answers. "Stuff just sits out here and rots." He lifts a painting from the pile and loads it into his cart.

James figures the people who lived here left with only what they could grab. No space wherever they were heading for things like paintings and dressers.

Dallas shakes his head. He walks over to a kitchen chair the men threw and raises it high in the air. In one quick motion, he drives the legs of the chair onto the street and closes his eyes as it splinters into pieces. Murray is already yelling at him.

"If they can't have it, why should you!" Dallas shouts. Murray raises his cane as if to strike them and the boys run for a spot to reenter the woods.

As they gain some distance from Motor Murray, they turn to watch him limp impotently after them. They can make out the round, ruined hole of the man's mouth and the muscles in his neck. As though his face is not large enough to expel the kind of venom he wishes to project across the impossible distance. Even the sound of his vitriol is flaccid by the time it reaches the boys, who stand at the entrance to a small trail behind a plot of abandoned property further up the road. They can only make out a few words.

"You're dead! . . . I'm . . . kill! . . . Little bastards!"

Is this exactly how they hear it? Have they perhaps filled in the actual words with a familiar sentiment? For how many times have they heard someone threaten to kill them?

"You're a dead man," Felix's older brother Bob said just last weekend when Felix used his shoes to catch tadpoles in the creek.

Yesterday James's father said that if he caught him pouring out his whiskey again there would be nothing left of him, which is the same as being dead. How many shouts from the neighborhood teenagers, after catching the three of them rolling their garbage cans down the street, end with the promise of murder? It isn't to be taken seriously, even if James's mother constantly pleads with him to avoid teenagers when he sees them in the street. To stay close to home. To be within shouting distance so she can presumably hear him and fly on mother's wings to his rescue.

In fact, it is so common that, for most boys in Turnbull, it has become almost the point. The game's end. The prize winnings. With each foul threat Motor Murray screams, the boys count little electronic points in their heads, like a game of psychological *Pac-Man*. Every curse, or rattle of his cane, means the boys are gobbling up the ghosts. And doesn't Murray's open gob sort of look like the ghosts in *Pac-Man*? Isn't Murray himself sort of a living ghost?

The boys watch him turn away and head back to his cart. He seems to do a dance with the ground. His cane, and the inward turn of his lower leg, flex in opposite directions as he steadies himself with his bent right arm, which extends outward as if he were about to escort a woman to the dance floor.

Felix thrusts his hands into the air and whoops loud

enough for Murray to hear. But he doesn't turn, and the three boys disappear into the thick of the woods, laughing.

The horseman—death—gallops. He is not supposed to limp. We gallop from death and it gallops after us. Time is described as a flighty thing. Fleets of angels reportedly sing us to our rest. A smooth ride across the Styx comes courtesy of a silent ferryman. It is a tidy affair. The universe ties off the end of a loose strand. And yet the boiling, disjointed barks of Motor Murray on his way back to his rickety cart are like a prophecy of doom.

The boys march down the sloping hill that ends at the shallow, cold stream, electric with energy. A fun sort of fear. Unaware of time, unaware of rules, and equally ignorant of the fact that in a few short knots down time's invisible strand, one of them will be dead.

The world's vague threats will suddenly sharpen, the way a soft rumbling thunder will focus into a deafening peal. And it will not be tidy. The bones in the neck will feel like they're cracking. The disbelief will quicken the process. Bloodshot eyes will fill the afternoons every day after this one. The sheriff will yawn and watch men drain puddles in the roadway and assume it will be the day's biggest task. But he will be wrong.

And yet, the boys can't see much further than the canopy of trees in the foreground that line up like soldiers at the creek's jagged edge. The boys leap like semicolons across the murky stream.

James, following the others, shorts the bank and his heels land with a mucky splash. He swings his arms to gather his footing and rights himself just before he hears his mother scream his name from atop the hill that leads to home.

CHAPTER TWO

"JAAAAAAAAAAAAAAMES!"

The sound of her voice carried through the treetops like a desperate aria.

He recognized the pitch of his mother's call more than his name, which distance had diluted. James stared up at the leaves stuttering in the breeze, as if they were the ones who'd called out to him.

"Jaaaaaaaaaaaaaaaames!" she wailed again. The same rising wave of sound upon the long *a* thinned out at the *m*, and crashing with an awful hiss at the end. The eight-year-old watched his friends Dallas and Felix clamber up the steep bank on the other side of the creek. His heels slanted gingerly at the edge of muck, his backyard rising through the trees before him. She would panic upon the third call, James knew. He gained his footing, overtook Dallas and Felix, and bounded up the steep hill to his house.

James could already hear the older kids in his neighborhood answering his mother with their best impersonations. It had become a ritual, the duet between him and his mother, that when she would routinely call out, "Jaaaaaaaaaaaaaaaames!" they would answer back with his trademark, "Yeeeaaaaaaaaah!" Even this block-wide mockery was not enough to deter him from answering this way.

His mother, Janet, was never fooled, and found the impostors funny.

His mother called out once more, and in unison, the neighborhood kids answered back, "Yeaaaaaaaaaah!" James kept running, up the steep hill, through the tall weeds that grew as high as his waist. He passed his favorite oak tree. From this vantage point, he could see the ridge of his roof, and of the roof that once served as a barn for Clover, his dad's horse, which had died when he was too small to remember.

James reached the top of the hill and used both hands to cup his mouth. "Yeaaaaaaaaaah!" he shouted.

His yellow shirt was soaked with sweat and water from the stream. It clung to his body, all ribs and pale flesh. His wild mop of curly brown hair was moist around the hairline, and sticking like wet noodles to his forehead and cheeks. James took some time to catch his breath before completing his jog to the back door. Moments later his mother pulled the door open. It was made of heavy oak, and had swollen over the years from water damage. He could see the upper corner of the door jerking inward, until it finally broke free. James was still out of breath.

"Oh, there you are," his mother said, planting a meaty fist on her hip.

"What's the matter?" James asked.

"Nothing," his mother answered. "Just wanted to know where you were, that's all." She raised her plump arms in the air, gathered her hair away from her neck, and fanned herself. Even in her thin housedress, the heat pressed down on her short, round frame.

James shook his head at her. "I ran all the way up here for nothing?"

"Not nothing," his mother said. "You're within reach, somewhere?"

"I'm in the backyard." One of the many lies he'd rather tell. A picture of where he had actually just been emerged in his mind.

"Oh," his mother said. Pausing for a moment, she asked, "With who?"

James looked exasperated. "With Felix and Dallas. Who else?"

"Oh," she answered and stood in the doorway. She peered at him—a smile forming at the top of her fleshy cheeks. "What?"

"You just called me all the way up here for no reason," he said and almost smiled. He could never really be angry with her. Besides, he was relieved to know she hadn't somehow learned of his spying on the sheriff through that odd network of moms that always seemed to teleport information across the neighborhood like magic carrier pigeons.

"I just like to know where you are, that's all," she repeated.

"I know. That's where I am."

"Okay. Do you want lunch?" she asked, keeping him standing there.

"I'm not hungry." He pushed his wet hair back from his forehead.

"I think I might have some corn chips."

James smirked, and started to walk back down to his friends. His mother stopped him again.

"Listen, don't get overheated, you know how you get. If you sweat too much, come up and have corn chips. It'll put salt back in your system."

"I'm fine."

"And don't go too far, I'm going to call out for you again."

James looked at his mother with a blank expression.

"I worry," she said. "There's a lot of crazies out here, you have to be careful."

"Mom. I'm fine." James turned to go back to join his friends.

"How far you going to go?"

"I can always hear you calling, and I can always run back here."

"Okay, don't . . . you know. Just be careful," she pleaded, but James had started running back down the hill before he heard his mother struggling to close the bloated door.

At the bottom of the hill Felix and Dallas were leaning against a tree. Even in a reclined position, Dallas Darwin stood over Felix, pushing his wavy black hair away from his eyes. His mother's new preferred haircut fell over his face, forcing him to smear it aside from time to time, but he never complained to her.

Perhaps it was all the Bible lessons. Through no effort of his own, Dallas knew the Bible like most kids knew baseball, or crude jokes. He knew Shadrach, Meshak, and Abednego, he knew Jonah, and Abraham, and the meaning of the twelve lamp stands in Revelation. He knew how many years is a "time and half a time." He knew the earth was supposed to be a place for perfect humans. He knew the healthy way to live was the Christian way.

"Yo, screw this, Jim," Dallas said, taking a leaf he'd rolled up like a cigarette from his thin lips. "We're playing *Star Wars.* Felix and I decided you're going to be Princess Leia."

James's face dropped in horror. Immediately he cast his memory back to the image of Princess Leia, clad in a leather bikini, crying out to be rescued.

"Why?" he whined.

Felix Cassidy smiled. "Because your brother is cooler, and you're chained to your fat mom like Jabba the Hut." All three dissolved in laughter. "That was Dallas's joke," Felix added.

James had gotten used to cracks about his mother's weight. Besides, Dallas always made up for it.

"All right, enough. James, you're Luke Skywalker," Dallas said. It was the first time James had ever been Luke Skywalker. Sensing Felix's jealousy, he glanced at him—his gold-colored eyes jarred open, looking like bright pennies in the sunlight.

"Fine, I'm Darth Vader," announced Felix, squinting at James.

"You can't be Vader," Dallas said, frustrated. "We're running from the Stormtroopers. Why would Vader run from the Stormtroopers?"

Felix shook his head, silenced by the unimpeachable logic. "All right, I'm Chewbacca then."

"Good," said Dallas. "That way you can't talk. Let's go."

They stalked through the woods following the creek back upstream until it began to dry out, and the land rose to a steep green hill. Beyond it, cars zizzed by on Turnbull Road. Once inside these dense forests, all three boys would leave their lives behind: their poor Long Island town—the fights over groceries; even the sheriff's evictions despite their potential for fun; the menacing kids on the corners; shouts from windows; mothers calling out in the damp air; stray dogs left behind by transient masters; police helicopters grazing the treetops in search of suspects. They would become their own rebel group. Make mud-bombs. Sharpen sticks into spears and plan wars, escape routes. Learn how to survive in the woods. They could pretend to grow vegetables, hunt for rabbits. Turtle soup. Build snow igloos in winter. A balloon would serve as their weatherman, or an inflated shopping bag. Climb a tree and let the bag free to catch a ride on the wind. Watch it float above Turnbull and imagine they were inside it. Swirling over Turnbull Road gazing beyond their neighborhood. Softly touching down somewhere remote and silent. Or they could shed themselves and crash-land on the moon of Endor, where they'd wanted to be since they first saw it back in May at the local drive-in.

Even though James was Luke Skywalker, Dallas led them through the shrubbery, squeezing deftly between the thorns. He pivoted away from the creek bed and the other two obediently followed him uphill. They marched behind Dallas in crouched positions—the house where they'd watched the eviction at their backs—straddling logs, ducking beneath sharp branches. James spooked slightly when a green butterfly came alive from its perch among the leaves and fled to another branch above him.

Suddenly, all three boys froze at a rustling noise in the deep brush to their left. Dallas motioned silently for them to get down. They all crouched in silence. In a burst of shaking leaves, a stray dog bounded over a small bush and tried to squeeze between Felix and Dallas, just as Dallas began to rise. Felix grunted. Dallas jumped to fill the small gap for which the dog was heading, and landed a perfect tackle around its front legs. His weight bore down and the dog was instantly on its side, rolling down the hill with Dallas's limbs wrapped tightly around its body. The dog's muscles bulged from under the boy's arms, and in a matter of seconds it began to whimper. Giving up the struggle to free itself, it merely wiggled as it lay unnaturally on its back, with its pink and white soft belly facing the sky. Dallas was under the dog, calling for the other two.

"Chewy, Luke, get over here! I'm not wrestling with this thing for my health."

James and Felix bounded down the hill to help Dallas. They were getting caught up in the sticker bushes, freeing themselves for the moment by twisting away, and getting caught up again, but they were too excited to care. Felix laughed aloud.

"You're crazy!"

"I can't believe you just caught a dog!" screamed James, pulling the final sticker bush away from his body and gripping a hand around the dog's left ankle. When Felix got there, Dallas slipped out from under the dog and got back to his feet. He dusted the dirt from his jeans.

"That's no ordinary dog. This is a spy."

"A spy?" asked James. Squinting in the sun, Dallas's silhouette stood over him.

"This dog is not flesh and blood. It's a robotic spy, sent by sentries. They want to know if there are any rebels left. We can't let this thing go."

"Well, what do we do?" asked James.

"We take Spybot with us. Spybot will lead us right to them so we'll know where they are." Dallas turned his head to the side to get a better look at the dog, which had twisted its body while listening to its fate. Its head was lying flat on the ground, tired and shocked from the wrestling match, but its eyes were rolling up, down, and around. Its brow wrinkled upward as it tried for an expression of bored concern, panting for air with his tongue lying limp and almost touching the dirt.

"Get him up," said Dallas as he turned back to climb the hill. Felix took his hands off the dog and immediately it sprang to its feet and strained at James's grip on its left ankle.

"Easy, easy, boy," said James as he looked at Felix. "You want to help me here or what?"

Felix wrapped his lanky arms around the dog's neck and chest. Felix was all arms, as if they were years ahead, waiting for the rest of his body to catch up. He could make a loop of them and jump through. Slam-dunk arms, his older brother Bob called them.

His face was near the dog's head, and each time it jerked to get away, Felix had to throw his head back to avoid getting hit with an errant floppy ear, or a nervous tooth. The force made his wavy blond hair swing back and forth across his face. He could smell the dog's breath. It was young looking, maybe two, and it wasn't wearing a collar. Dallas wandered off into the deep part of the brush and disappeared from view.

"What the heck are we going to do with a dog?" James asked.

Felix looked around as if the answer to this question was in the breeze. Dallas came back through the brush, holding a short, corroded piece of white clothesline.

"Found this tied around a tree," he said, kneeling beside the dog.

Felix loosened his grip around its neck. With a fast knot, Dallas stood up with the makeshift leash and handed it off to James, who took the rope and looked down at the pitiful thing. The shock was wearing off, and the dog was beginning to go back to its dog business, sniffing the ground, poking its snout into the boys' legs, licking the knuckles of the hand that gripped its leash. James had immediately recognized it by its color, but the power in its legs confirmed for him that this was the same dog they had watched leap out of the abandoned house and dash across the backyard just an hour ago.

"Let's let Spybot lead the way," said Dallas, stepping aside.

The dog led them back up the hill as Dallas guarded the rear of their small platoon. Spybot plowed through the sticker bushes without giving a thought to the person he was pulling behind him. He leaped over small logs and scurried under

thick beds of thorns without a single stem touching him. He
rounded trees and made trails of his own until he reached the
top of the hill. James was dragged through it all mercilessly,
thorns whipping across his face. He tripped over a fallen limb,
smacked his head into a tree, and stepped into a hole.

At the hilltop, James tied the dog's rope to an old stump
and sat down to catch his breath. The other two quickly joined
him. James was just about done with being Luke Skywalker.

The interruption of the game, and wrestling with Spybot,
had taken some of the fantasy out of them all. James could
see it on their faces. The top of the hill leveled off at the sandy
shoulder of River Drive, where James and Dallas lived. Dallas looked up at the old utility pole, where the men had come
to clip the wires. He reached down and grabbed two short
pieces of purple and white wire. Twisting the two together, he
quickly formed a small man—a loop representing his head and
the stray ends for his arms and legs. Then he wound the leftover wire tightly around the middle section for his torso. He
handed it to James, who smiled and tucked it into his pocket.

"A little man right next to your little man," Dallas said,
laughing. "Let's cross the street and cut through my backyard
for a soda at Nino's."

James rose to his feet and untied the rope from the stump.
Felix straightened up from his Chewbacca pose. The boys
spilled out of the woods and looked both ways. Dallas and
Felix ran across River Drive and hopped Dallas's front fence.
James dropped the leash and left Spybot to fend for himself.
The dog paced back and forth looking for a way to join the
boys, and eventually leaped over the chain-link fence, racing
ahead of them through Dallas's backyard.

One corner of the fence had been squeezed through so
many times that there was a wide opening for Spybot and the

boys to slip through into another section of woods. A trail led to Mayflower Avenue. Across the narrow street, the trail snaked between Zambrini's Brick and Masonry Yard and Tommy Means's house.

Tommy was gone. Left with his parents when they were evicted. The boxes of belongings remained in a pile at the edge of the street like a graveyard of animal bones. The back of the masonry yard was a thick sand trap that stretched almost the length of a football field. A faint path picked up again on the far side and led to another fence. Through the hole in that one, the boys could reach the parking lot between Nino's Deli and Zambrini's.

These were the side trails, the back ways, the hidden alleys. Adults were forced to stick with the main roads to get where the boys could go in a matter of minutes. As a test one day, James had set out for Nino's at the exact same time his father got behind the wheel of his truck and headed to the same place for a six-pack. James was sitting there waiting for his dad when he finally stumbled up to the entrance. His father fixed his blurry eyes on him and sent him home to his mother with a parting swat across the top of his head.

The boys ambled across Zambrini's sandy lot. James had regained his grip on Spybot's makeshift leash. Felix's shoelaces had come undone and flopped around his feet. He was still laughing and marveling over the way Dallas had caught the dog. The boys knew Dallas was lightning fast, faster than either of them by far. But to catch a dog was remarkable.

As they neared the entrance to the small path, all three boys instinctively grew silent. They spotted three teenagers sitting on the concrete bumpers bolted to the parking lot. The teenagers noticed them immediately. One was smoking a cigarette. He stood up and dropped it to the ground.

"That's those kids Matthew and Nick," Felix mumbled. "The kids who work in the video store by the library. They're jerks; one time they chased Tommy Means all the way—"

"Shh," Dallas whispered. "Be cool about it."

A small airplane roared overhead, just yards above the treetops. The boys looked up at its white underbelly as it soared north toward the small airport just outside of town.

They stepped through the hole in the fence and came out of the shade, into the burning sun. Felix tried to avoid eye contact, something his older brother Bob had taught him to do whenever he found himself outnumbered or outsized. James, however, glanced up at the boy who wasn't smoking. The teenager glared back at him and then down at the dog tied to the rope. Dallas quickened his pace, feeling all six eyes burning into his scalp; the heat of the day turned cold.

James tried to smile but he could no more feel the muscles in his face than the rope in his hand as Spybot strained ahead, unimpressed. When they reached the corner of Nino's store, it occurred to all three at once that the teenagers were only staring the way everyone did in Turnbull. They'd said nothing. Made no sudden moves. A collective exhale gave way to the joy of soda and snacks that awaited them inside.

CHAPTER THREE

FIFTEEN-YEAR-OLD DAVID WESTWOOD kicked an empty soda bottle across Nino's parking lot, stupidly tough. One hand jammed into his jeans pocket as he watched the bottle dance across the cracks in the lot and spin like a ballerina. It tipped over, rolled off the edge of the lot, and came to a soft rest in the grass. If he kicked it again, it would do something different. David knew this. A third time would produce a new result—the random outcome of an object put in motion by an outside force. What would it take to get an action to produce the same result every time? he wondered. A team of gods, working around the clock. He stood away from his friends, ignoring their conversation.

"She's waiting for you to say something to her," Nick Darcy said as he smoked his cigarette and swiped hair from his face. Beneath the shaggy, unkempt mop of brown peered a narrow set of eyes, set deeply into a hooded, distinguished-looking brow. Nick had taken it upon himself to speak for Rachel Saint James, the head of the yearbook committee.

"You're full of it," Matthew Milton replied.

"I swear to God, I would never mess with you like that."

"What am I supposed to do, go ask her about my picture?" He took a drag from his cigarette.

"Yeah, go tell her that you want to make sure it's the one your mother picked out."

Matthew made an instant frown. "No way. I'll sound like a spaz."

"Or whatever . . . just go talk to her. Ask her out for a cup of coffee."

"Never," Matthew protested, though beginning to believe him. "Coffee's cheap," he added.

"An insult," David Westwood suddenly interrupted. He was facing away from them, looking at the corner of the building where the three kids and their dog had just disappeared. He glanced now at Nick and Matthew. "On the island of Triobrand it's customary for a man to bite off the eyelashes of a woman he's trying to court. To take her out to dinner or coffee is considered an insult."

"Don't bite her eyelashes, dude," Nick said to Matthew. He made a face, even though he was secretly impressed by David's random knowledge. They'd both heard these kinds of things from David before. His calling card or something.

"What's the problem today, freshman?" asked Matthew, his brow loosening, revealing the chubby mirth that always lurked behind his brown eyes. Matthew always made it a point of reminding David that he was a year younger than him and Nick.

David held up a defiant middle finger. Nick laughed through his nose.

"Davey's in a mood because he didn't get a phone call from his little Julia," Nick said.

"Oh, we're back at this again?" said Matthew. "The missus not treating you right?"

David turned away and looked for something else to kick across the parking lot. He got defensive when his friends made fun of his love for Julia Dawson. They hadn't the slightest idea what she did for him. Didn't know the murmurs of fear and doubt that filled his head—that voice which seemed always to chant, *You're ugly. A no-talent. You'll always be poor, no one will ever love you.* A voice her smile could silence. Didn't know how much she inspired his paintings, those lonely moments at the canvas, when his mind would search for some kind of focus. They hadn't walked in the wake of her perfume and felt dizzy in its scent—hadn't wanted to be the person he wanted to be when he was around her. They were not complete, not at ease inside their own skin, the way he felt when he listened to her violin practice. Watched the instrument jump to life beneath her chin, while her long, slender fingers worked the fingerboard. They didn't understand the small indent where the instrument met her collarbone, and how this soft nook cradled all the things he'd ever felt. Just as they could never understand his torment when she became mischievous and whimsical, brushing aside his company whenever she felt like it. The two of them would never know the hardness of her cruelty. So much so that David privately wished they'd never get girlfriends. Never suffer the way he did, her name bobbing like an apple in the turbulent ocean of the day's thoughts. *I should get dressed . . .* Julia. *I wonder what's on TV tonight . . .* Julia. *If Mom and Dad can't pay the oil bill, I'll need another blanket in the studio . . .* Julia. Matthew and Nick are lucky, he told himself. They don't know what love is. David breathed deeply. His friends laughed and changed the subject.

"Check it out," said Matthew, nudging David's shoulder with a fist. "Tomorrow Darryl Knight's having a party. His mom's actually supplying the beer."

"Nice," David replied, "another thing to help us forget we're actually alive." *Julia.* He wondered if she would be there and what she would wear.

"Heyyy!" a voice boomed near the entrance to the parking

lot on Turnbull Road. The three boys turned and saw Darryl Knight heading toward them. The large varsity offensive lineman's arms were stretched open, a wide smile smeared across his face. Darryl had sweat rings under the arms of his T-shirt, and his hairline was damp.

Matthew's face lit up. "Speak of the devil!" he shouted, heading toward him. The two embraced for a second and backed off. Nick followed suit, but David kept his distance, giving Darryl the military salute.

"You talking nonsense about me, Matty?" asked Darryl, holding his smile. "You coming to my house tomorrow night or what?"

"Absolutely, are you kidding?"

"Bring these two losers with you."

Nick and David looked at him to make sure he was kidding. He was.

"Don't bring beer, my mom's taking care of it," Darryl added.

"We heard," Nick said.

"Nothing. You heard nothing, got that?" Darryl was suddenly serious, pointing a finger at him. Nick nodded. "Get there around six or seven, and get rides so you can crash if you need to."

"No way, Darryl," replied Nick, "I've heard things about your mom. I'm trying to keep my virginity, you know."

"Keeping your virginity's easy for you, try keeping your head attached to your shoulders." Darryl took a couple of mock swings at Nick, who smacked wildly at the air in defense.

A car pulled into the parking lot, and the four boys wheeled around. Through the window, David could see the long-haired heads of two girls. One of them was Julia. She stepped out of the passenger seat and waved. She gave David an extra look, with a tight grin, before she closed the door and disappeared around the corner and into the store.

The other girl got out. It was Krystal Richards. An incoming junior, and one of the front runners for junior homecoming queen. Krystal was a track star, and an honor student, acquainted with the boys from their long sessions of tutoring in math and social studies. Her hair was the color of vanilla ice cream, and she wore it back away from her face in a loose ponytail. Large blue eyes like a robin's egg framed by long, blinking lashes and a round, pouting face. She looked like one of the surfer girls that graced the magazines on the racks at Nino's. Lips pursed, or smiling out from behind the surfboard. Didn't matter.

Krystal was the most popular tutor in school and the administration loved her. They were convinced she was destined to become a great teacher. It would seem the administration would have caught on that all her students were boys, foaming inside their heads and dreaming about her when they hit the pillow, but for some reason they thought it was her teaching methods. Krystal had no reason to get out of the car, but she did, and leaned against the door, her long muscular legs bronzed and smooth, extending from her short shorts. Her legs told the whole story, a symbol of her determination, like when she took a stumble in the 440 sprint event, got back to her feet, and managed to pull out in front of all the other girls just before the finish line.

"Another exciting day in Turnbull," she said.

Darryl looked her up and down. "Town ain't so bad," he said. "Just got a lot more exciting."

"Hey, David!" called Krystal, as if Darryl and the other two boys didn't exist. David nodded at her. "When are you going to take some pre-sophomore lessons with me, huh?" She swung her left knee from side to side.

David started walking toward her, but turned to follow after Julia. "When I become as stupid as these guys," he said, and disappeared around the corner.

His mind swam. He didn't know how to interpret Julia's little grin. He wasn't sure what she was doing, brushing him off and heading into the deli. Was she saying something without saying anything? He walked up to the door and leaned against the wall. Waited for Julia to come out.

She stepped out carrying a Coke bottle in each hand, and stopped short when she saw him.

"Hey," she said, brushing her black hair away from her face with three fingers while the other two gripped a bottle. Her nails were bitten to the quick, a habit she'd formed in middle school, when she still had braces and worried over everything. She had a small, upturned nose that drew attention to perfectly round, deep blue eyes. Like the sea, David always thought, and when he looked into them, they always seemed ancient, and tragic. Her head was held high by a long white neck, smooth but muscular—so that whenever she threw her head back to laugh, she revealed the ribbed tube of her throat. And her laugh. David could sit for a moment in the noisiest of places and still conjure her laugh. It both maddened him and filled his heart with lust, to see those straight rows of teeth gleaming white beneath her red lips.

"You know, it's been scientifically proven that Canadian porcupines actually kiss on the lips," he said.

Julia seemed to sense something was on his mind.

"Why haven't I heard from you today?" David asked, looking at the ground.

"I was out with my dad all morning. He wanted me to run some errands with him."

David shook his head. "Why are you always spending time

with him when you could be talking to me? Does he do it deliberately to keep us apart?"

"I doubt it," she said, frowning.

"I know, because you don't see it, but I do. You're too close to the whole thing to see what's really happening. He's trying to hold you back. That's why you have to make sure you keep me around him, so he doesn't think I don't matter to you."

"He doesn't even know about you, David."

"See what I mean?"

"I'm not even supposed to be dating anyone; he'd kill me if he knew about you. What's the big deal if I don't call you every day?"

"Because that's not us, Julia. I feel like I'm speaking to your dad right now, it's like he's taken over your mind."

"You don't even know my dad," Julia protested as she began to walk away from him.

"I know his type. He's like all the other fathers in the world."

"You're being a silly boy," she said, and laughed. "And I have to go. I'll call you when I call you." She smiled that awful, cruel, and beautiful smile, and got back into Krystal's car. The passenger window was open. David stormed after her.

"I'll call you tonight, so be up," he said.

Julia stared at him silently, blinking her large, round blue eyes. The car slowly crept into reverse. Krystal leaned over to look at David through the passenger window.

"Bye, David," she said, wriggling her fingers at him. He ignored her and walked around the hood of the reversing car to rejoin his friends. Darryl was still there, following Krystal's car with his eyes, until it disappeared up Turnbull Road. He turned back to David.

"What's your story? I'm telling you, we work overtime on

that girl. Talk her up, take lessons with her. You just stand there and she's panting all over you. Son of a bitch looks like somebody just kicked him in the balls too. I should have your problems, Red." Darryl turned to Matthew. "He should tell Julia, *Listen, your friend is hotter, give me a pass here.*"

"She's a troll, Darryl, you can have her," David replied. He wandered toward the hole in the fence and kicked a large stone across the ground and into the woods. *Red.* That stupid nickname. His mood was mounting, he could feel it. It was that old feeling. Julia used to make it go away. Now she was making it return. He wanted to do something that even screaming, punching, and kicking could not satisfy.

"What are you guys doing? Go home to your fadders," David heard Nick shout behind him in a jovial mock-Italian accent. He wheeled around and noticed the three little kids heading toward him. The one with the dog was holding a brown paper bag.

"Lunch money. Gimme your lunch money!" Matthew demanded and grinned wildly.

"Nick, I'll put twenty dollars down, says that little one with the dog kicks your ass," Darryl challenged. David could see from the kids' faces they weren't getting the jokes.

"First of all, you don't have twenty dollars, and secondly, why you betting against me?" Nick countered, taking up a boxer's stance.

"I like underdogs," Darryl said.

David fixed his eyes on the dog as it strained forward on its rope. Its nose was an inch from the concrete, as if it were sniffing for a way out of its predicament. Out of the heat. Out of Turnbull.

"Whose dog is that? That's not your dog," David said, glaring at the animal's captor.

"Says you," snapped the kid's brown-haired friend.

"I can tell that's not your dog, you got a dirty old rope tied around its neck."

"So?" the mouthy kid retorted.

"*So?* You little prick, so you're going to choke it to death. Untie it."

The boy holding the rope stayed silent and didn't move. Just stared up at David as though he was a loose tiger. This time the blond kid with the long arms spoke up.

"We caught it, what's it to you?"

As if on cue, the dog coughed and opened its jaws as if it were about to vomit.

"Gimme that rope and get the hell outta here!" David yelled, lunging forward. The boy quickly released the rope, and with a collective yelp, all three ran past him, through the hole in the fence, into Zambrini's lot.

David knelt beside the dog and untied it. The dog took off in the opposite direction, disappearing back around the corner.

"Aw, c'mon," Darryl said. "They caught it fair and square."

"I like underdogs too," David muttered. Scowling at the wake of the little kids, he tossed the rope into the woods.

CHAPTER FOUR

DALLAS, FELIX, AND JAMES streaked across Zambrini's sand lot and took the long way back home, up Mayflower. Dallas thought it gave them a better chance of avoiding the older kids. He'd been warned by James's older brother Kevin that in Turnbull, teenagers, boredom, and summer break were a bad combination. Kevin always joked with him that, given his wise-ass mouth, he should stick close to home. Kevin told him he could piss off a Buddhist, and although Dallas wasn't really sure what a Buddhist was, he knew enough to understand that he needed to watch it.

"Learn to run fast or punch hard," Kevin had told him once, reaching out and mussing his hair.

This world theory was the opposite of what Dallas's father tried to teach him. Yet everywhere he turned he found himself getting pushed and instinctively pushing back. Throwing an elbow on the lunch line. Scratching at someone's eyes to get his football returned. There was the justice his father had taught him to wait for, and there was the justice of his impulses.

"Some kids down by Floyd's River are building a fort," Felix announced. "Let's go check it out and tear it down."

James lifted his head. One of his grandest pleasures was the thrill of spying on other kids building a fort and ransacking it. He loved nothing more than to spy on people. It was how he first learned what sex was, when he snuck up on Kevin while he was laid out in the flatbed of his dad's pickup truck with some redheaded girl James never got to meet. The girl's hair was the color of blood in the moonlight, and she was down near Kevin's belt buckle, moving up and down. Kevin was moaning as though he had a stomachache. James stalked off after a few minutes, amazed he hadn't gotten caught and beaten to a pulp. Kevin hated spying, and people who spied.

"How do you know they're building a fort?" asked Dallas, pulling open his soda can and taking a large gulp.

"Could be a house," said James.

"Maybe. But then at least there'll be a foundation for dirt-bomb fights," said Felix.

It was decided. The three boys stepped out of the woods, turned the corner, and headed east on River Drive, the road that led down to the Estates, a private, densely wooded development built on the banks of Floyd's River. It was one of the few pockets in Turnbull with higher-income residents. Snobs, the local kids called them. People who eat cold pasta on purpose, and send their children to private school. Forbidding them to hang out with anyone from outside the development. A refuge for upper-middle-class families, guarded with gates and large dogs.

On the way down the road, the three boys haggled over where to build their new fort with the wood they would carry off as the spoils. James thought it would be cool up in a tree in his backyard, overlooking the stream. Felix wanted the fort in *his* backyard. Dallas lobbied to build it in the small plot of woods behind his house, so they could be halfway to Nino's Deli whenever they slept in it overnight. After much discussion, the three boys went with Dallas's plan.

About a quarter-mile from their homes, the boys looked

through the trees and caught the first glimpse of a tree fort, in its early stages: the large support beams nailed into three trees to form a triangle, and a wooden platform of plywood and planks. It was only a few feet off the ground, the work of amateurs, they all agreed. The materials for the walls were piled on the ground beneath the structure. The kids who were building it were nowhere in sight. Dallas took the first step into the woods and crouched down. The other two followed.

"We should probably take all the loose wood first and drag it someplace safe. Then we'll take down what's on the trees already, since that'll make the most noise."

"How do we get all the stuff back to your house?" asked Felix. Dallas didn't know.

Suddenly James remembered. "There's a trail that runs through this whole stretch of woods, all the way to my back-yard!" He stared through the trees in the distance.

Dallas made a wry face. "How do you know that?"

"My dad," James whispered. "My dad used to take his horse through these trails. It comes out across the stream in my backyard."

"Get out of here," said Felix.

"I'm with Felix," Dallas added. "I never saw any trails on the other side of the stream."

"I'm telling you there's a trail. It runs right along the top of this whole hill."

Felix laughed sarcastically.

Dallas was deadly serious. "All right, let's get closer, and if we see the trail, we'll take it."

The three boys slinked through the low brush until they were right beneath the fort. Dallas looked at the pile of wood, and saw the hammers were still lying on it. He made a note of it. They would come in handy, to take apart what had already been built. James was looking around somewhat frantically.

"I don't see a trail," said Dallas.

"It's here, I swear." James's father had told him that James used to ride along on Clover—wedged between his dad and the saddle horn—when he was three years old. Never before had he so desperately wished to remember back that far. He was turning his head, hoping for the faintest sign of an opening in the brush. "My dad talked about it all the time."

"Your dad was probably on his second bottle of whiskey," said Felix, trying not to be nasty, hoping Dallas would laugh. He only smiled.

James crawled up further ahead, straining his eyes. He was horrified. Felix's words punched through him, and he began to remember that all the times his father had told him about the wild, long trails down to the water, he *was* drunk, his lips constantly dry and needing to be licked. But it had to be true. He crawled further ahead.

"What if we pile the stuff up out on the street and pull it with our bikes?" suggested Felix.

"Too much noise," Dallas answered.

"My mom can take us back to the spot in her station wagon and we can just load it up," Felix said.

"That's not a bad idea," said Dallas.

James sensed the other two boys giving up on his plan. Still, he kept searching for signs of a trail. Dallas called him over, and though James wanted to keep looking, in the end he knew it would be better to help, rather than spend all day trying to find something that didn't seem to exist.

James grabbed the largest plank he could and began dragging it through the woods behind Felix and Dallas. Dallas was almost jogging with his plank behind him, so he could double back quickly. The three boys kept this up for a good distance, until Dallas turned his head to speak.

"This should be far enough, let's head toward the street." Without question, the other two followed as Dallas turned and dragged his spoils out onto the shoulder of the road. The three piled the wood up neatly to give the appearance that it was meant to be left there, and headed back. James kept looking off into the distance. Through the brush. Between trees, as if he were hunting rabbit. His father's trail was not there.

"One more load should do it," said Felix.

"What are you talking about?" Dallas snapped. "We haven't even taken down the wood they nailed up yet."

"I think we have enough to build our own fort. Why do you want to keep taking chances?"

"We're going to take every last splinter," Dallas replied.

At the site of the fort, Dallas slapped James on the arm and motioned for him to help with a large piece of plywood. Dallas inspected the fresh, yellow wood and wondered how a group of kids could afford a brand-new sheet like this. His instincts told him that a construction site must be nearby.

James interrupted Dallas's thoughts when he lifted the other end of the board and started to push Dallas backward through the woods. Felix, as if motivated by his own impatience, grabbed a hammer that had been lying there and loudly knocked one side of the support beam off the tree with a single swing.

Dallas's eyes widened. "Felix!" he yelled. "What are you doing?"

Felix was looking at the tree with a grin. "Sons of bitches wouldn't have been able to climb on top of this thing anyway," he laughed.

The structure sagged from its own weight like a beaten

boxer. Dallas's eyes were burning into Felix—the mere image of him standing in the leaves with the hammer gripped in his right hand, and the structure swinging in the wind behind him, was enough to send him into fits.

"That noise just echoed, you idiot. Let's go." Dallas pulled on the plywood, and nearly yanked James off his feet. He was practically running with the thing, dragging James along.

James felt as if he were back on the end of that leash, struggling with the dog. He kept glancing around as he stumbled. Felix caught up with them, dragging the plank he'd knocked off the tree.

The three suddenly heard loud shouts, and wheeled around to catch sight of five boys hurdling through the bushes after them. They were many paces off, but all three boys dropped their cargo immediately and bolted into the woods. Dallas instantly put distance between himself and the other two, leaping and ducking as he ran.

James was frantic. The kids were getting closer. He knew this because he could make out some of the awful things they were shouting. He looked over his shoulder, realizing he'd outpaced Felix. He thought of his brother, who always talked about strength in numbers, but James kept his own course—a panicked direction, with its own strategies and justifications, known only to the impulses of his mind.

James watched Dallas leap between the forks of a tree. He could feel his lungs bursting, and his mind began to tell him that it was no use. He began to question the whole thing while he ran for his life. He was angry now. Why had Dallas gotten greedy? Why didn't they listen to Felix when he wanted to stop after that last load? He was running, yes, but part of him was also wishing he was not running at all. He was angry, even at himself. For being stuck. For being run down by a gang of kids who would surely beat him up. He could hear the rustling leaves getting closer, and occasionally a kid howling out in pain after bursting through a wall of sticker bushes.

He dared not look back and ran on, leaping and ducking and sidestepping. Trees were whizzing by, and shouts came at such different distances, he didn't know who was shouting. He didn't know if the other two had been caught. He kept his eyes forward. His terror had complete hold of him.

Suddenly, he hit a low stump, catching the loop of his laces on the rotten edge. He flew through the air, landing on his side and rolling backward, down into a slight valley. His world was tumbling. His eyes focused on the ground, until he saw the tops of the trees, and the blue sky burning above him, and the earth coming back to hold him fast as his shoulders hit the dirt. Then again he saw the sky. Then the trees and, after, the dirt. From the speed of his own momentum, he managed to find his feet on the ground, but the imbalance and the dizziness sent him falling back. The sky snapped into focus. He had run smack into Dallas and Felix, who were standing above him in wonderment. James reached with his hand and grabbed a handful of dirt. He heard Dallas's voice, panting.

"I'll be damned."

James sat up and looked around. All three were in the middle of the trail James had sworn was there. He took two deep breaths and the joy that had washed across his mind spilled out into a smile. But he had no time to bask in it. Dallas grabbed his shirt collar and pulled him up and he found himself on his feet. He was off and running again, toward home.

The gang of kids had burst out of the deep brush that lined the trail, and were now in a flat-out sprint. They had picked up sticks along the way.

Felix put his head down and began pulling out in front of

the other two. "They're coming," he breathed out. "They got clubs."

The trail bent around sharply to the left, and ran along the ridge of a steep hill. Felix stopped short in horror, skidding across the dry dirt. Dallas and James stopped behind him. They had hit a dead end. The trail had run straight into a stockade fence that couldn't be climbed. Behind the fence stood a brand-new house, with new windows and fresh siding. Dallas's mouth dropped open as he surveyed the fence. James's heart sank. He thought of his dad and felt betrayed all over again.

"No way," cried Dallas. "No, no . . . no way." He slammed his palms against the wooden fence.

"What do we do?" shrieked James. The gang was approaching the sharp bend in the trail.

"Fuck you and fuck your dad!" shouted Felix. His eyes were moving all over the place.

Dallas didn't say a word and reached for a fallen branch. He handed it to James and found another one for himself. Felix picked up a large rock, the size of a cobblestone. The gang of kids reached the dead end, and stood a few yards away. They were all panting. James could tell by their clothes that they weren't from the Estates. The biggest of the five kids stepped forward; he was barely out of breath.

"Tryin' to take our stuff?" he said, not looking for an answer. James, Felix, and Dallas stared back blankly. The kid glanced at his friends. "You're outnumbered. Apologize and we'll drop the sticks."

Dallas shook his head. "I'm not begging."

"If you don't want to get beat with these sticks, you'll beg."

"I don't beg," said Dallas. "So up yours, we're taking your fort from you."

The smallest one in the group struck first, swinging a large stick. He connected with James's arm, while James thrust his stick forward like a sword and caught him in the abdomen. Dallas swung wildly as he fought off two kids. The leader, who only a second ago was trying to negotiate, was full of fury, taking broad swipes at Dallas. Felix threw his rock, narrowly missing the leader's head; he lunged for him with the same motion. Felix got the kid around his neck and pulled him to the ground. Dallas stomped down on his chest as the boy howled.

James caught a sharp stick across his back and tears rushed to his eyes. He charged at the kid who had hit him. Once on the ground, James threw punches wildly, connecting only a few. The smaller boy backed off, looking frightened. The kid underneath James got hold of his throat and was trying to choke him. James wrestled his hand away, took the boy's thumb deep into his mouth, and bit down. The kid shrieked and flailed, wriggling under James like a fluke on the end of a hook. James threw a right cross and drove the boy's head back down onto the ground. He still had his thumb in his mouth.

Felix refused to let go of his older foe, and Dallas was holding two kids at bay with his stick. The older kid rolled over and got to his feet, with Felix clinging to his back like a bull rider. The kid bucked and twisted from side to side, trying to knock Felix off.

James was moments away from claiming victory, when suddenly, from the corner of his eye, he saw the smaller boy step into view swinging a heavy branch, the leaves still attached. The branch caught James in the side of the neck, and he fell and rolled over onto his back, blinking without making a sound, though he wanted to cry. His assailant stood over him, and James unleashed a swift kick. The blow landed in the middle of the boy's chest. It knocked him off the trail edge, and sent him rolling down the steep hill. James got to his knees and looked over the edge of the incline. The boy came to a halt at the base of the hill and lay there, motionless. After a minute James watched him push himself up into a sitting position, before giving up and lying back down on the ground.

As the older fighter jerked his body to get Felix off his back, he stepped right into the path of Dallas's swing. The tip of the stick caught him across his face, and, as if in slow motion, everybody turned to watch the blood spurt. The injured boy dropped backward instantly. Felix finally let go and pushed himself away. The kid rolled to his knees, holding both hands over his face. Blood was pouring through his fingers. He scrambled wildly to his feet, like a newborn calf, and without a look, a word, or a motion to his friends, he sprinted down the trail and disappeared. The other three dropped their sticks and ran to join him. The only ones left were Dallas, breathing heavily with the bloody stick in his hand, James catching his balance while still on his knees, Felix rising to his feet and dusting himself off with a deep sigh, and the small boy lying at the bottom of the hill.

They reached the bottom by using the trees to keep from slipping. When they approached the boy, he sat up with alarm and stared at them, his brown eyes blinking fearfully. James noticed for the first time how skinny he was. His shirt clung to him so that they could see his ribs, and his corduroy pants stuck like paint to a pair of bony knees. He had leaves in his hair and dirt on his face. James imagined that the leaves and dirt were caused by the fight, but somehow it seemed like they had been there for days. He looked starved and terrified.

Dallas was still holding his stick. The boy's eyes moved from Dallas to James to Felix. He did not know them. And they did not know him. He struggled to get a word out.

"My name is . . ." He stared at James. "Jason Brock," he said finally. Then he looked at Dallas. His eyes traveled down the stick, and his lips trembled when he saw the blood. "I'm seven."

Dallas raised his weapon slightly and pointed it at him. He looked over at Felix and James, who had not, since they reached the bottom of the hill, taken their eyes off the boy.

"We're taking your fort," Dallas declared, wiping sweat from his face with the back of his hand.

The boy nodded and bit his bottom lip. "I want to go home," he whispered, trembling in the leaves.

"So do I," said Felix.

Dallas let the stick drop to the ground. They watched Jason Brock clamber up the hill and disappear over the ridge.

C HAPTER FIVE

"LORD, WE PRAY THAT YOU WATCH OVER US at this time, as we gather as a family to enjoy this meal. We pray that we always remember to keep You in our hearts when we lie down, and when we speak, and when we go about the broad paths. Please, Father, send Your spirit to the grieving family members of those who lost their lives in the Beirut embassy. We know that You are now embracing them in the heavens, but we ask that You continue to watch over their loved ones who remain on earth. We also pray that You watch over Dallas."

Dallas opened his left eye and peeked at his father, hands clasped together at the head of the table, eyes shut tightly. Dallas closed his eye and kept his head down.

"We know that out of the mouth of babes, Your kingdom bubbles forth. He is a precious gift to us, given by the power of Your holy spirit, and we make this supplication so that he may act as a light to Your roadway. We pray that he resist the temptation to misbehave as other children do, and that he remain peaceable with all of Your creations, Lord. For these things we pray in the name of the Holy Ghost. Amen."

"Amen," Dallas and his mother said in unison. Dallas would not look up at his father until he saw him pick up his knife and fork and cut into his pork chop.

His father, Michael, was a frail man, with wiry arms and a

size-thirty waist. He wore thin-rimmed spectacles that sat on a small, slightly pointed nose. Though Dallas's hair was raven black, his father's was strawberry blond, straight as a pin, and parted to one side. His hairstyle hadn't changed in years. The dinner table usually remained silent until Mr. Darwin decided it was time to speak. Often he would tell a story about something that had happened at his job, distributing auto parts to area garages and private homes. Occasionally he would ask his wife, Rebecca, about her job, as a hall monitor and aide at T. Walter High School. He hadn't asked her about it lately.

Dallas was a picky eater, and moved the food around on his plate, hoping to give the appearance that he was digging in. He had lost his appetite, trying to shake the image of Jason Brock cowering under the bloody stick he'd waved at him. He heard his father's fork and knife drop onto his half-empty plate with a metallic jingle. He looked up, startled.

"I almost forgot," Mr. Darwin said, looking at Dallas. "Good deeds."

Dallas searched his mind for a moment. "I don't have one," he said with a heavy sigh, and went back to toying with his food.

"Come on," his father prodded, "you know that every Friday we share what good deeds we did for other people."

"I forgot it was Friday," mumbled Dallas.

"And why do we do good deeds?"

Dallas peered at his father to gauge if he needed to answer. A warm smile spread across Mr. Darwin's face.

"Because it's part of our worship to God," Dallas answered.

"Why is it a part of our worship?"

Dallas looked over at his mother, eating as if nothing was happening. "Because we are God's messengers on earth and everything we do we must do to prove our love and worship to God," he replied flatly.

"We must be without blemish before the eyes of unbelievers," said his mother. "So no one can say, *Oh, look at that Dallas Darwin, he says he's a Christian, but look at all the things he does,* right?"

Dallas nodded and looked down at his plate.

"You're getting almost to that age where you have to decide for yourself whether you're going to be committed to the Lord," his father tacked on. "Part of what identifies you with the Lord's flock are the good deeds you do. So let's hear it."

"I . . . I can't think of one, Dad." Dallas looked at his father, almost wishing he would ask him questions about his day, so that he could at least absolve himself of some of the guilt he felt.

"I'll go first," his father said. "Today I hand-delivered a carburetor to a customer who is restoring an old Buick, because the customer is handicapped and couldn't get anyone to drive him to our store."

Rebecca Darwin pondered this for a moment, looked at Dallas, and then back at her husband. "If he's too handicapped to drive, then why is he restoring a car?"

A short burst of laughter escaped through Dallas's nose. His father looked at Rebecca and shook his head playfully.

"He does it as a hobby, since he's stuck home most of the day." Mr. Darwin now turned his attention back to Dallas. "What's one good deed you did this week? Come on, they can be real simple."

Dallas thought for a moment. He couldn't get Jason Brock out of his head. The trembling little piece of humanity was standing in the path of every good thought. That soiled cherubic face shone like a bright bulb, exposing all the dark, dirty insides of Dallas's heart. He flashed back, quickly, to the bottom of the hill, standing there with a stick in his hand. A stick that had already flattened a nose. He had it in his hand. He raised it, with great menace. But he did not swing. A thought suddenly struck him with excitement.

"I didn't hit a little kid with my stick today!" he blurted out, before thinking it through.

His father looked at his mother. "He was in a fight today?"

"First I heard of it," she said, forking her peas away from her broccoli.

Mr. Darwin looked back at his son, eyeing him up and down. There was an angry, chilly look in his eye, a look that often unnerved Dallas to the point that he would almost beg for a spanking, so he could be turned away from his disapproving face. Dallas searched his mind for a way out.

"How is not hitting another human being with a stick considered a good deed?" his father asked. There was a long moment of silence. So long, Mr. Darwin picked up his fork, and with an angry sniff took another mouthful. He wouldn't make eye contact with his son.

"I could have hit him with it," Dallas finally mumbled, looking back down at his food. He heard the fork drop again.

"That is not the point. That is not the point, Dallas. You are a representative, not only of this household, but of your Lord God. Does this kid know you're a Christian?"

"No."

"Well thank God for that. At least you didn't bring reproach on the Lord's name. You're dismissed from the table, go to your room." Whenever his father passed a sentence, there was no appeal. Dallas got up without a word, and left the dining room.

Once inside his bedroom, Dallas laid down on his bed and

stared up at the ceiling, his right hand folded across his chest. He began to count the things he'd done wrong, not in telling his father, but in putting himself there, standing in the tracks of wrongdoing. Like feet that run to badness, his father always said. He thought about the kid he *did* hit with his stick, the bigger kid who ran off and was probably dealing with questions from his parents right now. Mostly, he thought about those few words from poor, quivering Jason Brock. And yet, Dallas couldn't beg God for mercy. He couldn't beg for anything. He'd almost rather go without than get that feeling in his stomach that he needed to rely on someone's kindness or mercy. He turned on his side, and rose to his knees at the head of his bed. Behind his headboard, a shelf held his record player. He pulled out the new album his mother had purchased for him. Billy Joel stood, legs apart in his leather jacket, with a stone cocked back in his hand. He placed the record on the turntable and turned the dial up. He laid back down. The speakers crackled a bit, but finally the guitar screeched out. Dallas stared back up at the ceiling.

Friday night I crashed your party
Saturday I said I'm sorry
Sunday came and trashed me out again . . .

Dallas listened to the lyrics, but still felt a great heaviness lying across his chest. His eyes filled with tears. *My name is Jason Brock. I'm seven.* Why am I like this? Dallas wondered. Soon, he broke into giant sobs, and covered his face with his hands, crying into them with the heavy kind of sorrow that not even a guitar solo, which normally cheered him up, could stopper.

* * *

Rebecca and Michael Darwin sat in the living room clutching their coffee mugs. It was a warm night, and Michael opened the bay windows that covered almost the entire front porch of the house. The breeze drifted in, but barely. He was discussing their finances.

"So three thousand goes into this investment account and it stays there for at least five years, untouchable."

"And it can be added to?" his wife asked.

"Any time we want, but the point is, we can't take away from it, and as it gains interest, you know, you never can tell how things will work out in the future, with interest rates and all that. We may end up tripling our money in no time."

"That would be nice."

Michael dropped back down on his seat next to Rebecca and threw his arm across the back of the couch. She reached for her mug and sipped piously.

"We should have started a long time ago," Michael added.

"And we can't go into it at all? That's a lot of money. What if we need it for something?"

Michael had already begun shaking his head. "Only emergencies, like if we have to total out one of the cars. This account is really restrictive, which is what we need."

She nodded, and sipped. Her husband played with the edges of her black hair, running a handful of it through his fingers, and twirling it around his index. She hadn't yet shown the early signs of gray that most raven-haired people get, and in the soft yellow light of the living room, she looked younger than she was. Her high cheekbones sloped inward to sunken cheeks, but the wrinkles that were beginning to form there weren't visible in the evening light, nor were the faint crow's feet around her eyes. She toyed with the rim of her coffee mug with slender fingers that tapered down to delicate polished nails. Rebecca hadn't gained a pound since high school, and her collarbones were white and visible above the neckline of her shirt. Michael wanted to dive into her neck when he saw her in this light. But he vanquished the thought with the more important consideration of their money. "If we don't touch it," he continued, "eventually we won't miss it, and then the sky's the limit. It may even pay for Dallas's tuition when the time comes."

Speaking Dallas's name seemed to have an effect on Michael. He strained his ears in the silence, while his wife took another sip of coffee. Michael had an odd habit of pouring an entire cup of coffee, and only taking a sip from it. He was always busy with something. "What's Dallas doing in there?" he asked, motioning to the bedroom.

Rebecca perked her ears up. "Listening to his record," she answered, sinking back down into the comfort of the couch. "That Billy Joel album I got him."

Michael exhaled through his nose and sank down into the couch with her.

"I wish you wouldn't buy him those kinds of things," he said absently, as if he were just looking to fill the air with his voice.

"Why?"

"I don't know. It's not good for him. Before the Lord found me, I was like an animal on all fours, doing all sorts of things—and I listened to all sorts of debased music. He's got too many things influencing him already . . . Those kids he runs around with. Did he tell you about this fight he was in?"

Rebeccca shook her head.

He glanced out the window, pondering. "I'll bet I know who started it, Rebecca. It was that Illworth kid, I can bet that dollars to doughnuts."

"How can you know that?"

"Kid's got no parental supervision. He's a bit of an idiot, really, a stupid kid. Probably shoots his mouth off and then Dallas gets in the middle of it."

"Supervision," Rebecca repeated, as though it was a dead word.

"With a father like his, how could he be expected to behave himself?"

"Janet's a nice woman, though."

"But the old man, Ivan? You saw him at the block party last month. Smashed the tables, and fell down. Threatened Minister Roberts." Michael got up from the couch, distracted by a noise outside, and went to the window.

Rebecca started to laugh, and raised her mug to her lips. "He said Minister Roberts was looking funny at his wife. Can you imagine? The size of that woman? His wife back home is a hundred pounds soaking wet, he's going to eyeball Janet?" She chuckled at her own observation, but her husband was intently watching Ivan Illworth across the street, as Ivan bashed his garbage cans into the ground, denting them.

"Here's a perfect picture right now, Rebecca," he said, waving her over to the window.

She rose to join him, and when she looked out, her mouth dropped open and she half-gasped, half-laughed. "What's he doing?"

"Smashing his own garbage cans, apparently."

They shook their heads. It was like watching a gorilla at the zoo marking its territory. Ivan's apelike, husky frame thrashed the metal cans, throwing them across the yard, only to retrieve them moments later. Michael and Rebecca watched from the comfort of their living room window; it was the first time in family history that Michael finished his cup of coffee.

Halfway through his tirade, Ivan Illworth began to shout in his slurred voice

He kicked one can over, and threw another across the street with more incoherent screams.

"What's he saying?" asked Rebecca.

"I can only make out the curse words," Michael answered.

CHAPTER SIX

IVAN ILLWORTH STORMED INTO HIS HOUSE and slammed the front door.

"Fucking cans!" he yelled.

James was at the kitchen table with Kevin, while Janet sat in the living room watching television. She rolled her eyes when Ivan walked past her into the kitchen. Ivan looked at his two boys. He gave them that familiar expression. James could tell what he wanted. He gave in.

"What's the matter?"

"Nothing," his father sniffed, opening the refrigerator door. James knew it would only be a few seconds before all his "nothing" poured forth a litany of grievances.

"Those fucking cans aren't worth a shit, that's the problem," he began. "I try to fit an extra bag into them, they dent. I try to take a bag out, the can falls over, it dents some more. I stand the can upright and leave it, it falls over and rolls out into the street." He paused for dramatic effect. "I went and threw the goddamn things across the street. We need plastic cans." He took a seat between the boys.

James sat with the collar of his shirt flipped up to hide the black-and-blue line that stretched across the side of his neck from the tree branch. He knew the collar would not escape his father's notice. His brother sat across from him; both had been

sitting quietly, eating egg noodles with baked beans and on-
ions. Kevin would be entering college after the summer, having
just graduated from T. Walter High.

Ivan searched his sons' faces for a sign of sympathy. He
noticed James's collar. "The hell are you wearing your shirt
like a greaser from the '50s for?"

His tone made James shrink a bit, and the lie he'd fixed on
telling flew from his memory. He felt his lungs fill with hot air,
and his mouth turned dry. His brother, seizing the moment to
make fun of him, unwittingly bailed him out.

"The Michael Jackson look is bringing it back," he imi-
tated in a high-pitched voice. His father looked at Kevin, and
then back at his youngest son.

"Christ, that fruit on the TV? You're imitating him?"

"No," James said before he realized he was undermining
his own escape.

"If you're going to wear your collar up, wear it like James
Dean, not like some fruity little black on the television." He
reached over and grabbed James's collar. James could smell the
whiskey on his breath, and felt his father's drunken momentum lean into his neck. A dull pain rushed through him. A faint
whimper escaped. His father narrowed his eyes and pulled the
collar away, exposing the dark bruise.

"Oh man! Bruiser," Kevin laughed.

"What the hell happened to you?" Ivan asked.

James looked at his brother, and then back down at his
plate. "Dallas got us into a fight. We tried to run, but we got
cornered. It was no big deal, this kid just hit me with a stick."

His father stayed silent for a moment, considering his son's
neck through one open eye. "I bet it feels as bad as it looks."

James glanced quickly at his father, and saw that he wore
a slight grin. He smiled back. "It hurts like hell."

"*It hurts like hell,* he says," chuckled Ivan. "I bet it does. Ha ha. That's a good boy." He grabbed his son by the shoulders, shaking him around. James felt the pain scorch through his body, but he dared not cry out. "Tell me, did you give it right back as good as you got?"

Kevin sat up, seizing the opportunity. "Are you kidding? James is too sensitive for that."

Ivan waved him off. "No, no . . . there's a little bit of rage in this skinny body. Christ, that bruise is bigger than your whole head." He started to laugh again.

Janet, meanwhile, had gotten up from the couch when she heard Ivan's laughter. She reached the kitchen doorway and gasped. "What happened to you?"

Ivan immediately turned away as if he'd been caught doing something he shouldn't. Soon enough he composed himself. "It appears that our baby son went three rounds with an armed gorilla, Janet."

"Shut up, Ivan," she snapped, "you're drunk." She turned to her son. "And you've been fighting. What have I told you about fighting? I thought you were with Dallas—wasn't he there?"

Ivan's eyes came alive. "Oh-ho, he was there all right, and it was him who caused the whole thing. The baby in the manger himself."

"Shut up, Ivan. Who did you fight with?"

"Me and Dallas and Felix, with these kids down the block," James said softly.

"He who lives by the sword, shall—" his father started.

"Why were you fighting?" his mother interrupted.

James looked back and forth at his parents. "They chased us through the woods," he answered.

"Love thy neighbor and all that," his father said.

"What were they chasing you for?" Janet asked. She moved toward him and turned his head to the side so she could inspect the bruise. She tried to run her fingers across it, but James knocked her hand away.

"We stole their wood and tools. They were building a fort."

"No, son." His father seemed to sober, his tone funereal. He reached over and grabbed his son's arm. "You never steal. There's plenty of wood and tools right here in your own backyard, no need to go and monkhouse with someone else's things. You should never steal. It's a chicken-shit thing to do."

"Ivan, shut up," Janet said, turning to her son. "You fight again, and you'll be grounded for the rest of the summer. Go to your room."

"But about the stealing, son—"

"Ivan, go somewhere. I don't care where, but go somewhere."

"All right, I won't get involved," Ivan replied, holding both palms out in submission.

James rose from the table and left. He disappeared down the stairs to his bedroom, a small space in the back corner of their semifinished basement. The walls were lined with a cold wooden paneling, painted blue for James, after it was originally pink when Janet used it as an arts-and-crafts room—a hobby she quickly abandoned when it didn't end up bringing in any extra money. The floors were made of a rough wood, painted a cool gray, with an area rug circling the center. His bed was pushed against the far wall, while a shelf hung just feet above it, displaying his small collection of books. A tome of fairy tales he hadn't read in a while. A 1982 almanac. A book about whales his brother had bought him three years ago. The spines were lined up, but tilted like dominoes, and James had used one of his dad's old cowboy boots as a bookend. Across from the bed stood his dresser and a small mirror hung on the wall above it. A dead plant sat in the opposite corner, a gift his mother had bought to "liven up the room," though James never remembered to water it. The thermometer mounted on the wall above the plant was broken, and in the winter, James had to manually connect the two wires for the heater along the baseboards to kick on. Often his father came down to do it, and nearly every time, he'd vow to have it fixed. "But for now," Ivan would say, "this'll take the chill from your little bones," while James clutched his quilt.

James didn't protest his banishment because that was precisely where he wanted to be, especially at night, after his father had had his fill of whiskey and his mother was empty of patience. Besides, with his neck throbbing, and the pain reaching up into his ears where he could feel his pulse, all he wanted was to lie down and close his eyes. He emptied his pockets and placed the little wire man Dallas had made for him on his dresser. Then he climbed into bed and softly nuzzled under the sheet he used as a blanket in the summertime.

He stared up at the ceiling and wondered what fate the other two were suffering. No doubt, Dallas hadn't told his father, because he would never hear the end of it. Maybe he would tell his mother. Felix's parents wouldn't care, so long as he didn't do anything that could get them sued. His father Simon would be concerned with who'd won—a competitive streak ran through him that often took hold of his senses, like the time the neighbors threw a block party and he'd joined in the three-legged race with Felix. To win, he'd dragged Felix crying down River Drive, while the boy twisted his body to soften the scrapes from the asphalt.

James wanted to avoid another fight, at least until September, for if there was anything he feared, it was the threat of losing the freedom of summer.

He began to think about his brother's comments, which seemed to increase the throbbing in his neck. I can fight all right, he thought to himself. But what did he mean by sensitive? I fought two kids today. Two kids, and I knocked over that little Brock kid. What was I supposed to do? He thought about this for a moment. He was confused. What am I supposed to do?

James heard two stiff knocks on his door, and he sat up and peered into the darkness. Switching on the light, he remained silent, listening. Then he heard his father's mumbling voice.

"Son. Open the door, son."

James wanted to pretend he was asleep, but he knew his father would persist. He always called him "son" when he wanted to complain. Reluctantly, James crossed the floor and opened the door. The light fell on his father's figure, swaying in the doorway. Ivan squinted, made blurry eye contact, nodded, and pushed his way into the room. He was carrying a small glass, and a clear sandwich baggy with white pills. Two spoons were lodged in his right hand. He crossed the room and sat down on the edge of the bed. James sat beside him and stared at him with curiosity. Ivan looked at James for a passing moment, before he nodded and burped as he spoke.

"Good that you're okay, son." He reached into the inside pocket of a nylon jacket he had all but inherited from Kevin and pulled out a blue bag. He broke whatever was inside it, and massaged the bag until it grew ice cold in his hands. "Whereabouts did they chase you?" he asked as he reached over and placed the cold compress on James's neck. The boy winced from both the pain and the cold, and then took over holding the compress.

"Back close to the Estates."

"Ah, there's tons of trails near those Estates. I used to take you on the horse through there."

James was already nodding. "I know, we ran down the trail when we started getting chased."

"It's a good length, that trail. The Indians used to use it for trade and travel. Back when I first bought this place, James, there were woods as far as the eye could see, and the stream opened up into the river, and we used to get the horse to pull firewood back from deep in the woods. All those fires we used to have . . ."

James nodded. He'd heard these stories. "Well, it's all houses now. We ran smack into a fence."

Ivan shook his head. Emptied two white pills onto one of the spoons and placed the second spoon over it. Crushing the white pills into a powder, he continued to shake his head.

"That's a real shame. Now when I bought this place, there were no houses back there at all. That's a real shame, to put a fence up like that." He emptied the white powder he'd made into the glass and reached into his other inside pocket to pull out a small pint bottle of whiskey. He poured some whiskey into the glass and stirred the drink with one of the spoons. "I don't understand it, myself. Why would you buy a nice piece of wooded property and then fence it all in? They could have owned horses, they could build a nice little boat house at the bottom of the hill to put canoes in, they could have cut a foot trail down to the water. What the hell's the sense in building a big fence right down the hill? Here, I want you to drink this." His father handed him the whiskey glass. James stared at it, then back up at him.

"That's alcohol," he said, stunned.

His father grinned. "It's got a couple aspirin in it too. It's good for these type of things. You'll feel better in the morning."

"Mom says don't drink alcohol," James muttered.

"Your mother says I'm a drunk, you're a drunk, everybody's drunk. I think she's drunk. Here, take this, it won't kill you."

James held the glass and peered into it. It looked a bit like iced tea, until he raised it to his nose and took a whiff. His body reacted with a chill that sent his small frame wriggling. His father laughed.

"Come on, now, get a good swig."

James raised the glass to his lips and started to drink.

"Good job, make sure you get the last of it, or you'll miss the aspirin. Atta boy."

James finished; chills ran down his spine, and he retched a couple dry heaves. He coughed, and cleared his throat.

"Good for congestion too," his father added.

The two of them sat for a while; Ivan told his son the aspirin and whiskey would help put him to sleep and take some of the throb out of his bruise. James could tell his father was still bothered by the fence, but now he was on the subject of Mr. Darwin.

"He goes about town with his Christian stuff, and that's all well and good, but . . . it's not what you need to know. It's not good for kids to hear about when they're so young. All that duty and all that heaven and hell. Time enough for counting when the dealing's done, that's what I say."

James stared blankly at his father, who by this time was rambling as if he were alone in a room somewhere, laughing at his own jokes. Then his face turned serious and brooding. "One day . . . one day he's going to push too far with me, that priest of theirs."

James knew he was speaking of Minister Roberts, the Darwins' spiritual counsel at their church. Every time his father would see the minister pulling into the Darwins' driveway, or ministering door-to-door on River Drive, he'd come barging into the house howling about it. James never understood why his father hated him so, but it was well known that this was the case.

Ivan's face brightened up again, as a new memory surfaced. "Did I ever tell you the story about what my father . . . your grandfather did to a priest a long time ago?"

James shook his head. This was a new story, one he'd never heard. He sat up, but his father reconsidered.

"Maybe we'll wait for another time," he said, slapping his son on the knee and rising to his feet. "If I speak too badly about religion and all that, you know who'll have my head in a jar somewhere?" He pointed his index finger to the ceiling.

"God?" James asked.

Ivan's face went sour. "God? Hell no, your mother." He took back the whiskey glass and swept away all evidence that he'd been there. "God," he repeated. "I'll take my chances with God."

After Ivan checked to make sure he had everything with him, after he told James to keep the cold press on his neck as long as he could, after he asked his son not to mention the whiskey to his mother because it was just better for both of them, just as unexpectedly as he had arrived, Ivan backed out of the room and closed the door, leaving James dozing off from the aspirin and whiskey. The raindrops hitting the window pane tapped a light rhythm, and sent James reeling off into oblivion.

CHAPTER SEVEN

NO MATTER WHAT MEDIUM David Westwood worked in, paint, pastel, charcoal, or pencil, he wanted to see the world in contours. The shape of an object, and its relation to other objects, was the most important aspect of reinterpreting reality. The way he saw it, humans were too self-absorbed to pay attention to the shadows and colors of a thing. Humans make out the shape of an object, and will only pay more attention if it moves awkwardly, or threatens to take their lives. A tiger is a collection of six cylinders with an oblong shape at the head, until, of course, it's bounding across the jungle, growling toward an unsuspecting village full of dancing little children. Then the tiger is ivory teeth, and fire orange—legs roped with muscle—and the time is late afternoon, as the sun casts a deep shadow across the scene, and "eyewitnesses" are able to describe every blade of grass. David Westwood believed this in his heart. He wanted his own work to bring it right to everybody's stupid little attention.

Across town, on the western side of Turnbull Road, David sat in the garage he had converted into a studio, and worked away at his latest still life. He propped up a cow skull, a tea bag, three jars of spaghetti sauce, a can of Campbell's Soup, and wrapped them in the American flag he'd taken down from his front yard. His father had displayed the flag with the rest of his neighbors in a spontaneous, communal spark of patriotism after what had happened three months earlier at the embassy in Beirut. It was the spirit of the times, the neighbors said. He'd had numerous arguments with his father over taking the flag down until he finally did it himself, while his father was pulling a double shift as a security guard at a King Kullen in a rich town further east. If worse came to worst, he thought, he could always sidestep a battle by telling his father that he needed the flag for a still life. His father wouldn't be any more impressed. He'd probably scan his eyes over the canvas, breathing through his mouth. Not getting it. But if the flag served some purpose, he'd most likely acquiesce.

Half his heart was in his work, but the other half was tormenting his mind over the fact that he had just called Julia and she hadn't answered. Was she practicing her violin? Was she out with some other boy? Who knew what she was doing. What brainless crap she was being talked into by her brainless friend Krystal. He took a thick charcoal stick and slid it across the page, lining the outer shape of the cow's skull. He didn't lift the charcoal from the page, but dragged it down to catch the contour of the spaghetti jars. Usually, when he drew, he would tap into a trance, as if he were hypnotized. He'd lock into the still life, running his fingers across the page, eyes fixed to the object, as if his hands were just physical manifestations of what he saw. He was left-handed, and used this advantage to smear his palm across the lines, to follow every curve his eyes followed, and blend it naturally into the paper. When he came out of the trance, he would be able to look down at the outside of his left hand and see the dark charcoal covering his flesh from the tip of his pinky down to his bony palm. It was the sign of a hard day's work.

But today, every time he began to fall into a rhythm, his

mind would snap back to Julia on the other side of town. The thought made his lines bolder. The charcoal sticks in his hand would break and roll to the floor. David felt a kind of sadness that had no beginning and no end. He felt a pain in the back of his eyes. His chest was heavy, and he didn't know exactly why. All the world was in order, as far as he knew.

Julia was likely at her violin, unable to hear the phone. Chin up to receive the wooden curve at the nape of her neck. Other wannabe artists at T. Walter High were probably running the streets, eating fast food, getting stoned with their friends. Not home creating more brilliant work than he was, which is what he feared the most. His mother was home from her work waiting tables at Windmills Diner. His father was out, probably sitting in his rent-a-cop car watching out for vandals at King Kullen. Despite these reassurances to himself that all was in order, there was still something deep down that scratched at his mind like a cat begging to be let in. The focus he had longed for was lost in this nagging mist of fear and sadness. He had taken his dinner out of the oven and brought it into his studio to eat. He had closed the door to keep the dog out. He had taken out the garbage, handed his mother her glasses, and told her to leave him alone for the rest of the night. All he'd wanted was to be left alone, and now he was. He could hear his ears ringing. He stood up, put the charcoal stick down, opened the garage door, and disappeared into the warm, wet Turnbull night.

David didn't know what he was going to say or do when he got to Julia's house, but he knew he was heading there. The rain was getting heavier with every step he took up Turnbull Road. Julia's house was to the north, a good mile after Nino's Deli. The rain was falling in fat, round, July drops, slowly at first, until the wind picked up, and David could hear it hitting the street hard. He hadn't thought to grab a jacket for his walk. He was wearing jeans and a light T-shirt, which was covered in charcoal dust, paint, and glue. The rain had made the charcoal run, like mascara, down the front of his shirt until it resembled the face of an old woman awash in tears.

By the time he'd reached Nino's Deli, he could look up at the streetlights and see the rain pouring in swirled sheets, twisted by the wind. Blown across the sidewalk. It pushed against his body. It was warm out, but he was soaked through and shivering. His clothes sagged heavily at his feet, yet he plodded along, bending his face to the wind, and ducking from cars packed with teenagers riding the shoulder, hoping to soak him with puddles. David endured this torment. He dared not reach back and give any of them the finger. They would surely slam on the brakes and make him eat that finger.

The closer David got to Julia's house, the more his heart raced. He became more hopeful with every stride that she would be home: that her parents would be out somewhere. He kept his mind focused on her face. The face she'd often give him at school, at the end of the hallway, when she hadn't seen him all day. Her eyes would come to life. He remembered how quickly he had fallen for her because of them. In fact, it was Julia and those splendid eyes that caused him to believe what he did about art. Before he had met her, he was just like the rest, obsessed with appearances. In May she emerged from a gaggle of cheerleaders in the hallway and fixed her eyes on his. They were locked. They stared at each other until they both disappeared from view, in the thick people-stream of backpacks and laughter. Before that day, David only saw the nameless faces of his classmates—ugly scowls, smug grins, judgmental eyes. But when Julia's eyes captured him, the rest fell away into blurry shapes, moving about in the hallways, stepping across his path. That moment changed his focus. Every time he dared to imagine himself famous, standing in the midst of reporters and in snapshots at the entrance to his splendid new show, he imagined himself giving credit to Julia, who'd be leaning on a wall off to the side, demurely smiling and sipping from her wineglass. Turning away from Warhol's offers to videotape her. Julia was in all of his daydreams.

But it never satisfied the urge; he had to see her in the flesh. And it never soothed the worry inside him when she played her little games, and vanished for days at a time without a phone call.

He could hear the water slush inside his shoes as he rounded the corner and turned left onto Adam Street, where Julia lived. He imagined her face once again, the surprised look she'd give him when she opened the door. It was late, but he knew she wouldn't mind.

His chest throbbed when he got to her dirt driveway and noticed there were no cars parked outside the house, though the living room lights glowed yellow through the drawn curtains. He decided to go around back, where the washer and dryer were squeezed into a small room with a concrete floor. He knocked loudly and pressed his ear to the door. Moments later he heard footfalls, and the back door was pulled open. The washroom light flooded David's eyes, and he shielded them for a moment. Julia was in her pajamas, peering out in disbelief. She stood squarely in the doorway.

"My God, David, what are you doing?"

He pushed his wet hair away from his face. "I had to see you. Why haven't you called me?"

Julia craned her neck to look outside, glancing up at the sky. "It's pouring, David. You're soaked." She pulled him into the house, just far enough to shelter him from the rain. "You didn't take an umbrella?"

David wrapped his trembling hands around her waist. She pulled away slightly. He noticed. "The umbrella was not originally intended for rain," he said. "It was invented for shade from the Egyptian sun."

"Why did you come out here? What's the matter?" Julia reached behind her and grabbed a towel, handing it to him. He paused as he took it, as though awaiting a response from her about the umbrella. Who else in school would ever think to tell her that?

"I wanted to see you," he eventually muttered. "My artwork was driving me up the wall, and . . . and I felt like such an idiot about today."

Julia cast her eyes downward. "I felt bad," she whispered to him.

David could no longer feel his knees, and he lowered his head to smell her hair. He inhaled deeply before she stepped back.

"My parents are going to be home soon," she said.

"Is that why you're not letting me in?" David's face was firm. Julia looked at the floor again. It was a nervous gesture, and David sensed it and tried to change the subject. "In many ancient Arab nations it was customary for a host to pour melted butter over a guest's head."

Julia glanced up at his hair, matted down from the rain. He looked at the towel in his hands. "I get crazy over little things," he added. "Everything to me is like a hint of some horrible thing that's about to happen."

"Nothing's going to happen."

"Right? Nothing bad's going to happen." He started to laugh a little.

"Nothing." Julia exhaled. Seemed to feel nervous again.

"I don't know what I'd do without you, Julia," David whispered. "You stuck by me through all that crap last year."

Indeed, she had been the only one who defended him, when he got the whole town into an uproar over a mural he had painted on the side of Tony's Pizzeria, just a few miles down from Nino's on Turnbull Road. Tony, the owner, had asked him to "paint something nice" for his customers, and David decided to paint paradise—American marines shaking hands with Soviet soldiers. Their weapons discarded at their feet. Russian and American children were sitting on the ground, playing. A turbaned little boy holding a lit match stretched on his tiptoes, reaching for the outer edge of the American flag. The flag was beginning to catch fire. Tony didn't seem to mind.

"It's like soon there's going to be no more countries and flags," Tony had said. "John Lennon. 'Imagine.' I dig it." David had been shocked at Tony's interpretive skills, though he didn't like the incredulous looks the guy had given him, or the way he'd asked if David could paint the shaking hands a little more accurately. The hands looked fine to David, who'd clenched his jaw and folded his arms across his chest. Tony had dropped the subject after that and walked away with a satisfied nod.

But his customers sent notices to the store, and it wasn't long before a letter appeared in the *Turnbull Times* calling the mural anti-American and demanding a boycott. What most burned in David's mind were phrases like "badly rendered," "ill-proportioned," "amateurish." For weeks he'd tried to start new projects, but those words, those words. They made his hands tremble.

Eventually Tony noticed his registers getting lighter with

each passing night, and finally he went out with a bucket of white paint to cover the mural.

The *Turnbull Times* printed letters claiming the boycott had been a success. They thanked Tony for coming to his senses. David still got dirty looks wherever he went. Even his two buddies, Matthew and Nick, kept their distance for a while. Soon enough it all blew over. The town went back to normal. Julia had gotten into some arguments with schoolmates. She called them all a bunch of conformists. They ignored her. By then, the painting had been covered over. The school halls quieted again. Except the whole school thought Julia was crazy for defending David.

Now Julia heard the neighbor's dog bark and a car door slam. Then another car door slammed. Julia whirled around in a panic.

"Oh crap, oh crap! My parents are home!" she exclaimed, nudging David out the door.

"Good, I want to meet your dad."

"Are you nuts? You can't stay here." Julia kept shoving.

"Why can't I meet him?" David protested, trying to fend off her pushing. She shoved harder, and began to panic.

"I told you, I'm not even supposed to date. If I have a guy in the house, they'll both kill me. Go!" She pressed against him once more and pulled the back door open with her free hand. David backed outside. The rain had slowed to a drizzle.

"Come on, Julia, how can we ever be free?" He leaned in to kiss her. All he got was a hand on his face, and it shoved him backward out of the house. He looked at her, startled, then heard Julia's father call out her name.

"When will I see you again?"

"I don't know, just go!" she whispered. She waved him away and closed the back door, locking it.

David stared at the door for a few moments. Then, still clutching the towel she had given him, he slipped along the side of the house, crossed over into the shadows of the trees that lined the property, and stepped out onto the shoulder of Adam Street. He looked at the soft yellow lights glowing behind Julia's front curtains. Then he scowled and turned away.

The walk home was long. David took slower steps down Turnbull Road. The rain had stopped. It had washed all the cars and the street signs. The streets glistened under the lights. Everything around him was refreshed. He stalked the mile and a half back to Lincoln Avenue recalling her words.

How did she tell me to go home? he asked himself. What was her tone? She was concerned, wasn't she? Yes, she was scared. Afraid of her father. Everything she does, he questions. He's a maniac, that father of hers. And she was only trying to protect me from him. That was sweet. That's the Julia I'm in love with. She said, *You can't stay here,* as if the police were after me. She was only worried. There was only worry in that sweet, sweet voice of hers.

He crossed the street to avoid a large puddle that had flooded the shoulder of Turnbull Road.

Still, she could have faced her father, he thought. Maybe she'd call and explain it all when he got home. Knowing her, that's what she'd do. He realized he probably wouldn't be home in time when she called, but his mother would come in and tell him that she had. They'd settle the whole thing out, he imagined. He'd tell her exactly what he thought—that her father was ruining their life. They'd laugh and agree. They'd run away from Turnbull. Return when he was a major artist doing an interview for *The Dick Cavett Show,* when they eventually came to their senses and put the show back on, like his father always railed about.

A car whizzed by and honked. David looked up.

Here I am, bastards, he thought, glaring at the fading tail lights. Come back and look at me. Here's David Westwood. Poor, crazy maniac, David Westwood. The artist who's getting out of this grimy, shitty little town. Turn the car around. Fight me if you want, I don't care. I'll bash and crush and smash and recreate this whole goddamn world. I'm going to get the best of you all . . . you sons of bitches.

He stalked past Nino's Deli, and on down to Lincoln Avenue, entertaining himself with thoughts of fame and wealth, and adoration, and the opportunity he'd eventually get to seize his enemies and ruin them. He interviewed himself, and answered his questions as if he were talking to Cavett. He jumped over puddles, and wandered around them. His hair was almost completely dry, but his clothes were still soaked. The towel hung over his shoulders and he occasionally put the end to his nose and breathed in the smell of Julia's house. He thought he detected traces of her perfume. David considered knocking on Mr. Hopkins's window. He lived across the street and was always good for small conversations about history or literature. But would he know anything about a young girl's mind? Would he be able to testify as to how it works? Was he even awake? Would he be alarmed? The questions drove David back toward his home.

He entered the house through the open garage door. He'd stopped dripping, but his clothes stuck to his body and sagged at his feet as he brushed past the easel and opened the door to the main house. His mother was watching *Nightwatch*; he could hear Charlie Rose talking about the homeless or something. He wandered down the hall and stopped at the entrance to the living room. There his mother sat. She was so engrossed in the television, she didn't look back to see him standing behind her. Her mouth was slightly open. David slid the towel off his shoulders and rubbed his hair with it balled up in his fist. The show went to a commercial.

"Anyone call for me?" he asked his mother.

She picked her head up, startled, and glanced over her shoulder. She didn't notice he was wet, and she looked back at the television. "No," she said, shaking her head.

David turned away. Back toward the other end of the hall, as if protecting his face from an explosion. He winced as though a sharp pain had sliced through his body.

CHAPTER EIGHT

JAMES'S BEDROOM WINDOW FACED EAST, so in the early morning, when the sun blazed, rising toward its noon peak, rays poured into his room more loudly than any alarm clock. He kicked the sheet off and shielded his eyes. His first thought was of his neck, and the fight he'd been in the day before. His second thought was of his father, visiting in the middle of the night. He sat up and reached for his neck. The pain was gone, though the bruise was probably still there. He stretched and felt good. Poking at his neck with an index finger, he felt nothing. He'd slept so deeply, he didn't remember any of his dreams. He glanced at the wire man that sat on his dresser. He pulled on yesterday's play clothes and headed upstairs, where he could hear the faint mumbling of his father at the breakfast table.

"I think I might like to get another horse," he heard his father say as he climbed the stairs. His mother said something inaudible. James appeared in the archway of the kitchen, and saw his father sitting before an open newspaper. His mother stood with her back turned, working at the kitchen counter. Ivan's eyes lit up.

"And in this corner," he announced, "weighing in at . . . Jesus, what are you weighing these days, Jimmy?"

James's mother turned around and told Ivan not to make

light of it. She gave Ivan a light slap on the back of the head. He smiled up at Janet, and sipped his coffee. Janet rushed to inspect her son's bruise.

"It must hurt like hell today," she said.

"No. It doesn't hurt one bit. See?" James poked the spot with his fingers. He saw his father nod to him knowingly. James turned his attention back to his mother.

"That's amazing," Janet said. "That kind of a bruise, you should be lucky to be walking around. Sit down, I'll get you some milk."

James sat across from Ivan, who was reading the sports section, one hand on his coffee mug.

"I'm going with Divine Mr. Smith," Ivan said after a long silence. He looked up from his paper at his son. James nodded. He always liked watching his father pick the winners at Belmont. He would get up every morning and make his predictions over breakfast, using a crude, mistrustful system. He believed most races were fixed and the winners were picked following some numeric pattern in which they appeared in the newspaper. Sometimes he chose on a hunch, but whenever he did that, it was always off a thirty-to-one shot. Ivan wanted to practice making predictions first, and see how he fared, before he actually bet money at the track. He always felt he had a calling for gambling, but never bet a dime.

"You think he'll win?" James asked.

"I have my reasons," Ivan said. "He's listed last here. It's a psychological thing, you know—you list a thing last and nobody pays any attention to it."

"When you see Mr. Darwin today, you apologize for that fight you were in yesterday," Janet said over her shoulder. "The last thing we need is him thinking his son's friend is a troublemaker."

Ivan slapped his coffee down on the table with a loud clap and twisted his body around. "Apologize? And what about his own son—the little darling?"

James's mother put an empty glass in front of him and reached for the refrigerator door beside him. "His son is no concern to us."

"The hell he isn't."

"Will you let me discipline my child, Ivan?"

"Fine, but I think you're crazy to give that bastard the satisfaction. What's he going to say to the man anyway? *I'm sorry your son started a fight and it nearly cost me my whole head?*"

"Ivan, go somewhere. Just go."

"I'll go somewhere eventually. But I think it's ridiculous. The missionary's son gets a free pass?" He looked back down at his paper.

"At the very least, the missionary's son is getting some instruction from his father," Janet snapped. After pouring milk into her son's glass, she sat down at the small chair beside him. The wooden chair creaked and strained under her weight. "Mr. Darwin's faith teaches that it's important to be peaceful even when someone else starts the fight."

"Don't listen to him, son," Ivan intercepted.

"It'll keep you out of a lot of trouble in life," Janet continued. "I used to be a pretty devout Christian back before you were born."

Ivan breathed a heavy sigh, then went back to reading his paper.

"Mr. Darwin says that if you live by the sword, then that's how you'll die," added James. "Like if you shoot someone, you'll get shot. Like that."

Janet nodded. "I remember once he said that if more people loved each other, we wouldn't have so much war and hatred. There's going to be a time when God takes over again and he's going to get rid of all the people who make the world such a bad place." She took James's glass after he was finished and brought it to the sink. "He says we were supposed to live forever."

"Fool's Paradise," Ivan blurted.

She looked down at him, and gave him a light smack on the head. "He happens to believe in *something*."

Ivan looked startled. "I'm talking about the horse, for Christ's sake. Fool's Paradise is going to come in eighteen-to-one."

Kevin appeared in the doorway and yawned a good morning as he poured himself a cup of coffee. James often wondered why his brother always grabbed what he wanted from the kitchen and then went back to lock himself in his room.

"Kevin, why don't you go to church?" Janet asked.

Kevin looked around at everyone in the room. "Why don't *you* go to church?" he replied.

His mother was silent, and stayed so after Kevin left. Ivan finished his paper and slapped it down on the table. He looked at Janet, who was lost in thought somewhere. Then he stared at his boy and, as if reminded of something he'd almost forgotten, shook his head.

"*Apologize*," he said, and sniffed.

CHAPTER NINE

JAMES DARTED ACROSS THE STREET to Dallas's house, leaped up the front porch, and hit the doorbell. He squinted in the early, wet sunlight as he peered across the street and watched the face of his own house. It looked peaceful from where he stood. Like all the other houses on River Drive. He heard the door open. Mr. Darwin was standing there, holding the screen door and leaning against the frame. He immediately caught sight of the bruise on James's neck and stood sternly over him.

"Come in, James. You get that thing on your neck from the fight yesterday?"

James stepped into the house, nodding and looking at the floor. He could feel Mr. Darwin shaking his head as he walked past him.

"You and Dallas have reaped what you sowed. Your violence has begot violence. Dallas is downstairs."

James couldn't get to the basement door fast enough. Mr. Darwin followed him there. "You two better behave yourselves today," he warned.

At the bottom of the stairs, James caught a glimpse of Dallas's bobbing head as he dug through a massive pile of clothes. The Darwins kept their washer and dryer in the basement, but more often than not, that was where the clothes would stay after they'd been washed. It was Dallas's morning ritual to rummage through the heap of shirts, skirts, socks, and towels to find his play clothes. He arose from the bottom of the pile holding a pair of green shorts. He wore a triumphant smile, and was startled by James standing at the bottom of the stairs.

"Jimmy, gimme a second." Dallas ducked behind the dryer and pulled on his shorts. He had no shirt on, and under the basement lights his skinny body looked like a tight wrap of bones and shadows. Dallas emerged from behind the dryer and started rooting around in the pile for a shirt.

James moved toward him. "You get in trouble last night?"

Dallas shrugged. "Sort of. Sent to my room."

James nodded silently. Dallas pulled a wrinkled shirt from the pile and stretched it over his head.

"What are we doing today?" asked James.

Dallas slammed the dryer door closed. "We're going down to the end of the block to get that wood."

"What?"

"Look at the bruise on your neck. I want that wood as payback."

"You're father will kill you. My mother'll never let me out again. Besides, they probably took it all back."

"Well, that's what we're going to find out."

"What about Felix?" James looked around, as if Felix were hiding somewhere.

"What about him? We'll stop by his house right now."

The way Dallas revealed his plan, as though it was a plan to play kickball, unnerved James. But he couldn't tell him no. All he could think of was what his mother would say if he were to come home with fresh bruises and cuts, and the possibility of another beating, if the gang they had fought decided to recruit some bigger kids from down the street. He thought there were times when Dallas was crazy. But he also knew he could not let him go alone—the first real friend he'd ever had. He was trying to think of more questions.

"How do we get past your dad?"

Dallas cocked his ear and listened for his father's footsteps. He could hear the floorboards creaking in the back corner of the basement. "We'll have to stash the wood at your place for a while before we start to build the fort. But we'll just tell my dad that we're going to Felix's house." Dallas looked down at the pile and saw the sleeve of a green shirt sticking out. He pulled it loose and threw it to James. "Here, when we get to Felix's house, put that on. You should probably wear green. Camouflage yourself a little."

James looked down at his orange T-shirt. He pulled it off, put the green one on, and then pulled the orange shirt back on to cover it. Moments later, the door at the top of the stairs opened, and light poured in. Felix scampered down the steps and stopped short in full sight of his friends. Dallas shook his head.

"Your dad just said we begot violence or something," Felix said. He looked confused.

"You just blew it for us. Why didn't you stay home?" cried Dallas.

"Just blew what?" Felix looked at James for the answer. Dallas went over to an empty folding chair that stood lonely in the center of the basement. He dropped down on it and crossed his arms.

"Dallas wants to go get the wood we took yesterday," James said.

Felix stared at Dallas, and then at James. He noticed the bruise for the first time. "Holy mackerel! Your dad do that to you?" Felix asked.

James looked surprised, and slightly hurt. "No," he said,

rubbing at the bruise and covering it with his shirt collar. Felix stepped forward for a closer look. James shoved him away and moved back. Dallas had been sitting quietly, trying to devise another plan. Abruptly, as if awakened from a trance, he unfolded his arms, slapped his knees, and stood.

"Well, we can still say we're going to your house, Felix. We hang out there for a few minutes, and then go get our stuff." Dallas nodded to the other two as if they understood his orders and planned to follow them. This was the way it was. Dallas had thought all through the night about what he'd done. He thought about their chase, about Jason Brock. He saw no reason why this little boy should have to ruin the whole plan. In some way, he saw the boy's tumble down the hill as a wasted tragedy if they didn't stick to the plan. He feared what Brock would think of him if, after telling him his fort was to be taken, he didn't make good on his promise. He was bolstered by the bruise on James's neck. This had to be done. He knew the chance was great that they would all drag themselves home with broken skulls and bleeding lips, but at least it all would have come to something. Even his father had to understand that. But when he looked at James and Felix, and their worried expressions, he felt they didn't understand.

"I don't know about this," said James, as if he had heard Dallas's thoughts.

"Those kids were crazy," added Felix, "I don't want to get my face broken."

Dallas tried to plead with them. He looked at James. The collar of his shirt had pulled away from his bruise, exposing the deep black and blue.

"When we're sitting up in our new fort, James, you're going to look at your neck and at least it'll feel like it was worth something."

James reached up and drew his hand to the crook of his neck where it met his shoulder.

They argued a little further. Felix wanted to know exactly what the plan was. James remained mostly quiet. He rubbed at the bruise every time the other two mentioned it, and he took Dallas's abandoned seat at the folding chair. Dallas was mapping it all out for Felix. James knew that sometimes Dallas didn't trust Felix. Other times the two were partners in crime, teaming up, even sometimes leaving him out. But Dallas was ranting now about how he needed both of them. He wanted James to be the lookout, so if trouble came along he could get a head start out. He told Felix that he needed him to convince his mother to come by with the car. He spoke in excited terms, waving his arms around. Like a general in the army, ordering his men. Rounding up their morale for a final push to the breach.

The boys finally agreed, and with a deep breath, James rose from his chair and began to follow the other two up the stairs. Dallas took the lead and turned around to say something when he heard the soft slapping sound of water on the basement windows. He crossed the floor, jumped onto a bucket, and looked out of the small window. Rain began to gently fall, like manna, and the drops ran down the window pane.

"Dammit," he barked under his breath.

CHAPTER TEN

WHEN DAVID WESTWOOD ROLLED OUT OF BED to answer the phone, his windows were rattling from the wind and rain. He pulled the blinds open quickly, but all he saw were blurry, foggy window panes. He let the blinds spring back into place and crossed the room. It was Matthew Milton on the line. When David heard his voice, his shoulders drooped in disappointment.

"What do you want?" he growled, carrying the phone over to his bed. He dropped down heavily.

"You coming to Darryl's party tonight?"

"It's raining outside, are you blind?"

"It's supposed to clear up before the party starts."

"I'm painting tonight," David explained.

"*I'm painting tonight*," Matthew mocked. "Come on, Darryl says he ordered an extra keg, and we're playing drunken piñata."

"Darryl Knight is a fool. His friends are fools too."

"Word on the street is, your little girlfriend's going to be there." David sat up straight. "She's coming with Krystal."

"Who told you she was going?" David asked, trying to be nonchalant.

"She called Darryl last night after she hooked up a ride with Krystal. It's like, the whole incoming senior class is going to be there. Give yourself a chance to meet some seniors, maybe the year'll go a little smoother for you."

"She called Darryl? At his house?"

"*At his house*? No, on the Bat Phone, what the hell? . . . David, she'll be there. Probably the only sophomore that'll be there, but who knows. I wouldn't be surprised if half of Turnbull shows up."

"What time?"

Matthew laughed. "Nick will pick you up. What are you doing today?" There was a long pause. "David, hello?"

David snapped out of his daze. "Yeah . . . um. Nothing."

"I'll see you, buddy."

Matthew hung up and David was alone again. It was nearly eleven thirty in the morning. He pulled some clothes on, and ran his fingers through his hair. He opened the bedroom door, walked down the hallway, and went into the garage to look at his painting. Half the American flag had come to life in its contour colors, but the other half was a vague sketch. He sat at the low stool in front of the easel and turned it sideways for a better view. Dipping his brush into the open jar of linseed oil, David fixed his eyes on the flag, but all he could think about was how Julia had called a buffoon like Darryl Knight, on the evening that he himself had braved wind and rain to stand before her and declare his love. She had kicked him out. And then, he thought, she immediately ran to the phone to call Darryl Knight.

She wasn't interested in art, or intelligence. She was interested in what Darryl Knight had to say. Meaningless concerns. What the team planned to do to beat Sagamore this year at homecoming.

It was as if she'd missed the whole point. How one track-minded those kids were, kids like Daryl, running around with erections, trying to make the world a liquid mass of sameness. How David was at least one voice shouting down the marching band sweeping through town, their stupid goosesteps—the same people who called David a traitor. A communist, and why, how, where's the reason? Fuck them, David thought, I'm not a communist, they're the communists trying to scare silence into everybody. You want real communists? Try calling Darryl Knight, and she did, that's exactly what she did, she called that communist while he had trudged home in the rain, soaking wet, half-dead from cars full of more communists trying to get a rise out of him with their honking and swerving, all so she can get right on the goddamn phone and call that traitor with the touchdown brain and yard-mark pecker, all sweat and jersey—him and his ass-slapping troupe he hangs around with like he's the king of Egypt. And what's freedom to those jerks?

David reached across his easel to grab the tube of black paint, but stopped himself. He was planning to use it on the flag. He was excited with anger. Too easy, he thought. He'd made a vow with himself to never paint when full of emotion. His work could not be happy, nor angry, nor jealous. He was interested in objects, and how they are seen. Last year, perhaps, he would have messed around with the flag, as he'd done with the Tony's Pizzeria mural, but not now.

Staring at the stripes on the flag, his mind reeled back to the beginning of last year, his freshman year. Ms. Merrick's second-period English class. She had asked everyone if they were afraid of nuclear war. He'd raised his hand, along with Hanna D'Amico, the class president. Ms. Merrick called on Hanna.

"I think nuclear war is scary, cause it only takes like one bomb, and that's it. So it's like . . . whoever presses the button first wins the war, you know? And this new guy is totally nuts. What if he presses the button before Reagan?"

The class nodded.

"What if Reagan presses the button first?" David asked. Hanna looked over at him and rolled her eyes.

The boy behind her spoke up: "Then we win the war."

"And it's all about winning and losing?" David countered. "What about their children and wives and innocent people? If a bomb drops on us it'll be terrible, but if it drops on them it'll be great?"

"Better them than us," another student chimed in.

"Yeah," another agreed, "what do you care what happens to those people, they started with us."

"Their children started with us?" said David.

"No," Hanna jumped back in, "but if their parents don't want their children to get blown up, then their parents shouldn't start with us."

"Get them before they get us!" someone shouted.

"Oh, that's great," said David. "If everybody does that, there won't be a human being left on earth."

"Don't be so melodramatic. Since when do you care about a bunch of freedom-hating Nazi communists anyway?" asked Hanna. "You know what they do to their children, don't you?"

"No, what?"

"They can't do anything. Right now, if we were over there you'd be taken out and shot to death, right, Ms. Merrick?" Hanna always had a nasty little habit of speaking her mind and then asking the teacher if she was right or not.

"Well . . ." Ms. Merrick said.

"I hear the communists got spies all over the country, and they record everything we say over here," a student in the back added.

"That is such BS propaganda," barked David, using a word he'd learned in world history the period prior.

"How do you know?" asked Hanna. "Did you see that movie *The Morning After*?"

"More propaganda."

"Yeah, they got spies all over the place, the communists. They want to make everybody like them," another student said.

"You're probably one of 'em," accused the kid sitting in front of Hanna. He made slits of his eyes and glared at David.

"Ms. Merrick, we got a communist in our class, kick him out!" another shouted.

"Get out of America, communist!" a quieter boy in the far end of the classroom yelled.

"Love it or leave it."

"Love it or leave it, yeah."

"Communists must die!"

"You're a goddamn Russian commie, Westwood!"

"All right, all right!" shouted Ms. Merrick, calming the students down. "Let's get ahold of ourselves."

David never forgot that day, because his classmates would never let him forget it. The rest of his ninth grade year, his nickname in English class became "Red," and it wasn't long before kids who weren't in his class caught on. Every so often he'd hear a voice shout, "Communist!" from across the crowded hallway. One day he went to his locker and discovered that his lock had been glued shut and the door was painted red with a yellow hammer and sickle.

After that, he came to class carrying a copy of *The Communist Manifesto*. Wore a T-shirt that read, *No Nukes*. He scrawled the words *Bash Reagan* on the cover of his binder, large enough for little Hanna D'Amico to notice and broadcast it to the rest of the class. David laughed at his new identity: the evil communist, plotting to blow them all up. But it bothered him still. To him it was all a misunderstanding. Yet he knew there was no way for him to turn back now, not after all he'd done to perpetuate the myth.

He could feel himself retreating. He first recognized it when he stopped saying hello to people he knew in the halls. Waited for them to say hello first, which they rarely did. To avoid the lunch room, he dragged a comfortable chair down to the stacks of the library and read everything he could get his hands on. Magazines, almanacs, outdated encyclopedias. Leeches and bloodletting were actual operations—how would future encyclopedias explain David's generation? Here were whole shelves of information most people forgot. It was as though David were tearing up the floorboards of the world and discovering what lay beneath. Donkeys tethered to stones to make wheat. New York City buildings held together by long rods capped on each end with an iron star. There is a city called Rome on every continent. The rule of thumb was a measure of thickness on a stick with which you were permitted to beat your wife.

Through it all, he began to read *The Communist Manifesto*, rather than just walk around posing in the hallways with it. Inside it he found ideas that thrilled him, ideas not far off from the religious sermons he sometimes received from a schoolmate of his who was also an outcast, and told him about the great lives people would lead where they'd all be living equally on a paradise earth. Food would be in abundance, and nobody would have more or less than others, and God would be the only leader. The kid always left David with tracts and scriptures to prove his point.

What the kid had said gave him his initial idea for the mural on the side of Tony's store. But David wasn't religious. He was only drawn to the kid in the way a dog wanders over to another dog, sniffing, investigating the similar "dogness" of the other. David felt somehow connected to this quiet boy— because he was also being called names, for not celebrating Christmas and for saying he would rather face jail than join the armed forces. They had an odd sort of understanding. They nodded to each other in the hallways, but never dared sit together or be seen speaking to one another for more than a few seconds. It was as if they both knew the inherent danger. It was never spoken, but they both seemed to respect the crosses they each had to bear, and neither wanted to make it any worse for the other. Then David painted the mural at Tony's. He'd painted flames on the tip of the flag. Russians shook hands and played with Americans.

One day, David's father returned from the mailbox raving in anger. "Come outside and get a good look at what you've caused!" David flew out of bed and pulled on a pair of jeans. He saw his father in the doorway, shaking a fist, telling him he had a good mind to hit him.

"I should crack you in the fucken head," were his father's exact words, which still rang in David's ears. He had stepped into the sunlight and seen the burn marks in the grass. Someone from school had burned the shape of a hammer and sickle into his front yard. His father had worked all year to get a perfectly green lawn. There was also a letter left in the mailbox:

DIE COMMIE SCUMBAG! YOU PEOPLE HAVE SUCH A PROBLEM WITH OUR FLAG, YOU SHOULD GO BACK TO THE COMMUNIST COUNTRY YOU CAME FROM. RED, COMMIE,

COWARD SONS OF BITCHES. I HOPE YOU ARE THE FIRST ONE TO GET THE OVEN WHEN THOSE COMMUNIST FUCKS INVADE US. I HAVE TWO WORDS: GET OUT. GET OUT OF OUR COMMUNITY, GET OUT OF OUR STATE, GET OUT OF OUR COUNTRY AND GO LIVE WITH THE REDS IN RUSSIA. I HOPE YOU DIE, YOU PINKO, COMMIE FUCK. DIE DIE DIE DIE DIE!

His father told him he had only one thing to say, and there was no discussion. He told David to act normal or get out of the house. When David tried to argue, his father slammed the door behind him. From then on, David kept all his literature in his vandalized locker, which he'd also learned to admire, until one day even that was gone. Over the weekend janitors had taken a fresh coat of green spray paint and covered the door. But the paint was a different tone, and the red beneath made the locker stand out from the others, so the symbolism remained. He was different, and his locker was different, and all the students knew it, and that was fine with him. At the very least, he didn't have to read the number to make sure he was at the right one. He could see it clearly from down the hall.

His father never heard another word about it, and all of David's thoughts were kept hidden, in his sketchbook and on his canvas. Painting was a way of making his thoughts known, though he cast those thoughts safely over his father's head.

Therefore, painting the flag black would be too obvious. Even his dad, an uneducated graduate of T. Walter High, would recognize it. He had to be smarter, more subtle. That was the way *they* had made it between him and his father. Secretly, and in his sketchbook, he confessed that he'd begun to hate people. He wanted to see them suffer.

* * *

David worked at his canvas while his thoughts wandered from Julia, to last year, to the party. He was growing nervous. He kept thinking about the coming September, as if it were a prison sentence he couldn't escape. David was never fond of light brush strokes, so at least the torment didn't detract from his style as he jabbed and smeared his brush down the canvas.

He worked in relative quiet for an hour or so, blocking out the rainfall that battered his door. His father had returned home sometime during the night, and was no doubt forced to park his car out in the driveway because of David's still life and easel. David could imagine him already complaining about it. Could hear him banging about in the kitchen, fixing his lunch. David knew he would be pacing around all day until the rain stopped, because he was an anxious person, always busy "doing." Another characteristic David didn't have, to his father's lasting disappointment. He heard heavy footfalls, and a shard of shadow appeared under the door leading into the house. The door opened, and his father stood there with a sandwich in his hand. He glanced around the garage, as if checking to make sure his son was alone. David sat there, almost dumbfounded.

"Time you get up this morning?" his father asked.

"I don't know. What time did you get up?"

"I didn't get home till almost five. I was out earning a living so I can put a roof over your head." The two remained silent for a brief moment. "Did you eat lunch yet?"

David shook his head.

His father nodded, and looked around the garage again. "There's cold cuts in the kitchen if you want."

David pretended to work on his canvas, but was really just toying with it, slapping at it with phantom strokes and then looking back at his father. He was inspecting David's work. For the first time, David grew self-conscious in front of his father. His eyes wandered over to the still life, and back to the canvas. David could sense he was going to make a comment about it, and they both silently recognized it to the point that his father smirked slightly before he spoke.

"That's just the outside of it, right? You just got the shapes down for now?"

"Yeah," David answered, and cleared his throat.

His father nodded, as if he was proud of himself for knowing something about art. "Got to fix the shape of that soup can, no? It's bigger than the skull. Paint in all the shadows and stuff?"

"I guess, sort of."

Again his father nodded, and seemed to be making his retreat. He began to close the door as he backed into the house. "Okay, good chat," he said. Just as he was about to close the door, he took one last glance at the still life, and noticed the American flag. "That goes back up when you're done with it."

David turned to look at what he was talking about, though he knew damn well. He rolled his eyes. "Whatever. What for?"

"What do you mean, *what for?*" his father barked.

"It's ugly and stupid looking," David said. "We look like all the rest of the idiots around here with that thing hanging off the house."

"Hey, some of the people around here ain't so bad. What's wrong with Hopkins over there?" His father pointed. "Guy talks to you all the time. Used to let you swim in his pool. Besides, that ugly, stupid-looking thing keeps my grass nice and green all through the summer."

David frowned at the obvious dig. "It's not my fault there's ignorant people running around."

"No, it's not. No, it's not," his father agreed. "But you can help keep 'em away from my grass, that's all I need to worry about. And you can stop antagonizing them."

"Why do you want to hang that thing outside, when you don't even care about what it represents?"

"David, there's no discussion. That flag goes back up on the house when you're done with it."

David's father closed the door, as if to flee from the argument, and David returned to his canvas, fuming. There was never a discussion. With anyone, David thought.

CHAPTER ELEVEN

BITTER, THIRSTING IVAN ILLWORTH poured his fifth drink of the day, holding it up in the weak light that bled through the dusty window of his horse barn. The mix of heat and rain outside hung fog on them the color of old curtains. After Clover died, Ivan hadn't the heart to completely revamp the barn into something more useful. Instead he'd built himself a small work bench with leftover planks from the split-rail fence, and used the horse's old grain barrel for the legs. It came up to Ivan's chest, and was just big enough for his newspaper, an old-fashioned vise he'd used to fix his horse's shoes, and his daily bottle of whiskey. He inspected the glass for a moment, and poured half of it into his mouth. He grimaced; it was not expensive whiskey, his desire having long ago outlasted his budget. Ivan was just a step above drinking Wild Irish Rose, claiming only hobos and welfare cases drank that rotgut.

He was still seething over his wife's demand for James to apologize to that preacher. As if he'd done something wrong to him personally! As if it were *his* son who came home with a welt the size of Texas on his neck. It pained Ivan to think of his boy, that frail skinny kid, withering under some preacher's hellfire stare. To him, the world had been a simpler place before people came around telling others how to live.

Ivan took another sip of whiskey. He was delighted, glad

that it was never his calling to go save souls, that he was born a horse man—that he had, all his life, left everybody alone and hardly ever questioned another man's motives. All that nonsense Janet was spewing in the kitchen was pure pie-in-the-sky. He was happy to not waste time hoping for a future that might or might not happen. He was content to just take his life as a series of moments. Bold laughter. A little meanness sometimes. He knew that the good and peaceable, the noble and mighty Michael Darwin, had it all wrong, and Ivan glowed in the idea that the man was over there forever wasting his time; him and that pale, medieval wife of his. But he didn't understand why his own wife had bought into it so heavily. Unless of course she wanted to know Michael in the biblical sense.

Bathsheba, he thought.

He opened his daily newspaper and read about some group's attempt to preserve a plot of land further east, a plot that was once a sacred Indian burial ground and now threatened to become a stretch of condominiums. He scoffed. Not that it was being fought over, or that the burial site was bound to lose to the developers, but at a deeper notion—that the debate should even have to take place. He was horrified at the way the world could so easily pave over its past. Park their cars atop sacred bones. The idea of it made him wonder if it wouldn't be such a bad thing to bury everything he loved in the backyard, where the family plot could never be disturbed. He took another swill of whiskey and read on.

It was not long before his thoughts returned to the preacher, and how he was probably at that very moment frightening his son with doom and damnation, and pinning the whole thing on his little shoulders.

Janet Illworth looked out the kitchen window and saw the

soft yellow glow of light from Ivan's barn. As long as he was out there it was peaceful. It was a gray day. So dark. She was heating water for tea, alone in the house. Kevin was off doing whatever Kevin did.

She sat down on her small kitchen chair. Ivan had woken her up early in the morning, blathering like an old man. She had turned on her side, but he sat at the edge of the bed and went on and on about the senselessness of people who buy houses and build fences around them, or something. She had tried to shut him out so she could fall back asleep, but his voice had lost its soothing quality years ago, and it grated on her—making it nearly impossible to block out.

He was talking about Indian trails, and although she'd told him to shut up and go to sleep, he went right on talking. He was constantly bothered by something, so much so that she now hardly paid attention. She knew when it was coming too, because he had that annoying preface. *Not for nothing*, he would always say, before he assailed her ears with all the things in the world that vexed him.

Janet yawned in the still afternoon, as the tea kettle began to rumble on the stove. She remembered when his temper was a blessing. That was many years ago, when they first met, in fact.

She was at a high school party, the last of her senior year. Buddy Hawkins was a football player and scholar, a business major heading off to Yale in the fall. Buddy talked to everybody, including teachers, so it was no surprise to young Janet Ulrich that standing by the makeshift bar, mixing a drink, was Mr. Stewart, her history teacher. Buddy must have stopped by his classroom to announce the party to the students, and invited him as well.

Mr. Stewart was a man who wandered the hallways looking down at his shoes, and rarely spoke when he wasn't teaching about history. Janet thought he was a bit strange, until someone had explained to her that Mr. Stewart had gotten very close to Lionel Lambert, one of his graduating seniors, the year before. They were nearly best friends by the time Lambert graduated in June of '64 and joined the army. Seven months after graduation Lionel Lambert was dead. Killed in action in some hotel barracks in a place called Qui Nho'n. It was north of Saigon, that's all they knew, for who could possibly make heads or tails of all those foreign places? His body had been incinerated, they'd heard. His boots and dog tags, all that was left of him, were shipped home. There was a quiet funeral for him, but Mr. Stewart had stayed away. He went out walking— to the Sands Point Bridge at the southern tip of Turnbull. He'd climbed to the edge of the bridge and stared down at the death plunge below, until a car full of his students happened to be out joyriding and noticed him. They stopped and asked him what he was doing, but he simply hopped down and walked away without saying a word.

Perhaps it was Lambert's death that fortified Mr. Stewart's resolve to know his students better. Perhaps it was because he realized their time could be cut short. Perhaps that was the reason he'd been standing there, alone at the liquor cabinet in Buddy's house, watching his students smoke and curse and make plans for the coming summer. Janet didn't exactly know why she had approached him. She vaguely remembered being drawn to his broken spirit, the way one would approach a person lying in the street.

Mr. Stewart spoke for hours with pudgy little Janet Ulrich, supplying her with all the details of his life. Never married. An only child. He loved baseball, and his knowledge of history made him very much afraid that America was repeating it. Meanwhile, every time Janet retreated to mix another drink, the older class of '63 graduate, Ivan Illworth, would ask her what her pretty name was. He shouted many times over the music, before Janet finally told him. He nodded as if he was right about her name being pretty, and went back to quietly drinking his beer. Janet was immediately intrigued by his behavior. Drunk, yet oddly in control of himself. She'd heard stories about him, but there wasn't a soul who passed through high school that didn't have stories—half-baked in the bleachers at football games, or inside the stalls of the girls' bathroom. She thought about Ivan every time she re-joined Mr. Stewart in the hall. He had urged her to escape with him there, where they could get away from the loud music and talk.

Leaning against the wall beside a hanging picture frame, Mr. Stewart started to reminisce about his youth, all the cruel and painful tricks.

"I was always scared," he said. "Always playing by the rules. Ah, yes, you know about playing by the rules, you're in high school, but you may shed all that when you graduate, and I hope you do. There's not enough time in life to stay so damned civil all the time. Especially now, for your generation. No, life expectancy is very short, very short."

His eyes were glazed in tears, like porcelain. All the while Janet Ulrich stood silent, as if he could be having this conversation with or without her. But she knew he was keenly aware of her, for after every new thought, and every pause, he'd look at her, red-eyed, and focus on her face with a familiar sort of prom-night stare. Janet straightened her clothes, and offered to refill his glass, anything to get away from him.

In the next room, tall, drunk, and wide-grinning Ivan Illworth watched her. He shook his head.

"What?" she asked, folding her arms across her chest as if she knew he was undressing her.

"I know you," he said, smiling. "You're scared of me, aren't you?"

She didn't deny it, but stood dumbly, allowing him to take another step, so he loomed over her. He shoved a hand toward her and introduced himself, shaking her trembling fingers.

Suddenly Mr. Stewart emerged from the hall. He squeezed between them and grabbed Janet's arm. "Come with me," he said, pulling on her. "I know what you're thinking, but don't. Just come with me."

Janet's mouth dropped open. She looked at Ivan, who was staring at Mr. Stewart as if he'd been insulted. Janet pulled her arm back.

"No, Mr. Stewart," she said. He reached for her arm again, but she snatched it away.

"Come home with me tonight, before it's all over," he urged.

"Hey, the girl said no. I think you ought to get lost!" barked Ivan, removing his hand from his back pocket. Mr. Stewart didn't look at him, a fact that Ivan certainly noticed.

"Don't go home with this loser," said Mr. Stewart, merely pointing in Ivan's direction. "Don't make yourself a whore by going home with him. Come . . . come with me now. Escape!" he exclaimed, and reached once more for Janet's arm.

Ivan saw his opportunity. He reeled back his massive left fist and let fly. The punch echoed sharply through the music, as if a balloon had popped, and Mr. Stewart fell hard against the wall behind him. Ivan grabbed Janet's arm and pulled her away, into the night.

She was stunned, and remained that way for days—oddly aroused, too, by the lingering sensation of Ivan's powerful hand gripping hers. As though gravity itself couldn't pull her down. And when she recovered from all the whispers and rumors and half-truths that were told in the days that followed, she found she had herself a boyfriend.

But years later, what she would remember most was poor Lionel Lambert, and the sound of that punch, and Mr. Stewart's eyes. The tea kettle screaming in the gray kitchen was the only thing that stopped her from sobbing.

As she took the kettle off the range, she heard the back door pop open and then, moments later, slam closed. She shut her eyes and drew a deep breath. Her husband's voice boomed behind her.

"Not for nothing, but it should be *him* . . . that rat bastard, who should be apologizing to *us*."

C HAPTER TWELVE

BENEATH THE SOFFIT David could see the rain falling, absent its usual rhythm. Who thinks like this? David wondered. But he couldn't deny his senses. One could smell dryness blowing in—one could see the leaves rising to look upward like a boxer released from the corner, and one could notice in the puddles how the rings were able to spread farther apart before another falling drop destroyed them—how the puddles no longer rattled, electrified by raindrops.

But he still remained tightly pressed against the house, beneath the soffit and the rusted gutter punched with decayed holes, dripping. He gripped the flag he had stashed beneath his shirt and pulled it out to arrange it quickly. If the weather had permitted, he might have succumbed to his rebellious heart and hung the flag upside down to set his father off. Instead he clipped the top left corner to the top hook on the flagpole and secured the bottom with a tight pull of the string. He wrapped the excess tie around a cleat fastened to the side of the house.

Across the street a mailbox squeaked closed. David peered over his shoulder and saw Mr. Hopkins thumbing through his mail. To David, his body looked as though he'd surrendered to the brutality of everything—a gust of wind, a rainstorm, cracked sidewalks. But as he watched Mr. Hopkins flip defiantly through the letters, he felt something like hope swell inside him. Old age had melted off the man's armor. But he was somehow still armed.

He liked the old man, as much as he didn't want to cede the point to his father. To David, Hopkins lived the encyclopedias he himself read in the library. He knew even now that the moment Mr. Hopkins saw him he'd quiz him on a fact, or invite him over to watch a show his grandson had taped for him on the Phoenicians, or the history of denim. David liked that he could still sometimes surprise the old man—liked that there was an infinite number of facts to know, and nobody could live long enough to know everything.

David cleared his throat, though there was nothing in it, and it was enough to grab Mr. Hopkins's attention. He turned and held up a trembling yellow hand in the diminished light. David waved back.

"The largest organ on the human body is the skin," Mr. Hopkins called across the street.

"Everyone knows that," David answered. The old man was slipping.

"Unfortunately it's not always the thickest," Mr. Hopkins added. "Come over here; I have something I want to show you."

"I got to get ready for this thing I'm going to," David said, jerking a thumb toward his house.

"It will haunt you, when you get to my age, the things you refused to witness." He was already turning back toward his house, waving David over, knowing he'd come.

Mr. Hopkins had a basement he'd turned into a smoking lounge. The sweet smell of pipe smoke seemed to coat the wooden paneling. Standing alone on a small table stood a statue of Buddha's head with an elongated left ear that served ginger ale out of the pierced lobe. Duck decoys lined a shelf on the far end of the room. A deck of cards collected dust on the nightstand beside Mr. Hopkins's orange recliner. There was a bar fully stocked just behind the recliner and Mr. Hopkins led David to it.

He opened a drawer and pulled out a cigar box. Inside the box was a piece of red cloth, and when Mr. Hopkins unfolded it, David saw a round, shiny piece of metal—some type of coin he couldn't quite identify.

"My son won this at some auction. He knew I'd fall in love with it."

"What is it?" David asked, as Mr. Hopkins placed it into his palm.

"This is a silver half-dollar piece from 1861."

David took the coin delicately between his thumb and forefinger and turned it over. A woman draped in a toga sat on a rock holding a flag and a shield that read, *Liberty*. She was looking over her shoulder. She seemed afraid. David felt like he knew her.

"A rare opportunity to do what you're doing," Mr. Hopkins said. "To think that may have been used to pay a shoeshine boy working on the boots of Abraham Lincoln."

"The month of February 1865 was the only month in recorded history not to have a full moon," David said, raising the coin to his eyes to inspect what he might have missed. The edges were serrated by age. The center, nicked with small divots. Perhaps the bite marks of distrust.

"Lincoln's not impressive enough for you?" Mr. Hopkins asked, grinning.

David took his eyes off the coin and made a face. "I'm more interested in the shoeshine boy," he said, dropping the coin into the red cloth Mr. Hopkins was holding out.

"A rotting piece of nonhistory, the boy." Mr. Hopkins patted a porcelain statue of a foot waiter donned in a red overcoat, smiling. David felt a chill.

"While I have you here, would you mind moving this chair over to that corner?"

And now the true purpose of calling me over is revealed, thought David. He marveled at Mr. Hopkins's knack for getting people to do things he needed done. David smiled to himself and gripped the backrest firmly, lifting it a foot off the ground.

"You know, it didn't take long for me to get used to not being able to do these sorts of things anymore," Mr. Hopkins said as he followed David across the room.

David waddled the chair into place, and as soon as Mr. Hopkins was satisfied, David dropped it.

"What I'm saying is, when I got older, what bugged me the most, what kept me up some nights, were the things I didn't do that I regret."

"How do you regret something you didn't do?" David asked. The old man was trying to stuff a twenty-dollar bill into David's pocket, but David kept covering it with his hand.

"You'll see, David. It's funny, but on a long enough timeline, the things you didn't do haunt you more than the things you did."

"So I get to spend the first half of my life regretting the stupid things I do, and then the last half envying the stupid things I wished I'd done?"

"And happiness is a thing in the corner of your eye that moves aside every time you try to look at it."

"Not me," David said, handing Mr. Hopkins back the twenty. "I'm going to do everything I set out to do. No regrets."

"You'll need money for that." Mr. Hopkins waved the twenty in and out of the light that glared from a sconce behind him.

"Money means nothing," David mumbled.

"Say the people who never have any," Mr. Hopkins replied, and, for the final time, stuffed the twenty into David's front pocket without meeting protest. "When you make the big bucks off your art, David, you'll become aware of the things that not having money took away from you. Let's have a drink." He gestured to the Buddha-head ginger ale dispenser.

David shook his head. "That thing creeps me out. Like I'm drinking his ear wax."

"See, now I'm brokenhearted over things passed. A couple years ago you could hardly control your laughter when I poured you a drink."

David let the comment linger between them like a moment of silence for a dead friend. He looked at his shoes. Mr. Hopkins shrugged and David glanced up at him. "A fresh egg will sink in water, but a rotten one will float," he said finally.

At the front door, David thanked Mr. Hopkins for the money and glanced up at the sky, which was now tattered with holes of sunlight. Rays draped over David's house. It looked peaceful. As he walked down Mr. Hopkins's driveway, he allowed himself to wonder if the remorse he felt for banging on Julia's door would eventually turn to anger that he hadn't done something more.

C HAPTER THIRTEEN

MICHAEL DARWIN DANCED AND SKIPPED across the small puddles forming in his driveway, and used his shirt to shield his head from the falling rain. He ran to his mailbox. Letting his shirt drop back down to cover his torso, he took the letters and used them as an umbrella before darting back up to the porch overhang. Once he turned the doorknob, he realized he'd locked himself out. Safely under the overhang, he rang the doorbell and flipped through his mail while he waited for Dallas.

He turned two bills over and slipped them behind the rest of the stack. Dallas was not coming. He rang the bell again, and knocked on the frame. He looked back down at a familiar envelope from the Walter School District, the third in as many months.

"They have persecuted me, they will persecute you too," he whispered under his breath, as he ripped it open and unfolded the letter.

Dear Mrs. Darwin:

The T. Walter High School Administration and its Board of Education wish to meet with you regarding the community's concerns. As you are aware, a disciplinary action stemming from the alleged incident of April 13 is still pending.

Michael heard the door unlock, and peered through the small panes of glass to see Dallas yanking on the knob. His son leaned closer to get a better turn, and soon the door creaked open. Michael pushed it the rest of the way. Dallas looked confused.

"Locked myself out," Michael explained, still thumbing through the letters. Dallas asked where Mom was, and his father told him she'd gone to the store. He turned to rejoin his friends but then wheeled around.

"Dad, we all want to go back over to Felix's house. Can I go?"

"I don't want you out in this rain. Why don't you play in the basement?"

Dallas nodded and turned away, trying to think of another excuse.

Michael tossed the mail on the coffee table and dropped onto the couch with a heavy sigh.

He looked back at the letter again. It had been a lingering ordeal ever since Rebecca had broken up a fight while she'd been working as a monitor in the hallways of T. Walter High. It was three against one, and the one getting beaten kept trying to run away. Kept trying to get to his feet so he could make it to where Rebecca sat petrified at her desk. Michael could still remember how her hands trembled when she got home and told him the story. The boy at some point had called to her for help; he'd reached his hand out to her. Seeing the look on his face had somehow stilled her nerves and she sprang into action. She rushed to the boy and draped her body over his. The three boys stopped kicking and Rebecca screamed at them to go away. They ran down the hallway, laughing.

Rebecca had sat with the boy in the nurse's office while his parents were called. His name was Odin. He wanted aspirin, but the nurse would only give him a cold compress and remind him to pinch the bridge of his nose to stem the bleeding.

Rebecca thought a hand on the boy's leg would calm him, but he already seemed eerily still. Like he'd been through this before. That was when Rebecca first noticed. She had been so frightened, so singular of mind to stop the beating, that she hadn't seen in the hallway that he was wearing a skirt. But now, in the nurse's office, with the boy out of harm's way, the world beginning to return to its predictable pace, the order of things took shape again, and she stared down at the skirt, clear as the nurse's indifference. The skirt was long and black. Like something a peasant would wear in the middle ages—ratty, with decorative black trimming at the hem. She looked at his hands. His fingernails were painted black as well. Rebecca thought he had to be the strangest child she'd ever seen. She thought his parents must have been working all day and night not to notice. She was horrified, but said nothing. Not even when the boy caught her looking and silently pulled the cold compress away from his eye for a moment.

After his parents picked him up, saying nothing to Rebecca, she resolved to call the cops. She got the boy's full name and made a report in front of the school.

Days later the three kids were caught. One of them, Joe Ragone, was the son of Mr. Ragone, the guidance counselor; the other two were Joe's friends—all three on track to get into college with honors.

Rebecca would have known none of this had Mr. Ragone not approached her in the hallway to explain the misunderstanding. You see, Joe's friend Alan, one of the other boys—who may be getting into NYU, isn't that something?—had thought Odin was trying to pick up his girlfriend. Alan had felt threatened; you know how boys are when it comes to their girlfriends.

When Rebecca cast her mind back to the meek child in the black skirt, she'd nearly laughed in front of Mr. Ragone. But what did all this mean? she wondered.

The police involvement was problematic, Mr. Ragone had said. In fact, if the report could disappear it would make the whole thing seem laughable. The trouble boys get into, he added with a dry laugh. But isn't it something—that three boys from this town could actually get into college with honors? It would be such a proud moment for the school.

Rebecca told Mr. Ragone that she was proud of the school no matter what college the boys attended. Shouldn't everyone be? she asked, before they parted ways.

Mr. Ragone came back the next day because the police report was problematic for Rebecca as well, he was sorry to say. It violated protocol. She really wasn't supposed to go outside of procedure. It could be grounds for a disciplinary hearing, and, after all, Mr. Ragone said he knew very well what a hearing meant for a hallway aide. But that could be swept away along with the police report. And, of course, Rebecca's testimony to the school principal that it was just a hallway scuffle would clean up the whole messy incident quite nicely.

Michael remembered the day she left for work, resolved to do what Mr. Ragone had asked, and how she came home that same day determined to do the opposite. Michael didn't press to find out why. He'd assumed her Christian conscience wouldn't permit her to lie. It was a sin, after all.

Now the school was entering into procedures to determine if Rebecca's violation of protocol was grounds for dismissal.

Michael was rubbing his eyes in the gloomy, gray afternoon, when he turned his head at the sound of a car door closing. He stood up and looked out the window. Rebecca was pulling two heavy grocery bags from the backseat, getting rained on unmercifully. He thought of how beautiful she looked in the gray light. His chest throbbed for her, and he leaped for the door to hold it open. She bounded up the front porch, and gave him a quick kiss on the lips before rushing her bags into the kitchen. Michael closed the door behind her and sat back down on the couch. Rebecca stood in the doorway after dropping the bags onto the counter.

"It's raining hard," she said.

"Yes."

She looked around, down the hallway, and into the den. "Where's Dallas?"

Michael pointed downward.

Rebecca smirked. "He's dead?" she laughed slightly.

"He's in the basement with his friends."

Rebecca smiled and sauntered over to him. Sitting beside her husband, she read the worry in his eyes, and asked him what was wrong. He leaned forward and lifted the letter with two fingers, holding it up to her. She read it wearily, as if she'd read it before.

"I'm not looking forward to September," Rebecca sighed. "I don't even know if I'll have a job."

In silence, Michael reached his arm across the back of the couch and pulled her into his chest. He twirled a lock of her hair around his index finger as she sank into his embrace and then slid down onto his lap, quietly; safely. She spoke a little about the crowd at the supermarket. Michael asked mundane questions. Before long, she was asleep, breathing softly and evenly. He sat and watched her. Petted her hair, looked at the clock on the wall. It was getting late. The rain continued. He listened to it tap on the window behind him, as the occasional car whizzed through the puddles in the street. The boys playing downstairs were soundless. He leaned his head back and prayed that all would go well for his wife and family.

CHAPTER FOURTEEN

THE MUSIC WAS BLARING THROUGH THE TREES, beyond which lay Darryl Knight's backyard. David, Matthew, and Nick approached from the street after parking around the block. The rain had tapered off, and sunlight was faintly pushing through the clouds in the early evening. A bottle hit the asphalt, exploding at their feet like a snowball in a winter fight. David adjusted the knapsack he'd brought along and peered through the trees to see who had thrown it. All he got back were the whooping sounds of teenagers from the backyard.

They rounded the corner and headed up the front path. Darryl's mother answered, clutching an empty garbage bag and blowing her blond bangs back from her face. Her smile revealed a perfect row of glossy white teeth that upstaged the deep laugh lines in her tanned cheeks. Her divorce had dragged on, while she and Darryl's father had tried to live together in the same house. She'd run to the neighbors' house on a few occasions, clutching Darryl's hand. There were calls to the cops. The boy would come to school yawning more often than not. But things had been calm since Darryl's father finally left. She'd been alone now for five years.

"More of Darryl's friends?" Mrs. Knight asked. "I know you, Matthew; who are these two?"

"This is Abbott, and this is Costello," answered Matthew, smiling back.

She shook her head and stepped aside. "That's nice to say about your friends," she bantered. Her blue eyes locked with David's stare and she winked at him. David nodded, and blinked. Something inside him had stirred. The boys stepped through the doorway and entered the house. "Darryl's in the backyard with everyone else." Mrs. Knight led the boys through the hallway and into the kitchen where sliding glass doors opened onto the backyard.

"We know. We heard," answered Matthew.

Mrs. Knight turned around and asked him what he meant.

"Some kids threw a bottle out onto the street in back of you," said Nick shyly.

Matthew shot him a look. Mrs. Knight's face sobered from its usual expression of mirth and she threw the empty garbage bag down onto the kitchen table. She stood by the sliding glass door and screamed for Darryl. He quickly appeared from around the side of the house with a curious look.

"I bought you and your friends beer because I want you to have a good time, but if you throw one more bottle out into the street, I'll kick everybody out of here!" she yelled, stepping through the glass doors and strutting out into the backyard. She was wearing tight jeans with a small halter top. The three boys followed her body with their eyes, speechless. She sauntered over to a table where empty beer bottles sat abandoned, and she scooped them up, inserting her slim fingers with their long manicured nails into their open mouths.

"How did Darryl come out of her? She's hot," said Nick, staring.

Matthew turned on him. "Nice going with the beer bottle story. Darryl would kill you if you blew his party."

"You started to tell her, I just finished," Nick said.

"I was talking about the noise and the music, you idiot."

David was staring at the crowd through the sliding glass door. He watched a kid about the same size as Darryl chug an entire bottle of beer and burp as he slammed it down. Then the kid looked into the kitchen doorway, and cupped his hands to his mouth to make a megaphone.

"Milton! Get your ass out here!" he shouted.

With a mischievous smile, Matthew stepped out into the backyard. "Joey Ragone, you bastard, you started without me," he said.

Nick and David walked outside as well.

"Ragone's such an asshole," Nick said. "You hear what he did to Odin Meuller last year?"

"I heard rumors," David answered. Nick shook his head.

A smattering of eleventh graders recognized Nick and made their way over to say hi. David slid away from the small group, found the cooler, and quickly popped open a beer. Then he sat down to drink at a lone table near the wall of the house.

Darryl's backyard was large for this development. A piñata hung from a low tree limb, and a quiet nook provided refuge for a keg and Darryl's closer friends. A group of kids were aiming to play drunken piñata, in which a player had to fail a field drunk test before he could take his whacks. It was still early, and nobody had failed the test yet. The stick leaned against the tree, and the piñata swayed in the slight breeze. A larger table had been set up in the far corner of the yard, and was now completely occupied; a group of kids sat silently, drinking their beers. Nobody paid attention to them, except when a beer bottle pyramid would come crashing down in a loud, rattling noise.

Darryl and his friends had moved to the side of the house

and were doing keg stands. Nick had been taken in by a small group of kids trying to fill up so they could hit the piñata.

David looked around to see if Julia had arrived but he didn't see her. More kids were pouring in by the minute. The yard was filling with everyone from his high school. Almost on cue, Hanna D'Amico—his foe from history class—came stepping through the doorway, smiling as if she'd just won a National Merit Scholarship. She looked around for familiar faces, saw David sitting at his table, and quickly looked away. She craned her neck to watch the boys standing around the piñata, until she recognized somebody in the crowd and screamed out his name. Behind her filed a small group of kids David also recognized from his history class. The air of conflict became so thick, David could almost reach out and grab hold of the comments they were sure to make about his political opinions.

The backyard was packed by eight o'clock, and David still saw no sign of Julia or Krystal. Even his lonely table had been intruded upon. Albert Sigorsky, a student in David's English class, had picked up some girl from the batch of hopeful, doe-eyed freshmen and had her draped over his shoulders and on his lap just a few feet away. The two were kissing each other all over the neck and mouth and earlobes. They paid no attention to David, who sat there watching them in a combination of awe and disgust. The girl had moved down to Albert's collarbone with her tongue, when Albert looked over and saw David staring.

"You watching us, you weirdo?"

David paused, allowing for the girl to stop what she was doing and give him a nasty look. The kind of look girls like her learn to give early.

"Yes, I am," David replied coldly. The kissers got up and shuffled off. David looked around; the party was filled to capacity, but still people managed to segregate into private groups. Miraculously, as if the phenomenon was not confined to the physical parameters of T. Walter High, the party began to mimic the exact social dynamics of the high school. As if they were all inherently aware of their place in society, and gravitated not only to their social groups, but even managed to cluster off into designated spots within the backyard itself.

To David's left was Darryl Knight's group of football players. They hovered around Darryl and the keg like a pride of lions. Whenever someone outside wanted to get to Darryl or the keg, they were circled and searched, as if entering the back lobby of the school, an exclusive hangout where the popular kids roamed. In the far corner sat all the kids who usually lined the walls of the main lobby. They accepted one another in rejected camaraderie. Some of the drama students were there as well, standing near the piñata, but off to the side, similar to how they hung out near the elevators at school, laughing loudly. They weren't with the piñata crowd, but they had picked a part of the backyard where they could be seen by everyone. The ROTCs and the blacks, true to their status in the school, were not invited.

David did not delude himself as to what his place was in the social scheme. He himself hadn't yet made up his mind where he fit in, but his classmates seemed to have made the decision for him. He wondered what he was doing there, feeling like a bird that incessantly slaps its wings against the window of a house. *Why do I even bother?* he thought.

"Red!" a voice called out. It was Darryl, arms akimbo. He was heading toward him. David wasn't sure what it was—the outstretched arms, the way he used his nickname as though it wasn't a put-down, or the way he seemed to genuinely love everyone around him—it could have been all those at once, but something in that instant made David smile slightly.

Darryl gave him a light punch on the shoulder. In doing so, he noticed the knapsack. "School's not for another two months almost, what's with the fag bag?"

David pulled the strap further up his shoulder, to where it met with his neck. "My sketchbook and stuff," he said.

"*My sketchbook and stuff,*" Darryl mocked. "You homo. What are you going to draw?"

"I also got a change of clothes. I might crash at Matt's."

"A go-bag," Darryl said. "Always good to have."

"You just said it was a fag bag."

"Well . . ." Darryl didn't finish his thought. The two held their silence like a hand of cards. David shifted in his seat, feeling as though Darryl was measuring him. Weighing him, like the choices at the lunch counter.

"You know, I used to keep a go-bag of clothes like that all the time," Darryl said finally as he picked up an empty beer bottle and pulled at the corner of the label. David watched him in silence. Darryl hooked his thumb toward his house. "Parents fighting," he added. "Sometimes it's better to stay away."

"Where did you go all those times?" David asked.

Darryl shrugged. Looked across the yard at two sophomores racing to the bottom of their beers. "My aunt's. The neighbors'. Wherever."

"I hear you," David said, as he clutched tight on the strap of his knapsack. He knew, but he didn't know. His parents didn't fight the way kids gossiped about how Darryl's parents had fought. There were no cops, no shouts of "Whore!" from the front windows. No midnight tussles in the driveway over the car keys. David's parents would go silent on each other. Ask David to pass messages between them. But Darryl was right: sometimes it was better to stay away. Silence, coldness, could be as loud as a fist through a wall.

"Anyway, Red, I just mean sometimes when you get away from these people you have some fun for a while, but it never really goes away unless you make it."

"What are you talking about?"

"People talk. People around here have nothing better to do sometimes, and I know what they say, but I figured out how to fit in. You will too, someday."

David kept silent for a moment and took a pull off his beer. "Did you know that humans are the only animals that will eat with an enemy?"

"I did not," Darryl answered. "But it makes sense."

"How does that make any sense at all?"

"Sometimes all it takes is for you to make them laugh," Darryl said. "And serve them some beer." He wiggled the empty bottle that he had dangling from his index finger.

David looked around at all the guests. Laughing, shouting, drinking Darryl's beer, while Darryl moved the empty bottle in slow circles through the air.

"I see your girl has arrived," Darryl said, as he began to drift back in the direction from which he'd come.

A wash of guilt pressed David to say something. "Thanks for inviting me here, Darryl," he blurted out.

Darryl stopped. A slight, sad grin tugged at the corners of his mouth. "Don't be a homo about it."

David saw Krystal Richards step through the sliding glass doors, into the backyard. Julia was right behind her.

Julia noticed David as Darryl crossed the yard. She waved to him with a smile and stepped down off the porch. Krystal disappeared into a crowd of boys all howling for her, forming a circle around her.

"All by your lonesome?" Julia asked. "You're a nut job, you know that? You nearly gave me a heart attack last night."

"Love makes me do crazy things," David said. He was happy. Bursting with hope. She'd walked over to him right away. He'd forgotten about her phone call to Darryl. Julia sat down at the small table across from him and held his left hand in her small, thin ones.

Moments later, Darryl and a couple of friends erupted with shouts and open arms. Standing in the doorway was twenty-year-old Bob Cassidy. A star running back for the Patriots, he'd single-handedly defeated Saybrook with a stunning three hundred–yard, five-touchdown afternoon, and at homecoming, no less. Saybrook High School, which spent so many years leisurely rolling over T. Walter with little effort, had been vanquished for the first time in Turnbull's history. And it was all because of Bob Cassidy, Felix's older brother. The town had saluted him for months on end.

Bob stepped down off the small porch into the pats of all his former teammates. Darryl and the rest of them had been freshmen when Bob starred in that remarkable game. Some players, like Darryl, had been riding the bench, secretly hoping someone would sprain his ankle so they could get a shot. Other players, now on the starting squad, had still been languishing as starters on the junior varsity team, where the only fans in the stands were their parents. But they all remembered and revered Bob. He was open with them. Helped them become better players. He took time with them, and even joined in fights between the athletes and the burnouts.

Bob spoke to one player while he was handed a beer by another. He hadn't been back to the school since the year after he graduated, when he performed the coin toss at T. Walter's homecoming game. He was back in Turnbull, home for the summer, after his second year at Rutgers University, where he'd earned a free ride by playing for the Scarlet Knights. With one swift motion, Bob cracked open the beer and started chugging. He finished it in mere seconds and reached for another.

David and Julia watched him from their little table. In the far distance, a few kids had started to take some shots at the piñata. Bob threw his head back and laughed at something and then, smiling, he turned to the small table and locked eyes with Julia. David shifted in his seat as Bob's face turned serious and he narrowed his sharp green eyes at her. David's own eyes burned into Bob's, and as if the guy sensed the suspicion, he looked at David. They stared at each other for a while, before Bob turned to one of his younger worshippers who happened to be in David's grade, and tapped him on the shoulder. Now they were both looking at the table, and Julia tucked her hair behind her ear.

"Who's that clown?" David asked Julia.

"I don't know. One of Darryl's friends," she replied.

"Stay away from him." David was too fixed on Bob to notice Julia shake her head and roll her eyes.

Bob strode over to them as he cracked another beer, his third. His friend was walking ahead of him, leading the way and waving Bob along. David stared at them all the way up until they hovered over their table. The friend spoke first.

"Julia, this is Bob Cassidy, *the* Bob Cassidy. The guy who beat Saybrook all by himself."

Bob nudged him on the arm. "Knock it off, she doesn't care about that," he said, smiling.

"What does she care about, if you know her so well?" David asked.

His classmate frowned. Bob just stared at David, sizing

him up. He looked very relaxed. His face was a stone. David's classmate cleared his throat and spoke blandly.

"This is Red," he told Bob. Bob's eyes never left David's. He held out his hand to shake it.

"Odd name," Bob said.

"David," he corrected. Glancing over at Julia, he felt compelled to shake Bob's hand.

"Why do they call you Red?" asked Bob.

"This is Julia Dawson," the classmate interrupted, as David and Bob broke their handshake.

David kept his eyes on Bob, but Bob turned all his attention to Julia. He took her hand delicately, drank a sip of beer, and told her that they would have to talk before the night was over. Then he walked away.

David followed Bob's back as he disappeared into a crowd of kids. Bob took the piñata stick away from a quiet drama student. Darryl spun Bob in six circles and released him, facing the wrong way. Bob took a large forward swing with the stick, and nearly drove it into a girl's face. The crowd scattered in a matter of seconds. Darryl broke into peals of laughter. David watched from his seat and huffed through his nose.

"What a jackass," he said.

"I want to go watch," Julia said, leaping up from her chair.

David simply stared at her. He was getting that feeling. But his heart jumped a beat when she reached out her hand, clasped his, and pulled him up to his feet. He abandoned his knapsack on the bench and allowed Julia to drag him over to the game. He reached toward a stack of beers standing on a table and cracked one open. He quickly chugged it down, then reached for another.

CHAPTER FIFTEEN

FELIX, DALLAS, AND JAMES CROWDED TOGETHER in the basement well into the late evening, entertaining each other with stories and games. Dallas rode his bicycle in circles around the lally columns, trying to pick up speed. Felix and James seemed to be in better spirits after the rain washed out Dallas's plan to go back for the wood. Only occasionally—whenever he twisted or contorted his body in a strange way—would the bruise on James's neck smart. Dallas would catch a glimpse of James wincing and shake his head in disgust, as if the two of them shared the same anatomy and the pain ran through Dallas's body as well.

"Dallas, do you believe in those *Ouija* boards?" asked Felix, as Dallas whizzed by on his bicycle.

"You mean that game where ghosts come down and spell things out?" he called back. "My dad says they're real, but I don't think so."

"I heard they can tell the future. Lottery numbers . . . stuff like that," said James.

"Please . . . then everybody would be winning the lottery," answered Dallas as he passed by again, faster.

"Not if you don't do it right," Felix defended. "I think it's real sometimes. We should get one."

Dallas shook his head as he circled. James and Felix were getting dizzy watching him.

"My dad would kill me if he caught me. He says demons get attracted to that stuff, and they'll come down and possess you."

James and Felix looked at each other for a moment before starting to giggle. Dallas stopped his bicycling, looking hurt. He stepped off and dropped his bike.

"Shut up! It's what my dad says, jerks!" He bounded toward them and lightly kicked Felix in the back of his leg as he rolled away. James jumped up to his feet and jogged away laughing.

"Dallas is afraid of a piece of wood," announced Felix.

Dallas frowned and looked over at James as if he'd understand. "I said *my dad* believes all that stuff. I don't," he cried. "You want to play with a *Ouija* board? I'll play with one."

"Where do we get one?" asked James.

Dallas shrugged.

"We can make one," suggested Felix. "All we need is a flat board and a black marker."

They looked around the basement. Dallas set his sights on a piece of plywood standing up against the far corner. He dragged the board over and let it fall with a loud slap onto the concrete where the two had been sitting only minutes before. They all stood around it, as if observing a dead animal. Felix asked Dallas to fetch him a marker. Dallas bounded up the stairs as Felix sat down Indian-style in front of the board.

James followed suit. "Isn't there a bunch of words on the board?" he asked.

"We have to write the alphabet across the top, and then the words *yes*, *no*, and *maybe*," Felix replied.

Dallas returned with a thick Pilot marker. He held it out to Felix. "I have to put this back in my dad's room as soon as we're done with it."

Felix nodded and took the marker from him. He began to pen the alphabet across the top in the thick black ink. Then he wrote the necessary words underneath, and leaned back, turning his head sideways to view his creation. He capped the marker, and looked up at the boys.

"Now we need a block of wood, or a triangle piece of metal or something," Felix said. Dallas and James got up and searched around.

"What about a hockey puck?" suggested James, holding up a dusty black puck that had been buried under a pile of sports equipment.

"That'll work," Felix responded.

The boys returned and sat down again. Felix took the puck from James and placed it on the board; he uncapped the marker and traced the shape of the puck onto the board, so they'd always know where to place the pointer. He turned the board so they could all see it, and scooted closer to his friends. "Now we put our hands on the puck, and ask the board some questions."

The three boys kept silent for a moment until Felix broke in with a question.

"Will James's bruise ever heal?" he asked the board, leaning his face down closer to it.

All three watched the board. After a moment, James looked at Dallas. Dallas looked at Felix. They were beginning to feel foolish. Suddenly, the puck began to move slowly across the board. It slid silently over to the word NO.

Dallas frowned. "Oh, come on, Felix was moving the thing."

"Was not!" said Felix.

"I felt you moving it, and besides, it's wrong anyway, his bruise'll be gone in a couple days. You're an idiot, Felix."

"I swear I didn't move it."

Dallas smirked and shook his head, looking down at the board. "Let's ask the board. Board, did Felix move the puck?" There was a long pause. Slowly, the puck slid over to the word YES.

"Now you're moving it, Dallas," Felix accused.

"No I'm not," Dallas replied sarcastically.

"These are dumb questions anyway, let's ask some good ones," said Felix.

James leaned in close and spoke to the board: "Will James, Felix, and Dallas be friends forever?"

All three kept quiet. The puck would not move. Dallas looked at Felix, as if he was waiting for him to cheat again. They stared down at their fingertips, joined across the top. They kept staring. They could hear the gutters dripping outside. Suddenly, the puck slid over to the word NO.

"Dallas, you moved it!" shouted James.

Dallas threw his hands in the air. "I swear I didn't move it, dude, I swear." His face betrayed him as he broke into a smile, and started to laugh.

"You're an idiot, Dallas," snapped Felix. "It's not going to work if you keep moving it."

Dallas still held his hands up. "Dude, I didn't move it, I swear." He laughed again, glancing from side to side at his friends.

"Nobody move it this time, I want to see if it works," said James.

Dallas was still enjoying his joke, when his eyes happened to fall on the marker lying next to Felix's knee. "Oh no, I got to put the marker back!" he yelped. He jumped to his feet and bounded up the stairs.

"If Dallas leaves it alone, it might work next time," said Felix.

"What do we ask it next?"

Felix searched his mind for a bit. "Let's ask what we're getting for Christmas this year!" Their faces lit up as James put his hands on the puck.

"Let's ask it now," James said.

Felix shook his head. "We got to wait for Dallas to get back, I don't think the board'll work unless everybody who helped make it have their hands on the pointer."

The two racked their brains to come up with more questions while they waited. Felix always wanted to know if he would be rich. James wanted to know if he would get married. They both wondered if they were ever going to get hit with a nuclear bomb. Felix wanted to ask if they would all stay friends and live next door to each other.

"We tried that already," James said.

Felix stared off into the distance, until a smile formed on his face. "A guy goes into a restaurant and orders a soup, and when the waiter comes with his soup he sees the waiter's got his thumb stuck right in it, so the guy says: *Waiter, why is your thumb in my soup?* And the waiter says, *I got this infection, and the doctor told me to keep the thumb in something warm, so here it is.* The guy says, *How 'bout sticking it up your ass?* And the waiter says, *I tried that already.*"

The two of them burst into laughter at the same time, and were only interrupted when Dallas tumbled frantically down the stairs and shouted: "James, your dad just banged on my door! I think he's drunk, and he's talking to *my dad!*"

James and Felix stared at each other; their faces sobered from the laughter, and they all three scrambled up the stairs to see what was happening.

Ivan Illworth had stumbled up to Michael Darwin's door and

took a moment to tuck his shirt into his sagging pants. He sniffed and smoothed back his hair. Then he opened the screen and banged on the wooden door three solid times.

Michael answered, peering through one of the small panes of diamond-shaped glass. He fixed his eyes on Ivan, who was swaying back and forth. Rebecca appeared behind her husband and asked who was at the door.

"Go back into the living room. It's Ivan Illworth."

"What does he want?"

"I'm going to find out, go back there."

Rebecca turned and walked down the hallway as Michael yanked the door open. Dallas breezed up to his father and saw James's dad standing there unsteadily on the porch.

"Can I help you, Ivan?" Michael asked.

Ivan recognized his impatient tone. He sniffed and smoothed back his hair once more before he spoke. "I just wanted you to know that it's okay, you know . . . All is forgiven."

Michael tried to smile. "What on earth could you be talking about?"

"Well, the fight your boy started yesterday," Ivan said. "The bruise James got on his neck, you must have seen it. But boys are boys, and I don't hold it against Dallas one bit."

"The fight Dallas started?"

"Yep. You should know, sir . . . you should jus' know, I don' hole it against Dallas one bit. Not one." Ivan's eyes darted past Mr. Darwin and landed on his son, standing there with his other friend.

"Hello, son," Ivan said.

Michael looked back and upon seeing the boys, pulled the door so only his body filled the frame.

Ivan went up on his tiptoes and raised his voice. "Jus' telling Mr. Darwin here, there's no hard feelings, son. Not for what his son caused to your poor neck."

"Ivan, are you feeling all right?" Michael asked. "Think maybe you had a little too much to drink?"

Ivan shook his head, still swaying back and forth. "I jus' wanted to put your mine at ease. There's no need for you to apologize for the fight or anything. Boys do boys things. And the same goes for Dallas . . . He doesn't need to be apologizing to me for anything."

Michael wrinkled his brow and shifted his weight to his other leg. "Ivan, Dallas is being dealt with for his part in the fight yesterday, don't you worry about it."

"But jus' pass that mess'ge to 'im, will ya? He doesn't owe . . . owe me an apology or nothing like that. It's all forgiven. Same goes for yourself."

Michael smiled. "Fine. Go home, Ivan. Go home and sleep it off."

Ivan stumbled backward and narrowed his eyes at Michael, inspecting him for a sign of insincerity. In the window beside the door, James's face peered into the evening dusk, watching his father. His face looked angelic in the late-evening glow of the living room lamp. Ivan waved to him.

"Have fun tonight, son!" he shouted, and staggered back down the porch, almost losing his balance entirely.

James watched from the window as his father straightened himself, and headed down the driveway. Ivan began to veer to the right, and compensated by staggering back to the left. Some other movement caught the corner of James's eye: trotting along, as ignorant as ever, was the dog from yesterday. Spybot. Looking nosy, bowing his head, and locking his dog eyes on Ivan as he reached the end of the driveway. James didn't see any hole in the ground, or anything else that could trip his father, but somehow he lost all balance and teetered to his left. He knocked into Mr. Darwin's mailbox, and bounced violently off it. Ivan reached both his hands toward the mailbox as if apologizing to it, and reeled backward before he finally hit the ground. He rolled over to his side. Mr. Darwin propped open the screen.

"Ivan?" he called.

Ivan got up on his knees and waved his hand in the air to signal that he was all right. James could feel his eyes widen as he stared out the window, and blood rushed to his cheeks. The dog had trotted up to Ivan and was licking his face with playful familiarity. Then the dog turned to Ivan's outstretched hand and starting licking that too. Ivan pulled his hand back and swatted the dog aside with a violent blow that sent the animal yelping across the street and drifting down the road. Then Ivan gingerly rose to his feet, and with an air of dignity, smoothed his hair, hiked up his pants, and continued home.

When Michael closed the heavy door by pushing his weight slowly into it until the lock caught, the three boys climbed down from the couch they had been kneeling over to watch. Michael looked at James. He took Dallas by the shoulder and drew him in. He smiled at James, a half-smile that looked like a nervous tick.

"I'm sorry you had to see that," Michael said.

James blinked up at him. Then he turned and climbed back upon the couch to look out the window again. To make sure his father had made it safely inside.

It was not the first time he'd seen his father drunkenly obsessed over something. Last month, at the neighborhood block party, he had gotten drunk before the food even hit the grill. Tables were lined up alongside the street. Janet had made a spread of side dishes and placed them on a table at the entrance to their dirt driveway. She had just finished putting down her last bowl of potato salad when she caught a glimpse of Ivan staggering through the crowd of neighbors, laughing and telling crude jokes. The neighbors were laughing too, but James watched his mother's face and could tell she wasn't pleased.

The only other person at the party who hadn't found Ivan amusing was Minister Roberts from the Darwins' church, a burly man with a boyish face, who blinked at Ivan with a sort of silent indictment. Ivan had noticed, and narrowed his eyes at him. "Do you know what Jesus did when he went to a wedding, Father?" Ivan asked, swaying before the minister with his fists clenched.

"I'm a minister, not a priest," he replied dryly. "You don't have to call me Father." He took a sip of his seltzer and looked away.

"You can look as bored as you want, Father, but I'll tell you what he did. He took water and made five barrels of wine. He was a regular vintner, your Jesus, always keeping the jugs full for the party. I'll bet you didn't think I had a knowledge for the Bible-type stuff, but I know plenty about it."

James noticed how the neighbors had grown quiet, and soon the only voices that could be heard were the minister and his father.

"I'm sure you do," replied Minister Roberts, looking down at his hands folded neatly around the seltzer glass.

"Okay, Brother Roberts," intercepted Mr. Darwin, "we have some food for you over by our table." He pushed the minister away from the conversation.

Minister Roberts allowed himself to be escorted, but waved his hand in the air. "It's fine, it's fine," he kept repeating.

Ivan had then turned to Mr. Frado, the neighbor who, at least to James, looked just as drunk as his father. Mr. Frado was swaying in the summer street. Ivan's face lit up to mirror his. He put his hand on the man's shoulder, and proceeded to try and teach him an old folk song.

Soon enough night had fallen, and Ivan was at his worst. All the humor had gone out of him. He was scowling in the dark, leaning against his own mailbox. He looked around at all the laughing neighbors as if he suddenly hated them. As if they had betrayed him somehow.

He'd had his fill. He had pushed off the mailbox and rounded the corner of the dessert table to go inside, but he did not make the corner cleanly, and he lost his balance. He crashed, facedown, onto the dirt driveway beside the table, and the neighbors let out a collective gasp. James rushed to his side. Ivan curled up into a fetal position and let his head rest in the dirt. James pulled at his arm until Felix's father ran and caught hold of Ivan's elbow.

"I'm fine," Ivan had said, still lying down. "I'm fine . . . I'll just sleep right here."

Mr. Cassidy pulled Ivan to his feet and gave his heavy arm to James. Ivan rested against James's shoulder, using him as a crutch, as his son led him up the porch steps and into the house.

Now, when Dallas put his hand on James's shoulder, it felt like his dad's and he startled. He crawled back down from Dallas's front window. Felix had already gone back downstairs to prepare more questions for the *Ouija* board. Dallas looked at his friend, who was trembling slightly, and was pale, his bruise darkening. Dallas made a face as if searching for something to say.

"Sometimes when people do things, they don't do it to be mean, they do it for no reason," he finally said. "Like they don't even know they're doing it."

James nodded and looked at the floor. "I know that," he said, breezing past Dallas and heading for the basement stairs.

Dallas glanced at his father, who had put his hand on the back of his neck.

"That was a good thing you did, Dallas," Mr. Darwin said. "That was a good deed."

CHAPTER SIXTEEN

BOB CASSIDY GAVE DARRYL A PUNCH ON THE ARM and demanded one more try, since Darryl had turned him the wrong way. The crowd that had gathered around the piñata grew in size with every second Bob held the stick, and with more jibes and joking, the varsity football team was spinning him around once again. They turned him seven times, and the crowd shouted off each rotation. When they stopped, he was facing the right way. Players were howling for Bob to take his swing. Bob was drifting and teetering around, dizzy, drunk, ecstatic from the attention. David stood with his arms crossed, but he stretched out his neck and went to his toes to get a glimpse.

"Hey, he's getting his balance back . . . Cheater!" someone shouted, laughing. Instantly, Bob reached back and came down hard with the stick. It made a loud whiffing sound as it glanced off the piñata's back side and crashed down into the dirt. The piñata bounced and swung on its string. Bob staggered forward. The crowd erupted and several of the other players lunged to pull his blindfold off. David seemed to cheer up a bit as he watched Bob search for his balance again. The guy was laughing with drunken glee, as people lined up to slap him on the back.

A smaller kid stepped forward and took the stick from him, wanting to get his turn. David watched Darryl try to put the blindfold on the kid, but Bob suddenly pulled on Darryl's shoulder and whispered something that drew Darryl's eyes to David. Their eyes met for a moment. Nodding, Darryl tied the blindfold onto the small kid, who looked eager to be taking his swings in front of Bob Cassidy. He volunteered his back to Darryl, who started spinning him around and around, while the crowd counted to twelve.

Entirely drunk well before he ended up on the edges of this circle, and well before Bob Cassidy showed up, the slight boy could hardly stay on his feet. A few friends were chanting his name, while Darryl and his crew stared intently, practically licking their lips in anticipation. David left Julia's side, and the closer he got, the more it looked like fun to get a shot at breaking the piñata open. The boy righted himself, and was just about to take his swing, when suddenly he staggered over to the other side of the circle. He lowered his arms and attempted to correct himself.

"Come on!" someone yelled from the back of the crowd.

"Swing, little man!" shouted another. Some of Darryl's friends started to boo and hiss.

"All right," said Darryl, "he's taken too long, we have to spin him again!"

The crowd roared. Even David smiled. The kid dropped his arms down and searched blindly for Darryl's hands. Darryl clutched the back of his shoulders and spun him another five times, as the crowd counted.

When Darryl was finished, the kid staggered about, and more people started to shout for him to swing. As if knowing he had little time, the kid took a moment to ground himself and raised his arms mightily. The crowd stopped like a watch. All eyes were on him. He reared back, and seemed just about ready to swing down on top of the piñata and burst its guts wide open, when he abruptly lurched forward and puked at his feet. The crowd groaned. David looked down at the puddle and scrunched his face. A dozen people moved away, as the boy, crouched with his head down between his knees, pulled off his blindfold and tried to regain his balance. Before he could, another wave hit, and he vomited again, as Darryl's friends pulled him away from the pen and led him off to the side of the house. The crowd was dissatisfied. Some more people began to turn away, when Darryl stepped into the circle and held his arms up in the air. David's heart was full—the boy had not broken the piñata.

"It's okay, it's okay. I prepared for this," Darryl announced. And with that, two of his teammates stepped forward with spades in their hands. They dug underneath the offensive pile and carried it off. The crowd had no problem parting the way for them to get by with their spades. With a divot left in the ground and nothing more, Darryl waved the blindfold around, searching for his next victim. Hands shot up in the darkness of the massive circle. His eyes locked on David, and he immediately pulled him by the collar into the empty space, to a few scattered cheers. David looked back into the crowd for Julia, though he could see nothing but a wall of classmates, all taller than he.

Darryl had his arm around David, and whispered into his ear, "Are you drunk enough?"

"Sure," David answered.

This satisfied Darryl, and he pulled the blindfold over David's eyes. David could feel the energy and space between himself and the growing crowd. He could also feel Darryl's hands tightly gripping his shoulders. He wondered if Julia could see this, if she was smiling. He imagined she was, since it was she who wanted to watch the whole spectacle in the first place.

David heard Darryl bark, "Let the spin begin!" and sud-

denly he was turning to his right. Clockwise. He heard the
roaring crowd count: "One, two, three, four . . ." He did not
feel as if he had turned around twenty times, but had lost his
own count by nine or so. He was reeling with nausea, and
he began to panic. Don't puke, he told himself as the crowd
chanted. He flashed back to the kid who had gone before him,
who was no doubt still crouched in the bushes somewhere. He
prayed that he not suffer the same fate. Please don't puke in
front of all these people, he repeated to himself. But his chest
was bursting with glee, because, even as he spun he started to
feel like for once the crowd was not howling names and labels
at him, or some other mean, hateful thing. He even started to
feel like he was a part of something, with each number the
crowd barked out: "Nine, ten, eleven . . ." He knew now that
Julia was somewhere, smiling for him. He knew she was looking at this turn as a crowning moment—the time when everybody in the school thought David Westwood was an okay
guy. These thoughts helped him to stay away from the other
thought—that he might vomit all over himself.

When the crowd barked out the number twenty, the spinning stopped, and David had no idea if Darryl had placed him
rightly in front of the piñata, or if he'd played another prank.
He tripped over his feet, turned once completely around, and
judging by the sound of the crowd, he turned back around
once more. He raised the stick in the air. God guide this swing,
he thought, trying to hold some semblance of equilibrium.
Then he reeled backward, and stepped down into the divot.
It wasn't much of a hole, but when David felt it under his
feet, the whole universe seemed to snap back in place like a
photograph. Suddenly David knew every object in the yard,
and where it stood. His mind painted the clearest picture in an
instant, the contours of every object.

He turned, righted his swing, and crashed down with the stick. He felt a slight paper resistance, and then the stick buried itself in the ground. Instantly, he heard the crowd erupt into a cheer. When he pulled off the blindfold, he looked up at the piñata, swinging from the tree limb in two broken parts, and the ground where his swing had ended was littered with candy, lollipops, and the occasional condom. Some of the candy had fallen right at his feet. The smile inside him reached his mouth, and he stood up dizzy, grinning over at Darryl.

Adding to his victory, he watched his classmates grovel at his feet for the candy, the way he'd imagined they all would one day for his artwork. He felt like a king who had just rewarded all his serfs with a feast. He spun around to catch the whole scene, his entire high school bowing at his feet and glad for it. In his moment of triumph, he had almost forgotten the most important element, and remembering, he searched the crowd for Julia. He looked to where he had last seen her, and then scanned to his left, but she was nowhere to be seen. He peered down at the ground to see if she was among those grasping for candy, but she wasn't. He looked up and around again.

The crowd dispersed after everything had been picked up, and David was still standing near the tree with the broken piñata swinging in the breeze. He glanced up at the head of the piñata; it was a paper horse. His eyes focused on its face, swinging in two halves with a dumb, happy grin. It seemed to mock him. He looked around for someone familiar and fixed his eyes on Nick heading toward him.

"Nice shot," he said, as he lightly punched him on the shoulder and took a swig of his beer.

"Where's Julia?" David looked over Nick's shoulder to see if he could catch a glimpse of her. Nick's eyes darted downward. "What is it?" David asked firmly.

After some hesitation, Nick bit his lower lip. "She's on the other side of the house with Cassidy . . . He—"

David didn't wait for Nick to explain. He bounded with long strides across the backyard. Halfway across, Krystal stepped deliberately into his path.

"You haven't said two words to me all night," she said, glaring up at him, smiling. Her white teeth shimmered from the spotlights affixed to the back of the house.

David looked down at her. "What do you want me to say?"

"Start with hello," Krystal said, placing her hands on her hips. She turned her head to the side.

"I'm not in the mood, Krystal."

As David started walking away, she yelled after him, "Get ahold of me later, I want to talk to you!"

David turned back to her. She was standing in the spotlight, and all the features in her face that made her the object of everyone's desire were illuminated. She smiled at him, but he turned and headed for the side of the house.

Darryl's friends were hanging out there, but David ignored all the proprieties of his social status and took a giant step into the shadows. Immediately Phil Massa, an offensive lineman who was always sweating, threw his damp hand up and placed it on David's chest.

"Whoa, whoa, whoa . . . Where you think you're goin', little man?"

The small crowd jumped into frenzy. They surrounded him. Nick caught up with David at that moment, but hung back. He lowered his eyes and watched nervously. Julia was standing by the keg next to Bob, and when the group of friends leapt to attention, they both looked up from their conversation. Bob was grinning at him. Immediately David regretted the intrusion.

He'd grown bold when he cut through the piñata. He had no means of cutting through the entire football team, and from the expression on Bob's face, it seemed Bob knew it too.

"I was looking for my girlfriend, that's all," said David, moving his eyes around at all the people who had surrounded him. Julia stared at the ground and nervously tucked her hair behind her ear. The side of the house was eerily quiet.

"She's in good hands," Bob said.

"David, we're just talking," said Julia, as a deep blush rose to her face. David clenched his fists as the circle of football players tightened around him.

"You like crashing parties, buddy?" Bob asked, taking a few steps toward David, who sized him up and down. "Because I know Darryl didn't invite you."

The small crowd moved in closer and they looked just about ready to seize him, when Bob broke them up.

"Easy. I can take this little guy blindfolded," he said, and turned back to David. "These guys tell me you're some kind of a wiseass? You like to start arguments with people all the time? Think you're some kind of fucking genius?"

"David, walk away, I hate fights!" Julia shouted from behind Bob. David looked confused.

"You walk away, I'll chase you," Bob said with a grin.

David glanced behind him. It was a long way to run. Feeling cornered made him angry. He could feel the warmth of the bodies behind him. A wall of flesh. Should he listen to his knees and buckle? Should he listen to his stomach and retch? Should he listen to his hands and tremble? Could he forgive himself afterward? The things you don't do are the things you regret the most, he remembered. He thought of the Vikings in that same instant. How they burned their boats after landing on enemy shores. Fight or die; there was no escape.

Burn the boats, he thought. You are a Viking; you hail from Vikings. Burn the boats. He closed his eyes and let fly with his left hand. He missed entirely. He quickly threw his right fist, a one-two combination his father had taught him. He opened his eyes for that, and saw Bob weaving his head out of the way as if David weren't even there, as if a mosquito was buzzing around his ears. Bob laughed out loud when David threw and missed with another left. Four straight misses, and Bob had not even taken his hands out of his pockets.

When David finally did connect, the punch landed square on Bob's jaw; a sharp pop rang through the air. Bob never moved an inch, and kept laughing even when the second punch landed on his cheek. Without taking his hands from his pockets, Bob bumped his large chest into David just as he was swinging with a wild right. The bump sent David flying backward. He landed on his back, but quickly rolled over and sprang to his feet. Bob laughed and turned to Julia. He winked at the friends who were standing with him, smiling their own little satisfactions. David charged at Bob; Bob didn't move. He braced his muscles for the collision, and when David's head drove into his stomach it was as if he'd rammed a concrete wall. David felt a bolt of pain run through his neck as he careened off the hard stomach and fell to the ground once again. Bob stepped lightly on David's back and then stepped off, laughing. David dragged himself up. He lunged with another desperate left, and punched Bob squarely in his teeth. Bob grimaced, but leaned back and kicked David in the backside. The momentum sent him flying. David landed headfirst into the fence that hemmed the side of Darryl's property.

Through the entire fight, Julia had her back turned, and she closed her eyes in pain each time she heard a crash and the crowd's laughter ring through the air. When she saw the fence beside her shiver from the impact of David's body, she finally turned around.

"David, stay down!" she cried out. The others jumped on the opportunity.

"Yeah, David, stay down," repeated one of the boys.

"Listen to your girlfriend," said another.

"Pretend girlfriend," corrected Phil Massa.

David heard this and sprang to his feet. He shoved Phil away from his path, and took a final swing. Bob stepped aside, and finally took his right hand out of his pocket to catch David by the collar. He spun David quickly to the ground. As if deciding she was nobody's girlfriend, Julia ran past the fight and disappeared.

The rest of the party had caught on that there was a fight and had gathered at the side of the house to watch, but since they had no sense of the history behind it, they gazed on in relative silence. Nick was waiting for his chance to break up the fight without getting hit. Bob had David pinned on his back, and placed his heavy knee on David's chest. He used his weight to crush the air out of David, who began to quickly feel his lungs grow heavier. He struggled to escape from under the pin, wriggling like a worm on a hook; Phil Massa stood over him laughing, looking around as if to see if he was the only person who saw the humor. Bob Cassidy smiled at David. David was getting light-headed, and was beginning to panic. He was convinced that Bob would kill him.

"Here's how it goes, buddy," said Bob. "You get your sorry ass up and get out of here, or I'll personally tear you to pieces, understand? Can't talk? You're losing your breath by the second, aren't you? I'll let you up, just nod that you'll get the hell out of here."

David made one last try to shove Bob's leg aside, but failed.

"I can stay here all night if you like. Just nod, and it'll be over with."

David stared up at his nemesis, who was grinning in the moonlight. The last thing he could imagine doing at that moment was giving him the satisfaction of a nod, but the pressure on his lungs had built up so intensely that he began to feel his life slipping away. He knew he would go unconscious soon, and yet believed he had one last punch left in him. He wanted that chance. He nodded to Bob Cassidy. Bob laughed, tousled David's hair as if he were a little child, and got off him. He stood up and jammed his hands back in his pockets. David rolled to one side, coughing and trying to suck in air.

Bob looked around for Julia. Phil Massa was standing next to him, staring down at David, who had rolled over to his stomach and was up on his knees gulping at the air. Nick helped him to his feet.

"Don't come around where you're not invited," Phil said.

David took his chance. He wheeled around with a steady right fist, and drove it into Phil Massa's face. Bob looked stunned as he jumped back. Phil hit the ground. Then his body sat upright. In a daze, he looked around at everyone, before he lay back down clutching his nose. Immediately the team pounced on David, but Nick had a good hold of his waist, and yanked him back. They both turned and ran.

Leaping through the bushes, Nick found his keys and they bolted for the car. David, though exhausted and furious, began to smile. He slid across the hood of Nick's car like he'd seen on *Dukes of Hazzard* and jumped inside through the open window. Nick tore off, and watched the football team grow smaller in his rearview mirror as they futilely chased the car down the road.

"We left Matthew there," David said, still catching his

breath and rubbing his constricted chest. Nick glanced into the rearview mirror and nodded.

"Matt's got no enemies. I'll call the house and arrange to pick him up out front."

David stared at Nick. "Now *you* got enemies," he said.

Nick shrugged, looking over at David with a smile. "I never liked Massa anyway. We call him Masshole."

David stared out the window. It wasn't Phil Massa, or the fight, or the chase, or Matthew that was on his mind. He rubbed his chest softly as he stared at the trees whizzing by. He could see the flash of Nick's eyes as he repeatedly looked over at him.

"Hold the wheel," said Nick.

"What?"

"Hold the steering wheel for a second."

David grabbed the wheel and trained his eyes straight ahead, concentrating on the yellow lines in the road. Nick reached both hands down underneath his seat and dug around for a few seconds. He came back up and took the wheel again with his right hand. David let go and sank back into his seat. He looked at Nick as he raised his left hand, holding a large, black gun with a wooden handle. David sat up.

"Why do you have a gun?"

"Relax, it's just a BB gun. But it looks real."

"Where did you get it?"

"Picked it up at the flea market. The pump's right on the barrel. It's already loaded with BBs."

David stared as the weapon glistened in Nick's hand every time they passed under a streetlight, growing dark and ominous between. Nick spun the gun around grip first, and reached it over to him. "Take it. It's yours."

"What do you mean?" David took the gun and laid it in

his lap. He ran his fingers across the cool metal barrel.

"If I know these football players, they'll be after you for a couple days. Least Masshole will be. You're going to need protection. Anyone comes around, starts static, just wave that thing at 'em. They'll go running for their mommies."

David looked back down at the gun and raised it to his eyes. He felt the pump action, gliding his hand down the wooden handle. He shook the gun to hear the BBs rattle in the handle where they were stored. He wanted to turn around right there and use it on all of them. He wanted to put a couple between Bob Cassidy's eyes. The way he'd grinned the entire time. He'd been fearful throughout the entire fight, and now he felt only rage. They all saw it. They all watched him nod to Bob Cassidy so he could breathe again. He'd done nothing to Bob; done nothing to deserve that. He wished he were holding a real gun. He looked back out the window.

"Thanks," he finally said, as they pulled up in front of his house.

They shook hands, and Nick told him not to worry; it would all blow over before school started. Nick tore off and David stood on the curb holding the gun with two hands. He looked down at it again, switching it to one hand and holding it like Dirty Harry. Glancing across the street he was reminded of Mr. Hopkins. He narrowed his eyes at the front of Mr. Hopkins's house, dark and peaceful looking. The low shrubs like black cotton balls were lined up beneath his windows. He took aim at Mr. Hopkins's front window. He could see the man sitting at his La-Z-Boy, his pale face awash with the blue light of his television. *The things you didn't do haunt you more than the things you did.* Great advice, old man, thought David. What did Mr. Hopkins have to say for himself now? He drew his bead on Mr. Hopkins's bald head and pretended to squeeze the trigger, then let the gun drop to his side.

He thought about Julia, and that bastard Cassidy. He wondered if she was trying to help when she told him to stay down, or if she was deliberately making it worse. He wondered where she had run off to. Thoughts of the fight made him angrier by the second. His punches should have done something; was he that weak? How could Bob Cassidy stand there and laugh? Why couldn't David drop him the way he'd dropped Phil Massa? And why couldn't he have hit Massa when Julia was actually standing there? How could he make it un-happen? Was it over now between him and Julia? Was she with Bob Cassidy tonight? Now? Was Bob explaining himself away? Was she just now believing him? Smiling at him because he went to his knees and begged forgiveness or something corny like that? Was she buying his lines? As David stood here, this very minute?

He glanced around. He was alone. The street was quiet. He looked at his watch. It was still early for a Saturday night. He peered down the street, and then back down at the weapon. He raised it to his face—suddenly so empowered with a gun, even if it was only a BB gun. He took the barrel and slid it down his pants at the small of his back, like he'd seen done in movies. He pulled his shirt over the handle, concealing it. Then he walked off down the road with no particular destination in mind. No companion but his own thoughts, which burned like white coals.

C HAPTER SEVENTEEN

THE SUN WAS BACK OUT AND BURNING HOT when James Illworth awakened. He rolled over to his side and lifted his head. He was alert enough to know that he was not in his room. He was on a strange floor. Gradually he sat up to see he was near the foot of a bed, and it finally dawned on him he was in Dallas's room. Then he remembered his father falling in the driveway, and Mr. Darwin giving him permission to stay over to "let your father sleep it off," as he put it.

James rubbed his scalp, yawning. He got up slowly, staggered a bit, and then stretched his arms up to the ceiling. Dallas had opened his eyes, and was moving around under the covers. A stir caused James to turn. Felix was sitting up, looking around as if he shared in James's initial confusion. The room began to come alive. The bedside clock read 8:07 a.m. Dallas sat up and pulled the covers off. He stood, crossed the room, and opened the door. Sunlight poured in through the glass doors that led to his back porch.

Dallas stretched in the doorway and looked out into the kitchen. There was a half wall that divided it from the dining room, and Dallas could see that his father was at the counter making sandwiches for lunch. This was how Dallas knew it was Sunday. His father made all the preparations early in the morning so that there could be no excuses or hold-ups for church service at three thirty. Dallas frowned, and looked over at the couch in the living room. Sure enough, his clothes were hanging, pressed, over the arm of the couch. His father must have snuck in while they were all asleep and picked out his Sunday outfit. The little black clip-on tie hung from the top of the hanger. He sighed, and wandered into the kitchen. His father noticed him, and glanced over before returning to his work.

"Morning, Dallas," he said. "Mom's still asleep. We have church today."

Dallas yawned, and looked out at the gorgeous day. Such a contrast to the day before. "Not till later, though, right?" he asked. He could sense his father grinning, though his back was still turned.

"The answer is yes. You can go outside and play, but I want you back here at one thirty to get ready."

Felix and James both stepped into the dining room. They were still in their clothes from yesterday, while Dallas was wearing his pajama shorts and no shirt. He stared at his two friends, dressed in shorts, socks, and T-shirts, and suddenly moved toward the bedroom.

"Go outside, I got to get dressed," he told them as he breezed past and closed his bedroom door. Felix and James said hello to Mr. Darwin and filed out onto the back porch to wait for Dallas.

Impatient, they jumped down from the porch after a minute and started kicking around a basketball they had found under the bushes. Soon enough Dallas emerged from the house, all in green. James took it as a bad omen. Dallas trotted down the steps and joined them by kicking the basketball clear across the yard where none of them would bother to retrieve it.

"We're sticking with our plan," Dallas said.

Felix rolled his eyes. James squinted at the sun and looked at Felix. It was a beautiful day, but James began to feel no different than yesterday.

"Why don't we build a fort using branches and sticks?" James asked. "My dad says we can use all his tools; we don't need to bother with their stuff."

Dallas was already shaking his head. "No way, we're going down there."

"Why?"

"Pride," Dallas answered. "You get pushed around here, and everybody thinks they can take a piece. Then someone comes along and takes another piece—and another piece until there's nothing left."

Dallas looked agitated, which didn't happen often. Even when fighting, he remained silent, and never raised his voice, but now he was practically yelling, and blood rushed to his cheeks. James looked down at his shoes, as if in compliance. Felix kept quiet as well. Dallas started walking toward the side of the house, and the other two followed obediently, looking across at each other, as if hoping the other would say something to stop it.

Suddenly James perked, hearing his mother's booming voice call, "Jaaaaaaaames!" Felix turned around and answered: "Yeaaaaaah!" Dallas shook his head. James frowned, and when he heard his mother finish laughing, she called out again: "Jaaaaaaaames!" He answered, and jogged across the street to find out what she wanted.

Near the driveway, Dallas leaned against his parents' car and dug his hands into his pockets. Felix followed James with his eyes until he reached the bottom of his front porch. Then he turned back to Dallas.

"I don't think James is going to do this," Felix said.

"What do you mean?"

"He keeps acting like he's going to back out at the last second. I think he's a fraidy cat, I think he's going to chicken out. Maybe we should do it without him," he suggested, knowing that Dallas would never leave James out of anything if he could help it.

Dallas shrugged at the notion. "He seemed all right the other day."

Felix shook his head and looked at the ground. "I don't think he's going to be a help. I think he'll chicken out and leave us hanging when we need him the most. You know what he's like."

Dallas watched James talking to his mother and didn't say anything. He figured she was warning James to be careful and not to stray too far. The two waited in silence until a green Chevy Nova went by, slammed on the brakes, and backed up at the foot of Dallas's driveway. The passenger-side window was open. The front bumper rattled where rust had eaten away the brace it was bolted to.

"Hey, pissant!" shouted a voice from inside the car. Felix walked down the driveway and leaned into his brother's window.

"What's up, little man, what are you up to?" Bob asked.

"You picking me up?" Felix asked.

"No. Just saw you standing there, figured I'd stop. What are you doing today?"

"Tell Dallas that you want to take me somewhere," Felix blurted, hoping to escape Dallas's plan.

"Get lost, go play with your friends."

Felix looked down at the door panel and noticed a wide smear of dried blood. "The hell's this?" he asked, pulling arms away in fear that he'd touched it.

"Friend of mine hurt his nose last night," Bob answered nonchalantly. "Had to take him to the hospital." The two brothers remained silent for a few seconds as Bob stared out through his windshield, down River Drive. "Well, I gotta go," he said, pulling the gear shift down, "see ya later."

Felix stepped back as Bob tore off, burning rubber in a screech of wheels. Felix turned back up the driveway.

"What's up?" asked Dallas.

Felix frowned. "He wanted to take me to Sports Universe to play some games. I told him no way, we're stealing some kids' stuff today."

CHAPTER EIGHTEEN

THE PHONE RANG LOUDLY in David Westwood's room while he was trying to sleep. He rolled onto his back, and pulled the covers off his face. He'd gone to bed wearing the same jeans from the night before, but his shirt was lying crumpled on the floor. The phone sang out again. He sat up, dropped from the bed, and grabbed the receiver before it rang for a third time. It was Julia. When David heard her voice, shaky and soft, every painful detail of last night crept back into his mind. She said she wanted to know how he was.

"I've been better," he answered. A long moment of silence. David looked around the room, and then dropped down on the edge of the bed. He rested his elbows on his knees.

"I want you to know that I didn't want anything bad to happen to you when I went back there."

"Are you seeing that guy? That Cassidy guy?"

"He was drunk. I swear he wasn't acting like that before you showed up." David could hear the tears welling up in her voice. "I'm real confused right now," she said. His heart stirred for a moment, but sank back to stone.

"If you're confused, then obviously I have my answer."

"It's not that simple. I was flattered, and he was being so sweet. He was just drinking too much."

"But you were flattered."

"He's, like, twenty years old, and he was the most popular guy at the party . . . Put yourself in my shoes."

"What do you plan on doing, that's all I want to know," David blurted out. There was another long pause, and David stood, letting the phone cord dangle at his knees. He almost fell in love with the silence. The dread of what her next words would be made music of the empty buzz in the handset. It was clear where it was all going. He waited. He just had to know. In words. Though he didn't want to know.

"David, I don't know what I'm going to do, I can't think straight right now."

"Fine," he said, slamming the receiver down.

He sat back down on the bed and pressed his face into his hands. He sat there, with every intention of staying that way for the rest of his life. His mind could not rest long enough to orchestrate his next move. Every option was dried up. He no longer had Julia. He no longer had any incentive to paint. He no longer had even a shred of pride, the way that bastard had manhandled him in front of everybody, laughing the whole time. He no longer had safety with his friends for he had gotten them dragged into a mess when he hit Phil. Like chess, every thought about his next move became checkmate. At every turn, there was a rook or a bishop in his path. So he sat there, stubbornly, the way the king sits on the board and the players shake hands before leaving the table. Even his tears had stopped. Every time his lip trembled he could feel tears building. He'd think of that bastard smiling with his hands in his pockets, and the hurt would subside to rage. He had no energy to get up and punch the wall. All the rage was compact, pumping through his body as he sat there on the bed.

He looked up when he heard a knock at his door. The knob turned and his father stepped in, glancing around at

David's room. He locked eyes with his son, and nodded.

"You're up," he said approvingly. "I need you to go to Ni-no's and pick up milk and butter."

"Send Mom," David answered.

"I'm not sending Mom, I'm sending you. Get dressed and go to the store." Mr. Westwood watched his son grudgingly get up and root around for his shirt. "Oh, listen, under no circumstances are you to take that flag down off the house for your still life." David looked at him in disbelief. "Last night, and this whole morning, I been seeing cars full of kids driving by the house real slow and then taking off," his father said. "What've you been up to out there?"

"I haven't done anything."

"Yeah, we'll see. For all we know, you still got people pissed off about that mural. I'm sorry. If you want I'll get you another flag."

"Forget it," said David.

"Butter and milk," his father repeated. "Half a gallon's fine."

"Great, I'm going right now."

Mr. Westwood dropped a five-dollar bill on David's dress-er, took another look around the room, and disappeared. Da-vid pulled on his T-shirt from last night, and put his sneakers on. He swiped the fiver from the dresser and stepped out of the room. Just then he remembered the cars full of kids. He went back, reached under his bed, and pulled out Nick's BB gun, stuffing it into the waistband of his pants the same way he had the night before. He left the house for Nino's Deli. Movement was his only solution to keep from crying.

C HAPTER NINETEEN

JAMES TROTTED BACK ACROSS THE STREET and rejoined his friends. Dallas and Felix stared at him, as if expecting him to waver and go home.

"What did your mom want?" asked Dallas.

James shrugged. "Be careful. Don't go too far."

"There's lots of crazies out there," finished Felix.

James looked at him and smirked.

Dallas stepped away from the car. "We're going to wait till around noon before we sneak down there," he announced. "That way they'll probably be inside eating lunch."

"I think we should get there early and stake the place out," said James. "Who knows if they'll be eating lunch or not? If they're not, we'll be screwed again."

"I like that idea," Dallas said.

"Let's go to the deli. Load up on drinks and snacks, for the stakeout," offered Felix, as if any delay might derail Dallas's plan. They all agreed, and headed for the trails behind Dallas's house, intending to take their usual path to Mayflower Avenue, and cut through Zambrini's Brick and Masonry Yard.

As they rounded a bend in the footpath, Dallas glanced up into the trees and fixed his eyes on the spot where he wanted to build his fort. Immediately, he began to have daydreams about the nights they'd all spend up there, overlooking his backyard. Late nights under the full moon. There would be no rules. That would be the attraction. And whoever wanted to be in their club could be in it. The kids from the estates. Even Jason Brock. They would only have to swear their loyalty and they'd be members.

As they walked, Dallas's eyes wandered up to the tops of the trees, and up farther to the bright clear sky, with its golden throb of light creeping toward noon. After scrambling across Mayflower Avenue, they ducked into the back lot of Zambrini's and spied a gray corner of Nino's roof rising over the treetops just a football field away.

CHAPTER TWENTY

MICHAEL DARWIN FINISHED PREPARING LUNCH for his family and packed it away in the refrigerator. He double-checked to make sure his clothes were laid out and ready for ironing. Rebecca was sleeping late, and he let her. Earlier, he had crept down the hall and put his ear to the closed door to listen to her steady breathing. A comforting sound.

Now he was rubbing his hands nervously, and checking the time. He pulled out his Bible. This week's discussion was on Job, and the suffering he had to endure for his faith. Michael was always moved by it. He knew, and it saddened him, that even under a tenth of what Job had suffered, he would have surely cracked. He would have cursed God, and died, just like Job's wife had told Job to do. He prayed for that kind of strength, but he never felt it would be granted to him. He thumbed through the book, and put a mark on the opening page of the account. Then he closed it and sat quietly, looking around as if he'd forgotten something. He searched his mind for anything that still needed doing.

Abruptly, he remembered his son playing in the basement the night before, and he jumped up to see if it needed straightening. He scrambled down the stairs, and switched the light on. The basement looked fairly clean, except for Dallas's bicycle lying on its side in the far corner. Some empty potato chip bags and a glass were scattered around a small scrap of the plywood he'd used to block up the basement window when it had broken a few months back. The small board, which was normally leaning against the far wall, was lying flat in the center of all their debris. He walked closer to it. It was not a complete mess. Still, he made a note to himself that he would have a chat with Dallas about tidying up after himself.

Mr. Darwin stooped down and picked up the plywood to put it back against the wall. He frowned, noticing the writing. Stepping further into the light, he saw the alphabet drawn neatly across the top, along with a string of numbers. The words YES and NO drawn underneath completed the image in his mind. He gasped and looked around.

"Lord, Jesus," he whispered under his breath, "he doesn't know the power of the demons he mocks." As fear turned to anger, he bounded up the stairs and ran to the front windows— the *Ouija* board tucked under his arm. He searched the front of the house for his son. Then he crossed through the house and searched the backyard. He wasn't there either. He stared at the *Ouija* board his son had made, this time in the bright sunlight. He shook his head and scowled in disgust. He would have to discipline Dallas, there was no doubt. He'd spank him good for this, and explain to him how real the demons were, how *Ouija* boards were a sure way to attract them. His face burned. He considered for a moment cutting the board up and using it as a paddle for the spanking. The message would certainly be carried. He wanted to wake up his wife, but decided not to. Instead he took the board into Dallas's room, and threw it on the bed. Better that he sees his shame in broad daylight, he thought to himself. It's because of his influences that he does this, he thought. Dallas had a poster of a Ferrari hanging on the wall. He reached over and tore it down. Then he flipped through Dallas's record albums. He took everything but an old storybook album of *Peter Rabbit*. He pulled every book off the shelf and carried everything out of the room in one bulking, awkward pile spilling over his arms. He laid out his case on the dining room table. Even his wife needed to be made to understand the dangerous path Dallas was taking. Then he sat down at the dining room table and waited for his son to come home.

CHAPTER TWENTY-ONE

DAVID WESTWOOD STORMED DOWN THE STREET toward Nino's Deli, his eyes darting to every car that passed. There was no way he was going to let them catch him unaware. He could feel the awkward metal of the gun jabbing into his lower back as he walked. He kept looking behind him, and every time a tire screeched, he'd reflexively reach back for it.

Deep inside, he hoped they would come driving by, and that damned football star would be riding in front. He'd put one right between his eyes, or better yet, right *in* his eye, so a football star he'd be no more. He'd only see half the field. He robbed me of Julia; I'll rob him of football.

He rounded the corner and headed down Turnbull Road, the way he had last night, and the night before, when he visited Julia in the pouring rain. Already he felt foolish for that, and wondered if she would tell her new boyfriend about it. The concept burned his mind—her new boyfriend. In one day, *bam!* She had a new boyfriend, and naturally it was a guy with none of David's attributes. This was not a kid interested in art, or music, or love—who composed poetry for her. This was a kid who ran around, and sweated, and bled, and whose job it was to crush people, and destroy confidence, and bash, and ruin, and wreck, and conquer, and to make sure that somewhere in the world, there were people humiliated and injured.

This was a kid like all the rest, and that realization made David rethink how he looked at Julia; perhaps she was like all the rest—a person who paid no attention to anything beautiful. The outer lines.

David's thoughts were interrupted by the screeching of tires as a car stopped short behind him. Immediately he heard the driver's-side door open and he spun around with the gun in his hand. He pointed and fired a BB before realizing it was Nick and Matthew. Nick ducked down behind his door as the shot ricocheted off his windshield.

"Jesus, Dirty Harry, what the hell?" Nick barked.

David tucked the gun back into his waistband, embarrassed. Matthew was laughing loudly in the passenger seat. David saw the shadow of a female form in the backseat.

Nick approached him. "Little nervous, are we?"

"Who's in the backseat?"

Nick looked back. "Krystal Richards. Picked her up at the beach this morning. She asked for you." He punched David lightly on the arm. "How you feeling, slugger?" Nick crouched down and shadowboxed at David.

"Did she tell you Julia dumped me for that guy last night?"

"Bob Cassidy? No, she never mentioned it."

"Just got off the phone with her. She won't give me a straight answer, but that's the way these things go."

Nick nodded solemnly and looked down, then back up at David in time to see his eyes filling up with tears. He turned away and gazed down the street. "Where were you going with the gun, David?"

"My dad sent me to the store. Says kids've been driving past the house all day."

"Massa's buddies. Come on, get in the car; we'll drive you to the store." Nick turned back toward his car. David drifted to the other side. "And forget about that girl. She doesn't know what she's doing. We'll get you a nice girl, no worries." Nick motioned with his head toward Krystal, who was sitting quietly in the backseat. David frowned and shook his head before ducking into the car.

CHAPTER TWENTY-TWO

SINCE THE PREVIOUS DAY'S TORRENTIAL RAIN had kept the nearby airport closed, the small vintage planes were now out in full force, taking advantage of the wide, clear blue sky. Siemens-Schuckert biplanes, Albatros-D.Is, single-passenger Cessnas, and Glider planes zoomed about, crossing over Turnbull to land at the local airport. James, Felix, and Dallas were halfway across Zambrini's Brick and Masonry Yard when a biplane roared overhead. Dallas leaped into the air and screamed out, looking up at the fishlike body streaming through the wind.

"I bet you could hit that plane with a rock, it was flying so low," said Felix.

"I'm going to fly one of those some day," Dallas said as he watched the plane glide over the treetops and disappear. They all stared up at the point in the sky where they'd last seen the plane, as if its ghost was still hanging there.

As they approached Nino's, something caught James's eye and he glanced across the way. Peeking out from behind a rusted, disabled bulldozer was the forlorn face of Spybot. James nudged Dallas and pointed.

"Stupid dog doesn't know when to go away," Dallas said.

"I like him," said James.

They approached the bulldozer slowly, and James could

see the dog was leery of them. He bowed his head and watched them silently. The closer the boys got, the lower the dog stooped, till he began to back away. He was shaking and his hind legs wobbled slightly. He turned to trot off, and as he did, the boys saw his tail was pulled tightly against his legs. His jowls were wrinkled and sagging with distress. He started to jog. James made some kissing noises and the boys stopped their advance. The dog stopped in his tracks. James made the noise again. Spybot's tail relaxed and he took a step toward them.

"He's scared of us," Dallas said.

"Yeah, well, if you didn't tackle him and tie a rope around him . . ." said Felix, crouching in the dirt.

"Maybe if your dad didn't hit him," Dallas countered, looking at James.

"My dad didn't mean to hurt him," James said.

"Yeah, well . . ."

They stared at the dog again. They were, all four, squatting low in the middle of Zambrini's lot. If it weren't a Sunday, if this were a weekday, and the yard were open, the workers would have surely chased the boys out of there by now, threatening all sorts of horrible things as they ran. The boys knew this. It was one of the things they did when they were bored.

But all that moved in the back of the yard was them, and the dog, shivering and frightened. James made the kissing noise again and held out his hand as if he had food. The dog's tail began to rise skyward. Another kissing noise, added with a slap on his knee, and the tail began to wag. The dog continued toward James with mincing steps. James crept closer. The two were like a teenage couple, shyly crossing the dance floor. The dog's eyes shifted from James, to Dallas, to Felix, to the ground, and then started back with James.

"Come on, boy," coached James. "Come on. Don't be scared."

Finally, he crept within a foot of James's outstretched hand and James took him into his arms. All three boys converged and started to pet him, as his tail relaxed and wagged freely. He licked James's hand and James scratched under the dog's chin, allowing his floppy left ear to drag across the back of his fingers. As he moved his hand to the top of the animal's head, he noticed bright red blood smeared across his knuckles.

"Aw, gross," said Dallas, stepping away.

"You cut yourself?" asked Felix.

James looked at the blood on his hand. "No, I'm fine," he answered, confused, staring at the dog. Clearly Spybot was favoring his left side, pulling away from James. James kept him calm and grabbed his left ear. The dog struggled. "Help me hold him."

The other two crouched down and each grabbed a part of the dog's body to help hold him still. Turning the ear over to expose the soft, white flesh, James saw it had been bleeding for a while. Dried blood had crusted at the ear's edges, and fresh blood had clotted slightly near the pointy tip.

"What happened to him?" asked Felix.

James shook his head. He reached with his two fingers and touched the wound. The dog jerked and tried to get away. James and the boys calmed him down, petting him gently. Once more, James reached for the wound, and felt a small ball under the skin, just below the raw cut. He squeezed on the dog's ear, and as the dog yelped in pain, James caught a small silver ball that dropped from the wound.

"Let him go," said James. When the boys let go, the dog took off running. James stared at the object in his hand. He wiped away the trace of blood and exposed the shiny round pellet.

"That's a BB," said Felix, who was leaning over James's shoulder.

Dallas nodded in agreement. "Someone shot him. Probably got into someone's garbage last night. *Pow!* Took a shot at him." The three boys looked at each other.

"Where'd he go?" asked James, glancing around.

Dallas shrugged. "Strays get shot all the time around here. Lucky he didn't get shot with the real thing."

James dropped the BB into the dirt and stood up. He looked around for the dog, but he was gone. Dallas and Felix had already walked away and were continuing toward Nino's. James stepped on the BB, pushing it down deep into the earth. He rubbed his hands clean on his shorts and ran to catch up with the others.

C HAPTER TWENTY-THREE

DAVID STEPPED OUT OF NICK'S CAR and stood on the empty curb. A slender arm reached out from the backseat. David knew immediately what Krystal wanted. He huffed slightly and took her soft hand into his. He pulled her out of the car the way a fisherman grabs the lead and yanks the great fish over the side of the boat. She noticed, but thanked him anyway and linked arms with him on their way into the deli.

"I'm just picking up some stuff for my dad," he told her.

"I'll walk with you," she said.

Nick and Matthew trailed behind as they rounded the corner of the building and David pulled open the door. Three kids spilled out of the store and brushed past them with cans of soda and candy bars loaded into a small brown bag. Matthew Milton looked down at them—the same three who'd been yanking that dog around the other day. The one carrying the bag had a bruise on his neck. A devilish grin stretched across Matthew's face. He made a sudden false lunge at the kids, and they jumped back.

"Aaaaaaaarghhh!" Matthew screamed at them. The three boys took off around the corner and ran past Nick's car. They kept running down Pinelawn Street and disappeared into the woods, near the back of Nino's parking lot. Matthew laughed loudly, and held the door open for Nick to walk in.

"What is your obsession?" Nick asked as he leaned against the candy rack and watched David and Krystal disappear into the back by the refrigerators.

Matthew shrugged. "Hate the little punks that run around here," he said.

Nino, the old man who owned the deli, popped his narrow, angled head up from behind the chest-high meat counter. He'd been cleaning the roast beef racks when the boys filed in. Nino was from old Europe. So was his wife. She worked part-time, helping out wherever she could. He leered at Nick and Matthew. Two lazy troublemakers, in his opinion.

"Boyce," he said, snapping his fingers at them, "get offa da candy rack. This is no playground, this is biziniss."

The two boys stood up straight and stepped away.

"Relax, we're waiting for David. He's in the back," Nick said.

"What's he doing in the back?" Nino leaned over the large counter and strained to see down one of his aisles. The boys could more clearly see the bird shape of his head, as if he'd squeezed it through the bough rails on the boat that had brought him to America as a young man. An arm was missing from his eyeglasses, and they kept sliding down his bony nose and away from his wrinkled face; he had to keep reaching up to right them. He stared back at the boys who were on the verge of laughter. "It's not funny," he barked. "Many a things go missing from here. My wifey says she sees you and de odder boys sneaking around."

"We never stole a thing in our lives," Matthew said, holding his hands out in earnest.

"So you say, but I suspeck different. My wife, she watcha you like a hawk."

"I don't know what she's seeing cause I never took a thing," said Nick.

"Just know. In the future, I watcha you boyce like a hawk. And if I see anything missing," he waved his finger at them menacingly, "I'll mayka you pay faw times as much. Faw times," he repeated, holding up four fingers, before reaching up to catch his falling glasses.

David came back from the refrigerator with a tub of butter and a half gallon of milk. He looked at his friends, and then at Nino. Locked in a duel of scowls.

Nino slowly peeled his glare off the boys as he rounded the counter and stood behind the register to ring up David's items. Even while he pressed the numbers on his old-fashioned register, he darted his hazel eyes up at the other two. They stood there like wooden soldiers. Nino's narrow face had reddened from the argument. Even as he read David's price aloud and bagged the two items, he kept his eyes on Nick and Matthew. They flinched, and left before David had received his change.

C HAPTER TWENTY-FOUR

At the Pinelawn Street entrance to the southern path that led to Zambrini's, the three boys ducked into the trail and looked back. Matthew hadn't chased them.

Panting, Dallas peeked through the trees. "Coast is clear." They stepped further into the woods, but Dallas stopped short. "Check to see if you dropped anything," he said to James, who was holding their bag of food. He rooted through it obediently.

"Don't think so," he said.

"What about my PayDay, check for my PayDay," ordered Felix, who had nearly tripped over his shoelaces when he ran with the others. He was kneeling down to tie them finally. James checked again.

"It's in here," he said while they continued down the path.

Dallas was grinning, as if he held a secret he was struggling to contain. "No worries, even if you did drop some stuff," he said as they emerged from the short path where Zambrini's yard opened up. He reached back to the elastic band of his shorts and pulled out two Milky Way bars, holding them up and then dropping them into the bag.

"Man, that's like your fifth time doing that and getting away with it," said Felix.

"Piece a cake, the old man's cleaning his shelves, he's the

only one in the store, and *boom*. It's better in wintertime, I got more pockets." The other two laughed in awe.

As they trekked into the sand of Zambrini's yard they could see the back of Nino's Deli—a dull gray box—through the trees, and the chain-link fence that bordered the parking lot. Straight ahead, about sixty feet away, they glimpsed the broken-down bulldozer where Spybot had been shivering. Dallas reached blindly into the bag and pulled out the Milky Way he'd stolen. As they passed the back of Nino's, he was about to rip the Milky Way open with his teeth when he saw Matthew and his friend leaning against the building. They looked agitated. Dallas immediately thought it was because of them. He dropped down, and the others followed suit.

C HAPTER TWENTY-FIVE

NICK AND MATTHEW leaned against the wall and waited for David and Krystal to come out of the store. They couldn't stand to be there another minute, being accused by some old man of something they didn't do.

Matthew shook his head with anger and spit. "I don't give a crap what his wife sees, she's as blind as him."

"Screw that bastard and his fat little wife, I didn't steal anything."

"They figure, *Oh, they're teenagers, look at 'em; they must be criminals.* Pisses me off."

"We got to get out of this town," said Nick as he stepped away from the wall and stood up on one of the concrete parking curbs bolted into the lot. He pivoted, doing a balancing act, and lost his balance when Krystal appeared before him. Nick stole another look at her short green shorts, the way they exposed her slender legs. Her tight T-shirt. In the bright, sparkling sun, Nick could see the pattern of her bra through the thin material, something the back of his car hadn't revealed. David emerged from the store and put his father's groceries down on the ground. He looked at his friends.

"What are we doing? Car's on the other side," he said.

"You got somewhere to be?" Nick asked. "Let's hang out awhile."

David frowned. "What about Phil Massa and the rest?"

"Buncha fags," Nick answered, leaning against the wall again. "They're not going to do nothing."

Krystal whistled and David turned to her.

"I can't believe you took him out with one punch like that, holy crap!" she said, laughing. It wasn't funny, but David started to laugh a little anyway.

"It was the least I could do, I was getting my ass kicked." The other two started to chuckle.

"Bob Cassidy's a jerk," Krystal said. "Guy's four years older than you, he's got nothing better to do than hang at a high school party and pick on a sophomore?"

David watched Krystal as she shook her head. He noticed how kind her face seemed when she smiled, genuinely indignant. Did he have the wrong impression of her all along? he wondered. He noticed the softness in her voice, but his face dropped when over her shoulder he noticed a Chevy Nova slowing down on Turnbull Road. It appeared to be pulling into the parking lot, but suddenly stopped, then kept going. David's hand snapped quickly to feel the gun in the small of his back. He peered into the car window and saw Bob Cassidy driving, and lost all feeling in his feet when he saw Julia sitting beside him. The car peeled off, disappearing from view, and he whipped around to face Krystal.

"Did you know about this?"

"Oh, Christ, here we go again," announced Matthew.

David darted his eyes at him. "The hell's your problem?"

"Not everything is about you. Jesus, can't we go one day without you moping over that stupid bitch?"

David stepped toward him. "Call her that again, I dare you."

"Oh, knock it off," barked Nick, stepping between the

two. They glared at each other. Matthew was getting angrier.

"You know, everybody's got problems. We just got accused of shoplifting in there. You act like you're the only person on earth and I'm sick of it. Let him come at me, Nick, see what the tough guy can do."

"Up yours. You want to go?" David held out his arms. Nick put his hands on David's chest to hold him back.

"Let him go, Nick," Matthew taunted. "See what he can do. You're such a tough guy, let's see you be tough."

David pulled away from Nick and kicked a rock across the parking lot. His eyes were searching for some rational explanation. On the ground. In the lines painted across the asphalt. In the broken glass. She was in his car. She was sitting in his car, and she must have told him to drive off when she saw David. He glanced toward his friends. They were silent. Matthew wiped the back of his neck and stared at his sweaty hand in disgust.

Krystal watched a change wash over David's face, from an expression of outward rage, to one of calm, inner madness. David was standing near a disabled shopping cart lying on its side. He stared at the ground in silence. His mind was no longer racing, but in a flash he imagined Julia wedded to Bob. Their three kids; the family photo standing in a frame on their coffee table. It gave some sort of permission in his mind to wreak all the damage he could.

His arms and legs bent obediently to the will of his rage. In one violent motion, he kicked his leg into the air and crashed his foot down on the side of the metal cart. The cart dented. Another wild stomp and it dented further. He picked it up, slammed it down. He picked it up again, and hurled it across the parking lot. He let out a guttural scream, grabbed an empty Budweiser bottle, and fired it against the wall of the deli. The bottle shattered into pieces. Then he was silent again, staring at the ground. The others didn't move, but Matthew rolled his eyes. Nino stepped outside to see what all the noise was about.

C HAPTER TWENTY-SIX

FELIX, DALLAS, AND JAMES were lined up side by side, watching the one kid throw his fit. It was nothing like the other day when he yelled at them about the dog. They saw the cart sail across the parking lot, and they ducked further down to hide. When the glass bottle shattered, the three boys looked at each other in fright. They knew it was time. Felix put his finger up to his lips to signal quiet, and began to creep away, staying low, but lifting his feet so they wouldn't drag. Dallas followed after him, making long silent strides, until he reached the soft sand. The two turned around and looked at James. James glanced over his shoulder and saw the teenagers were sitting quietly now. Nino had come out to yell at them, and then had gone back inside. James took one step noiselessly, but on the second step, his sneaker came down upon a dead pine branch, which snapped loudly. James looked at his friends, his eyes wide with panic. Dallas and Felix started to run.

"Little bastards!" James heard behind him, then dropped the candy bag and took off. Felix and Dallas were well ahead. In a matter of seconds, he heard heavy breathing behind him, and a firm hand grabbed his shirt, shoving him facedown into the dirt. He looked up from his belly and saw the bottoms of two pairs of shoes streaking after Felix and Dallas. Suddenly a knee dropped painfully down into the middle of his back.

"Stay down, little prick!" David yelled, holding James fast to the ground. James rolled his eyes upward to see, in desperation, as Felix was dragged from behind by Matthew and Nick. Matthew rolled on top of Felix and rubbed his face into the sand, laughing. Dallas stopped running and turned to look at his friend, who was screaming when Matthew started to rake his knuckles hard across his skull.

"You like spying on people?" growled Matthew. "You like spying?" He knocked on Felix's head like a wooden door.

"I'm sorry!" screamed Felix, clawing to wiggle away.

Krystal had caught up and was standing in the space between James and Felix, both pinned to the ground. Dallas stood untouched. Nick was kneeling beside Felix, pouring sand in his hair. Dallas picked up a short piece of pipe and hurled it at Nick. The pipe missed.

"If you'd hit me with that, I would've killed you," Nick said, with a mildly suppressed laugh.

James had his eyes turned up the whole time. His heart was exploding. He couldn't breathe. He was choked with fear. Run, Dallas, he thought. Run for help.

"Run!" he heard Felix cry out. Dallas turned on his heels.

"You want me to go get him?" Krystal asked. Matthew nodded, and she took off.

For a moment, James smiled inside. Though he was still fearful, he knew she would never catch Dallas. This was a kid who ran down a dog. She was only a girl. He knew the shortcuts. He'd escape the yard and get help.

Dallas blazed across the yard and frantically searched for the open spot in the fence. He had glanced back for a fraction of a second, and seen that he'd gained some distance. He kept looking for the hole, and finally found it. Suddenly his heart leapt. She was already on him. Krystal had her hand only a foot away from his shoulder. His soul deflated. He let out a whimpering shriek and crumbled to the ground. Krystal straddled him and pulled his arms behind his back.

"You're not fast," she said. "Who told you that you were fast?"

Dallas couldn't believe he'd been caught. He was panicked for the first time in a long while. She wasn't even out of breath.

James let his eyes drop; their hope was gone. He felt as if he was crying, though his fright had stopped up his tears. His mind flitted over a thousand things. David pulled James to his feet when Krystal rejoined the group, holding Dallas's arms behind his back. With a little force she threw Dallas away from her, and he put his hands up in a defensive stance. Matthew got up and circled behind him. Nick pulled Felix into the same circle forming around Dallas, then James was thrust into it as well.

"What were you guys doing? Spying on us?" yelled David. "You want to get smacked around some more?"

"Screw you!" barked James, though he looked as if he couldn't himself believe he'd said it. David stepped toward James and smacked him across the top of the head. James took it and glared back. David shoved him angrily.

"Yo, we should make these kids fight each other," Matthew said, tapping Nick on the arm.

Nick nodded. "I'd like to see that one fight him," he said, pointing first to Dallas and then to James.

"Yeah, David, let's shove 'em at each other and see what they do," Matthew ordered.

David pushed James toward his friend until they bumped chests. Dallas put his arm across James's shoulders, turned him aside, and kicked sand at David.

"All right, let 'em go," said Krystal.

"Should we let you go?" David asked. "What do you think, should we let you go? Why don't you beg us to let you go?" But in that instant, James remembered Dallas's credo, and kept quiet. The kid looked like he was getting angrier. "I don't hear you begging," David said, circling closer to James. He grabbed him by the collar and shook him.

James found that he couldn't move his arms; some force was holding them down, and he felt ashamed. He was allowing himself to be pushed around. He did nothing, even when David lifted his small body in the air, and threw him to the dirt.

Nick and Matthew surrounded Felix, who was limp with fear, staring at the ground. The two boys pushed Felix, laughing. They kicked him in his butt every so often, and stuck a foot out to trip him. Felix flailed his arms and scowled like a trapped raccoon in a garbage bin, which made Matthew laugh harder.

"He's in a panic," he said. "Relax, little man, it'll go faster that way."

Matthew shoved him to the ground. Felix scrambled back to his feet and threw a fistful of sand at Matthew. It was Nick's turn to laugh.

"Little fucker," Matthew snapped. He grabbed Felix's shoulders and swept his legs out from under him. Felix jumped up again.

"He's like a weeble-wobble," Nick said. The two shook their heads in amused disbelief.

Felix ran off to the edge of the sandlot, where a patch of trees gave shade to the men who worked there. He grabbed a stick, holding it like a light saber, and stared back at them. They looked bored and turned their attention to the other two boys.

Dallas had reached down and grabbed a large rock.

"All right, enough," Nick said. "Run along, little beasts."

But Dallas stepped forward and fired the rock across the circle. It bounced loudly off David's head. David stumbled back. "Goddamnit!" he yelped.

"Ooh, you're going to let him get away with that?" Matthew taunted. Then he grabbed Dallas by the shoulders and pulled him down. He put a foot on his back. Dallas wiggled away, grabbed another rock as he rolled, and slung it at David. This time it hit him in the elbow. David jumped back again.

"Will you get him under control?" he screamed.

Matthew started to laugh, as if the threat of Dallas's stones wasn't serious. David was on the verge of losing a battle with a little kid. He turned red in the face. He looked at James, who was slowly stepping away from him, and grabbed him by the collar. James allowed himself to be yanked around and kept quiet.

"Your friend likes throwing rocks?" David said, using James as a shield.

Dallas looked around. Grabbed a handful of igneous rocks—he'd remembered more than he realized in science lab. They did the trick nicely. They were not the same rocks washed smooth from the ocean. They were jagged. Bits of quartz that sparkled in the hot sunlight. A few were chunks of mortar and concrete left behind from the brick pallets. Black pebbles from asphalt and tar.

Dallas began throwing them, in rapid succession, aiming for David's head so as not to hit his friend. David twisted and ducked. Some of the rocks found their mark and each time, David grew angrier. Matthew and Nick kept laughing as they watched the scene unfold. When a sharp corner of cinder block struck David on the chin, he kicked the back of James's knees and dropped him so his head was near his own knees. He reached back with his left hand and grabbed the gun he had tucked away. The weapon was then at James's temple, and James shut his eyes. He squirmed as he felt the cold barrel touch his sweating face. Dallas stopped throwing. He heard Nick chuckling behind him, telling Matthew he'd never heard of killing someone with a BB gun. Dallas stared at David, snarled, and threw another rock.

"Stop throwing rocks," David growled.

Dallas threw another one. It missed, and sailed past David's head.

"Tell him to stop throwing rocks or I'll shoot you," David commanded. James didn't even open his eyes. "Tell him," he said again. James kept silent.

A smooth skipping rock hit David on the shoulder. He pulled James up, turned him around, and James opened his eyes. The barrel was in his face, waving from his left eye to his right. "Tell him to stop or you'll lose your fuckin' eye, I swear to God." He let go of James's collar.

Though he was free, James didn't move. Another rock whizzed by David's head. James looked blankly back at Dallas. It was as if he was somewhere else; indeed, as if he'd abandoned his own flesh in the middle of Zambrini's.

Krystal was creeping up behind Dallas. Nick and Matthew stopped laughing and turned to Felix, who was sliding away to make a run for it.

"Where you going?" asked Matthew. "You going to hit me with that stick? Your friend throws rocks, two can play at that game." He picked up a handful of stones the size of golf balls.

Felix, shivering with the stick raised in the air, stared at Matthew's hand. Matthew reached back and threw the first stone. It missed. He threw another one, and Felix swung the stick and knocked it to the side.

"Oh, you little wiseass," Matthew said. He threw another one.

Felix swung the stick and batted the stone clear over their heads. Matthew craned his neck and watched the rock fly out of sight. His scorn deepened, and he threw another. Felix fouled it off. Matthew and Nick looked at each other, slightly amused. Felix bit his bottom lip and squinted. Eyes darting side to side, he watched to see where the rocks would come from next. In his head he made a quiet prayer that he could see each rock and knock it away. Two went flying at the same time. One missed, the other, Felix just got a piece of and knocked it weakly into the air. It was as if there was a force field. When Nick threw another one, more on target, Felix sent it into the trees some thirty yards in the opposite direction. Matthew and Nick began to whoop and holler at him, trying to distract him. Felix swung the stick with passionate abandon. It was as if every swing was a plea.

Another rock came at his head; he fouled it off. One came at his knees; he golfed it into the air. Finally, Matthew threw a stone that curved toward Felix's stomach.

With a desperate swing, he hit a line drive back at Matthew, and it hit him square in the chest. Now enraged, Matthew and Nick bum-rushed Felix, throwing him on the ground. They squished his head into the leaves. Matthew got up and told Nick to back off. He had gotten hold of the stick Felix was using, and he raised it over his head.

James had his eye on the barrel of the gun; it seemed to eclipse the world around him. Out of the corner of his eye, he saw Matthew hit Felix with a stick. He saw Nick step on his head to keep him on the ground. David was still ducking rocks from Dallas, growing impatient.

"You do realize I got a gun in your face, are you going to tell him to stop?"

James stared at him defiantly. Just as the last rock hit David in the chest, Krystal tackled Dallas.

Seeing her holding the boy steady to the ground, David let out an awful, guttural noise that made James flinch, and suddenly the gun was driven into the side of his face. James staggered back, eyes closed, and fell to the ground. He lay on his back. Stared up at the bright sky, as the sweat from his face rolled down and stung his eyes. A warm, thick liquid poured into his left ear. He heard David storm away from him.

David grabbed Dallas by the collar and rolled him over onto his back. The veins in his temples were visible. Something in his mind raced at that moment. He thought of all the taunts at school. His fight the night before. Bob and Julia. He was always being made the fool. Even by little kids. He could only hear white noise inside his ears, and feel the blood pumping through his head.

"You want to throw rocks? I'll make you eat 'em! Open up!" he screamed. He grabbed Dallas by the throat and Dallas reflexively opened his mouth. "Here." David stuffed a rock into his mouth. Dallas spat it out. David held his throat tighter and cracked him on the jaw with a clenched fist. He felt the boy go soft in his hand. "Here, and here," he offered, stuffing rocks that were lying around Dallas into his open mouth.

Dallas tried to spit them out again, but the earth had fallen out from under him. He couldn't hear. He could only feel the jagged edges of a stone cutting into the roof of his mouth. Another, smoother stone clanked against the back of his bottom teeth. His head felt like an empty coffee can being filled with rattling marbles.

"Here, eat rocks . . . Here's another one." With each rock

stuffed into his mouth, Dallas's face turned redder. "Here, and here!" shouted David. "Here, here's another one. Eat it. Here's another."

Matthew and Nick had walked away from Felix, leaving the little boy sobbing at the edge of the woods. Krystal stood behind David, somewhat in shock. She brushed some hair back behind her ear and stood there, mouth agape. She looked at Matthew and Nick, who were drifting over toward David. Matthew still held the stick he'd used to hit Felix.

"Here. Eat this," they heard.

"He can't breathe!" Krystal screamed.

"David, that's enough!" shouted Matthew. But David had pushed Dallas's chin closed so the rocks were completely in his mouth. Dallas's eyes had turned red, and he looked up at David with muted fright.

"That's enough, for Chrissakes!" yelled Nick, as he lunged and tackled David away from the boy. David was panting. He looked down at what he'd done. Dallas was squirming on the ground, clutching silently at his throat.

"He's choking to death," said Matthew.

"Oh my God," Krystal cried. She turned and ran out of the yard, into the street where Nick's car was parked. Matthew kneeled at Dallas's side, but Dallas jerked away and knocked him onto his back. Matthew got back up and reached for the little boy. His face was turning purple.

"What did you do?" yelled Nick, shoving David away from him.

"I don't know the Heimlich," announced Matthew, looking desperately at the boy. His convulsions were slowing.

"Do something!" yelled Nick.

"I don't know what to do!" Matthew screamed back. Nick turned and ran away. Matthew stood up. "I'm . . . oh God . . .

I'm sorry," he said to the boy, and ran off as well. David stared at the three little kids in quiet shock. It was as if a shell had exploded between them, and they were all just beginning to realize they were hit. Stumbling to his feet, he tucked the gun away, turned, and ran.

James had opened his eyes when he first heard the kid stuffing rocks into Dallas's mouth, but his heart was so heavy—his mind so petrified with self-preservation—that he dared not move to stop him. He'd listened to the kid counting off the rocks as he stared up at the sky.

It was a bright sky, cloudless. It was muggy. Desperately trying to find a place of calm, James listened to the silence with relief.

Some blue jays were disturbed, screeching in the treetops. From the left side of his peripheral vision, a glider appeared in the sky, drifting soundlessly over the yard. Even as he heard Dallas kick with a weak leg, and heard a mute squeal rising out from his friend's red face, he watched the plane with envy, soaring beautifully.

He was afraid to move, for the kids could come back. Maybe they'd stuff rocks in *his* mouth. He could tell Dallas was crawling toward him. A slight squeal escaped from his body. James could see he was rapidly scratching at his throat. Then Dallas rolled over to his side, and lay there, motionless. James watched the plane glide over the yard, and disappear behind the tree line.

When Dallas kicked and convulsed for the last time, the yard fell silent. James could feel his left eye swelling shut, but the pain didn't follow. A blue jay chirped. A slight breeze rushed through his hair. He dared not move. Finally, he rolled his head to look at Dallas, whose red face had stiffened, and his eyes had reached their resting place, the outer corners dragged down toward his mouth. His face wore an expression like he'd been sent to his room for the night.

James heard Felix roll out of the woods and flop over on his back. He was still crying, and covered his face with his hands. James turned his head back to the sky and watched the blue expanse blaze over him in mockery. A shadow jogged into James's view. When he looked up, Spybot was standing over him. The dog rooted his nose down into the dirt and sniffed at James's neck. He sniffed the wound across his face, and licked it. James reached up and shoved him away weakly.

The dog trotted over to Dallas, sniffed him, and as if he'd smelled something entirely unholy, left the boy lying there and sat down beside James. He felt the dog's warm body nuzzle against his side. The heat grew more intense. Felix stopped crying and pulled his knees into his chest. Suddenly, James heard his mother's voice crying out into the air, "Jaaaaaaames!"

He was too weak to answer. He listened to the older neighborhood kids on River Drive answer with their sarcastic imitation. "Yeeeeeaaaaaah!"

CHAPTER TWENTY-SEVEN

IVAN ILLWORTH STOOD BEHIND HIS LITTLE BOY in the full-length mirror in their bathroom, adjusting the boy's black tie. It had been years since Ivan wore a tie, but the memory of how to tie one never left him, though so many other memories had. He crossed the tongue over the knot, pulled it through and tightened it, like a noose. He flipped the boy's collar down to frame the knot, but left the top button open. James watched him in the mirror. Ivan's eyes fell upon his boy's face for a moment. His mouth turned down in a solemn frown.

"So you can breathe in this heat, son, we'll leave the collar open slightly."

James looked at himself from head to toe. Other than the stitches above his right eye, he looked like a respectable old man in his little black suit bought special for the occasion. He glanced back up at his father, who had taken his hands off his shoulders and was adjusting his own tie; he hiked his all the way up and kept the top button fastened. James made a curious face.

Ivan looked at his son in the mirror. "People are less forgiving of adults," he said. "I'd look disrespectful if I didn't button all the way up."

James stared back into the mirror at himself, and his father. "Button mine up too."

Ivan stared straight ahead and nodded. It had also been a long time since he'd looked into a mirror sober, a vow he'd made to himself that morning. He'd spent most of the ordeal glazed over—through the police questions, the hospital, even sitting in Michael Darwin's living room while the man rocked back and forth in his wife's arms. But today he'd keep the bottle capped. He was surprised at how bad he looked—the broken capillaries in his face and eyes, and the dogged, wrinkled skin of his cheeks. It would almost amuse him if . . . He looked back down at his son and put his hands on his bony shoulders. He hoped his expression said all the apologies he could muster, because he couldn't speak them.

James sat in the backseat behind his father on the way to the funeral across town. His brother sat silently beside him. Ivan drove slowly past the Darwins'. Their car was already gone. They drove past the patch of woods on the corner of River Drive and Mayflower Road that was supposed to be the home of their new fort. James looked into the trees, blinking, and turned away. His brother put his arm across his shoulder and patted his back. His mother sniffled in the front seat.

The doors of O'Shea's Funeral Home were packed with people from the Darwins' church. When the Illworths arrived, all heads turned and watched them climb the steps. They didn't move until there was some whispering, and they saw the stitches on James. Then they parted down the middle of the porch to make way. Everybody stared as they passed and entered the building; Ivan nodded silently.

In the foyer, more people from the Darwins' church were gathered in small pockets, some sobbing, some consoling one another. A couple of grown men wandered about with Bibles in their hands. Ivan lowered his eyes as he passed them and soon they were in the chapel room, where Dallas's coffin rested, closed, on top of a bier ringed with flowers. There were so many flowers they formed a teepee, piled at the base of the bier. James peered out from behind his father, who was clutch- ing his hand. The grip grew tighter the closer they got to the coffin. James heard his mother gasp.

"Oh God," she cried, and rushed out of the room. Kevin followed after her.

Ivan and James continued along the crowded wall, weav- ing their way to the front. Ivan turned, still holding his son's hand, and cast his eyes over the crowd. He saw, on the far side of the room, Minister Roberts clutching his Bible, speaking to a small group of ladies. Ivan looked down at his son, who stared wide-eyed at his friend's coffin. Pictures had been put together in a collage. James looked for his own face, but he couldn't focus. Ivan glanced over at Minister Roberts.

"Looks like there's not an ounce of blood in that minis- ter," he said absentmindedly. "Like all those priests when I was growing up in the Bronx."

James looked up at his father and watched the muscles of his jaw tighten. He didn't appear to be talking to anyone but himself.

"All bloodless and constantly shocked by everything. Ev- erything surprised them. So why did they ask so many ques- tions, if the answers were going to take all the blood away from their face?"

Ivan and James crept closer, pressing against the wall.

"I think that's why they drank so much," Ivan continued, "to keep some color in their cheeks. But this one, this one here doesn't drink. He asks the bloodletting questions, but he doesn't drink. You must think I'm half out of my tree," he said to his son. "Why do I keep talking about drinking? It's just . . .

to look at him, even now he looks like he's asking questions he shouldn't be asking. I mean, why talk at all? Just say the prayer and let everyone be to themselves."

Ivan moved James aside when a man, reduced to tears at the bier, fled past them up the aisle.

"Reminds me of the priest my father hated when I was just a boy. Same heavy, colorless face. We'd pass him on Fordham Road, and he'd shift his eyes from us, on account of my father, and this one time when he went to confess. That's where I've seen that face before, that horrible look—from the priest on Fordham Road.

"My father had gone to confession one day out of the blue. He hadn't been to church in years . . . but he sits in this confession booth and he says all that *Forgive me, Father, I haven't been to confession in six years*, or whatever it was. He confesses to the priest that he made it with his wife, my mother, before they were married, which is supposed to be a sin. So, first the priest asks him: *How many times did you make it with her?* And my father starts to get annoyed. But he answers anyway. Then the priest asks: *What kind of things did your wife do for you before you were married?* My father bangs on the side of the confession, gets out of the booth, goes around to the other side, and tries to reach into the curtain to yank the priest out. Took six guys waiting on line to pull him away. They ask questions they don't want to know. Or shouldn't know." Ivan nodded to a man as he passed him. The guy's face looked like a wilted hydrangea. "My dad never stepped foot in a church again, and I never did either." They stopped short behind a crowd of mourners blocking the aisle.

Janet had stopped crying and rejoined Ivan at the front of the chapel. He looked at her and pulled her into his side with his left arm. Kevin leaned against the wall and peered around.

In the back of the room, there was a sudden disturbance as the crowd made way for Mr. and Mrs. Darwin. Rebecca walked in front of her husband; her face the color of wax paper. Ivan saw Michael and shook his head slightly. Michael lagged behind, his eyes bloodshot. He used the shoulders of some seated people to guide himself along.

"Will you look at this poor gentleman, good Lord," Ivan whispered.

The people gazed up with saddened surprise, and helped Michael Darwin along by patting his hand as it pressed against their shoulders. He made it to the front, locked eyes with Ivan Illworth, and was pulled to an empty chair next to Rebecca. He rocked slowly from side to side. It was the same condition Ivan had seen him in when he'd sat in the Darwins' living room on the day of Dallas's murder.

Someone from the church had stopped at the house and given Michael something to calm his nerves. He had taken it, and chased it down with scotch. It seemed as if Michael's state of mind had not changed since then. He looked as if he were about to fall flat on his face, but for his wife holding him up with her arm hooked under his. Ivan watched with pitying eyes, and rubbed his son's shoulders.

Simon and Anne Cassidy arrived, but stood in the back with Felix and their other son, Bob. Anne was holding a tissue to her nose, and clutching Felix by the shoulder as if she would never let go of him again. Felix stared around the room dumbly, and when he saw his friend standing there looking back at him, he made an odd face, and looked away.

More people filed in. They stared at each other, with nothing to say. Finally Minister Roberts cleared his throat and approached the podium. He dropped his Bible on the spine and let it flop open, a third of the way. He closed his eyes for a moment, then looked up at Dallas's parents. He grimaced.

"Family. Friends. When we read the account of Job, it brings many things to mind. Thoughts of suffering. Interminable suffering and hardship—but also of strength," he began nervously—his voice soft and quivering, seeming to melt under the fluorescent bulbs above him.

Ivan watched the minister look mournfully upon the Darwins. He wanted a drink.

Minister Roberts cleared his throat and resumed: "Job asked his Lord the Father why the wicked of his day go about earning money and having wives, gaining in health, and living happily, while they practice wrongdoing? And we too, we often question why so many good things happen to bad people." The minister cleared his throat again and coughed, as though to expel the whisper from his voice. "Rich people gain riches through unjust means, and show their wealth in all sorts of flashy ways. Men and women in Job's day acted similar, and yet here was Job, a faithful servant of God, suffering immeasurably, as we all suffer on this day. In this parlor."

Ivan's ears perked up. He tightened his grip on his son's shoulders. It was the first time in his life he'd felt included in any group. If suffering were collective, then others suffered with him. The hairs on his neck and arms stood on end. Minister Roberts took a deep breath. He wiped sweat from his face with a folded handkerchief he had tucked into the side pocket of his suit jacket. Ivan could see his hands were vibrating at the podium.

"Job asked God: *Why is it that the wicked themselves keep living? Have grown old? Have become superior in wealth? And their offspring are firmly established with them in their sight, and their descendants before their eyes? They keep sending out their young boys just like a flock. They spend their days in good times.*"

By the time Minister Roberts finished his passage, the strength in his voice had returned. Not the sonic boom of his reprimanding sermons, but at least the shaking in his chest had steadied.

"Job had everything taken from him in an instant, when God allowed Satan to remove all protection. His livestock were killed. His belongings sacked by neighboring tribes and barbarians. All ten of his children—yes, seven sons and three daughters—were killed in a sudden windstorm." Minister Roberts risked a glance at his audience. Many had begun to cry, but they were all still watching him. He looked back down and wiped away more sweat. "But Satan wasn't done. He then struck Job's very body, from head to toe with malignant boils. Painful to the touch," he added, and paused. He closed his eyes. "Job spent days sitting in ashes to soothe his pain, scraping the boils with pieces of broken earthenware. But Job endured. He never wavered in his faith."

The minister opened his eyes again and stared out at a rapt audience.

"With all that had gone terrible for him, he never turned his faith from God, even when his wicked wife said to him: *Curse God and die!*"

At these words, Ivan's mouth dropped slightly. He absorbed every syllable. Every pause.

"*Curse God and die,* his very own wife told him," the minister boomed. "Adding to that, three of his companions began to convince him that God was doing a wicked thing. Yes, they began to blame God for this great tragedy." He shook his fist in the air, as if to emphasize the rage of Job's companions. "And many of you may be doing the same thing, blaming God for this awful, awful tragedy," he said, now gesturing with an open hand toward the casket behind him. "This sweet child, taken before his time. What a wicked thing has happened here, to our beloved Darwin family."

Sobs became audible among the crowd, and Ivan looked at them. He reached up for his tie, as if checking to see if the knot had found its way inside his own throat, for it certainly felt like it had. The minister filled his lungs and gripped the sides of the podium. He was getting bolder.

"Job understood so little about what was happening, but he knew one thing: wisdom is hidden from among all men. Who in this room can question the doings and the allowances of Almighty God? Mortal man has not come to know the value of wisdom. Job believed this. And none of us will ever find it by land, or by sea, or by riches. Pure gold cannot be given in exchange for wisdom. It cannot be paid for with gold, or Ophir, or the rare onyx stone, or with sapphire. Gold and glass cannot be compared to it. A bag full of wisdom is worth more than one full of pearls."

Ivan nodded and pulled his boy in tighter. The audience took a collective breath, as though relieved from the burden of wisdom.

"Let's not question God's motives. Let's have faith that our little brother who lies here will be remembered by God, and that God will someday call upon Dallas Darwin."

Minister Roberts twisted his large body and extended his open hand out toward the casket. "God will say: *Dallas. Wake up from your sleep, little one, and return to your parents.* We all look forward to that day."

Rebecca sobbed upon the first syllable of her son's name, the hard *D* like a trumpet call in the distance. Her husband stared off into oblivion.

"So let us contemplate our suffering, and know that this world is not in His power, but the power of the wicked one, who first stripped Job of his children, and now has stripped the Darwins of little Dallas." The minister moved his grip from the sides of the podium to the top. "Do not get caught up in anger," he warned loudly. "And don't call for violence against that young, violent man now sitting in prison, for God has a place for all sinners.

"Job understood that all wrongdoing was going to be punished in God's due time. Job says: *At daylight the murderer gets up. He proceeds to slay the afflicted and the poor one. And during the night he becomes a regular thief. They do not know daylight.*"

He wiped the corners of his mouth with his handkerchief and deepened the lines in his soft face.

"But let it be known," he continued, "that Dallas will be in our midst again, because the last book of God's word promises at Revelation, where we read . . ." He flipped to the back of his book while the audience nodded. Rebecca's face was buried in her hands. "*And God will wipe out every tear from their eyes, and death will be no more, neither will mourning nor outcry nor pain be anymore. The former things have passed away.*"

His voice broke, and he straightened his tie. Ivan's own eyes watered as the minister looked up.

"Take comfort, all you mourners here. Let this boy's life, and tragic death, be a symbol not of God's disappearance, but of His very existence. What a wonderful God—that He's allowed us to love this big."

These last words weren't in his notes. Somehow they poured from him. He was staring back at the room. Their eyes filled. He felt it. He almost seemed trapped inside that instant, feeling his own transformation. To love was not a commandment, suddenly, but a gift!

"You've got to believe this," he said, pounding on the podium. "I know, I know, it always seems like we don't count, but we do. He speaks to us through his word, he cries like us!"

He didn't really know what he was saying, but each idea that dripped from his mind burned to be released by his tongue. He wiped sweat from his head. "He gives us defeat, so we can learn to know victory; He gives us darkness so we can love the light. Our hearts break so the better when they mend. I'm telling you, He's real, and He sees us, and He knows. You've got to believe me!"

Myriad eyes, wet in the dim light, flickered back at him. He couldn't tell if they understood. Their faces were like cornstalks. He felt like he could wade into them and they'd simply bend to the side without resistance. Then he remembered himself.

"For Job's endurance," he said, clearing his throat, "he received all the things he'd lost in double amount. He was awarded ten more children, and he will be reunited with the ten he lost. Consider all of this, and find comfort."

Ivan's mouth had dropped completely open.

The minister stepped down and received Dallas's parents into his arms. Michael staggered when he wasn't being held, looked disinterested when he was.

Ivan pulled on his son's shoulder, but James yanked away and headed for the casket. Ivan watched his son run his hands over it. Ivan wiped his eyes, looked at the preacher, wiped his eyes again, and began to shake. His wife put her hand on his back.

"I'll be in the car," he said in a trembling voice, and ran from the parlor, hiding his face with his hand.

That night, Michael and Rebecca Darwin sat in their living room holding each other while members of their church made coffee in the kitchen. Minister Roberts rubbed his mouth. He sat on the couch across from them, his eyes occasionally darting to the people in the room, then lowering solemnly to the floor. Rebecca's best friend in the congregation, Mrs. Waring, sat down beside her, massaging her back. Immediately, as if her touch had granted some sort of permission, Rebecca began to cry. Mrs. Waring helped her to her feet and guided her out of the living room while Mrs. Waring's husband drifted in with two glasses of scotch; the ice cubes clinked softly in the dim living room. He handed one to Michael, who took it as if by rote and immediately began sipping.

"Brother Waring, I'd like to take one myself, if that's okay," Minister Roberts said. Mr. Waring quietly handed him the glass. "If this is okay with the congregation . . ." the minister added.

"Under the circumstances," Mr. Waring answered. He turned back to the cabinet to make himself another drink. Michael was already finished with his scotch, and was waving the empty glass in circles.

Another man from the congregation wandered in and took the glass. "I'll get you a refill," he said.

Minister Roberts bit his bottom lip and glanced up at Michael, whose eyes were red. He looked as if he'd aged fifteen years.

"We know," began Minister Roberts, "that alcohol can temporarily lighten one's spirit. But the word is *temporarily*."

Michael received the refilled glass of scotch.

"You go ahead and have your fill," the minister encouraged. "Get good and drunk. Then, in the morning . . . Remember the beautiful morning, and bend your will to the purpose of doing good in the world. Live with the memory of Dallas as a young, inquisitive boy, who passed into God's keeping with full knowledge of your love for him," he said, as if he were finishing his sermon from earlier.

Michael was only half-listening, staring into his glass. "I was mad at him," he said softly.

The minister shifted forward on the couch, so that he was barely seated on the edge of it. He took a nip off his drink and leaned his large head forward. "What's that, Michael?"

"I was angry with him. While he was dying, I was angry, and I was planning to beat him. He was taken from me because I was angry at him." His last word strangled in the small space between the two men.

Minister Roberts shook his head gently. "You know that God doesn't work like that, Brother Darwin. God blesses us with offspring. He doesn't punish us by taking them."

"I don't know how God works," replied Michael, and he emptied his glass into his mouth.

"Remember Job," Minister Roberts said, and he set his glass down on the table.

Michael looked up at Mr. Waring and held up his own empty glass. Without hesitation, Mr. Waring took it and headed to the cabinet. Michael nodded to his minister with a faint smile. Remember Job, he thought.

After a short while, the friends filed out of the house. The Warings were the last to leave. Mrs. Waring turned on her way out the door and hugged Rebecca. She kissed her on her tears, and wiped her hair back away from her face. Then they stepped out of the house, and the Darwins closed the door tightly and locked it.

When Rebecca fell asleep, after taking two sleeping pills with a glass of warm milk, her husband rose from the bed and headed down the dark, silent hallway. He went to the cabinet and poured himself another scotch. He hated sleeping now, for every time he or his wife would wake, the first thing that came to their mind was Dallas, and they would immediately begin to cry. He hated to sleep because he hated to wake. He took a sip of his drink, looked down the hallway to hear if his wife had stirred, and then stepped into Dallas's bedroom for the first time since the day he'd left the house with his friends.

Michael turned on the light, and immediately noticed the bare walls where all his music records were once stacked. The sight of it choked him up, and he regretted entering the room. On the bed lay the *Ouija* board. The crude thing seemed to mock him from its place on top of the small quilt. He reached down and picked it up, then sat down on the bed where it had been lying. He ran his hand across the letters. He couldn't tell if the letters and numbers were in his son's handwriting, but he knew somehow that Dallas had helped create it, and therefore, it was a part of who he was. Michael took another sip. Stared down at the board for a long time.

I can't believe I was so angry with him, he thought. That I waited for him to come home so I could beat him. I was going to use the belt.

At this thought, he began to weep, and his sobs made his shoulders shake violently. He tried to remember all the good things he knew about his son, and all the things he had taught him. He hoped that Dallas knew to pray to his God. He dropped the board and the scotch glass, and covered his face with both hands. Somehow he knew that his son didn't pray, and it occurred to him that over this entire course of days, he hadn't prayed either, and the idea that his faith, at this most crucial time, seemed to have flown from him, made the sorrow deep and unending. There really is no hope, he thought to himself as he wept. My son is really gone from here, and I'll never see him, and I believe that, and so I believe in nothing.

Oh God, I believe nothing happens after death, but rotting and decomposition, and then eventually . . . yes . . . eventually everyone will forget. And when I die, and she dies, everybody will forget. In a hundred years, the Darwins will be nothing, like a family of trees fallen in the forest. Yes, we existed, but what good is being alive? It's all emptiness. It's all absurd. My God, I can't believe it. In the end, Dallas has taught *me*. He has become the teacher.

"This is too much, too much," he cried out softly, and buried his face in his hands once again. His chest ached. He lay on the bed sobbing like a newborn, curled into a fetal position, until he fell asleep on his son's pillow, clutching at the quilt. He slept on the edge of the bed, worried that sometime during the night, Dallas would return and want to slip in beside him.

The *Ouija* board lay on the floor alongside the empty scotch glass, until he awoke in the morning and started over. Not by bending his will to the purpose of doing good in this world, as the minister had suggested, but by going to his bank and withdrawing the three thousand dollars he'd saved, in order to help pay for his son's burial.

CHAPTER TWENTY-EIGHT

THE WORDS *IN THE BEGINNING* STARED UP AT IVAN from his kitchen table and he recoiled. Was it that simple, such an old book? Something that was supposed to be so life-changing starting so simply almost made him laugh. It was the middle of the night and Ivan was alone in the kitchen. The funeral had ended earlier in the day and James had finally fallen asleep downstairs. On the drive home from the funeral, James had turned down every offer of comfort. McDonald's, Carvel, pizza—Janet called them out from the front seat as their car cruised past the storefronts. After a while James just stopped answering.

Ivan had told Janet a couple of years ago that James never asked for anything—that it wasn't healthy. She told him James knew they couldn't afford much; but still, Ivan agreed, it couldn't be good for a child not to want things.

So the boy went without supper. He went downstairs claiming he wasn't hungry, though he kept coming back. His head hurt and he couldn't sleep. Janet gave him some aspirin and went downstairs with him. After a while she came back up.

"He's asleep at last," Janet said. "He cried."

Ivan nodded. Janet made some comments about the service. After a silent moment Ivan asked if she had that old copy

of the Bible her father had bought them as a wedding gift. She
got it down from the closet and said goodnight. Now alone in
the kitchen, Ivan noticed it was bookmarked to a page where
some scriptures were underlined. *Love is long suffering.* He
tried to find Job, then thought it best to start at the beginning.
He thought it odd that people skipped around the book—even
Minister Roberts. Echoes of the sermon came back to him.
None of this was supposed to happen. That's what Ivan took
from it, and the thought of himself one day inevitably lying in
that coffin—of Kevin, and then James, sinking silently into the
grave after him—had made him run from the funeral parlor.

He remembered sitting in the car, feeling ashamed, as he
wiped his eyes with the back of his coat sleeve. The way Job
had put himself back together made Ivan wonder why he never
questioned his own misery. Did Ivan imagine this for himself?
Did he lie in bed one night and dream of endlessly needing a
drink to steady his nerves? Of marrying his high school sweet-
heart and then spending most of their marriage being angry
with her because his life hadn't gone in some other, better direction? Had he honestly hoped for all this? For odd jobs to
get fired from, and mortgage payments to fall behind on? For
his wife to go to work, first as a housekeeper and later as a
manager of a convenience store on the east end of the island?
For them to never take a family vacation? To be displeased
with everything? Had he desired to live in a poor, depressed
town; had he wanted to live the experience of dashing down
the street barefoot when the cops came to tell him something
had happened to his son behind Zambrini's Brick and Masonry Yard?

On the day of the murder he had run down River Drive
despite the cops cruising alongside him pleading with him to
get in. He wasn't thinking; he was doing. If he could, he would

have grabbed the earth like an anchor rope and pulled his son toward him.

The cops at the scene must have been expecting Ivan to arrive in an orderly fashion, for they were sharing a cigarette and trembling over Dallas's body when he burst from the hole in the fence and sprinted across the sand yard to his son. James was bleeding from his head, and when Ivan saw Dallas lying dead a few feet away, and some cops crouching beside little Felix, he reacted as if they were all dead and started clutching at James screaming, "Not everyone, not everyone!" The cops pulled him off. James was shoving him away. Ivan struggled with the cops until one of them yelled that he was trampling on evidence.

He had followed the ambulance out of the yard and had seen Janet and Kevin. The cops had set up tape and were holding the crowd at bay. Ivan went frantic again when he saw her, and they rushed toward each other. The cops nudged Ivan back under the tape and Kevin sprinted home to get the car. Ivan was hesitant about getting in, not without his flask. But he'd left everything back at the house when he ran out. He certainly couldn't demand to go back home for it. But knowing where he was headed—not knowing what would await when he got there—made his mind itch more intensely. He needed to coat his fear.

At the hospital, when he'd learned James would be all right, when the doctors said they were just stitching his eye, Ivan slipped past the din of the Cassidys, family, and friends filing into the waiting room, and bought a three-dollar pint of Fleischmann's. He had guzzled it down in the hospital parking lot, trying to keep his eyes open in the searing sunlight. Every time he closed them he pictured Dallas's stiffening arms. Covered in dirt. Swelling in the heat. His fingernails had looked purple. His neck as thick as a grown man's thigh. The boy's mouth had been open. Stretched downward, almost like an old man, really. And not seeing him breathe, the finality of it . . .

Ivan had been crouching between a red Pontiac LeMans and a black BMW, tipping the pint bottle upward. When he'd finished, he had leaned against the whitewall tire of the Le-Mans and wiped his forehead. The shaking in his hands had begun to ebb.

Had he called out to God then? No. But he hadn't yet heard the minister's sermon. He hadn't realized yet that there was such a permissible thing as complaining to God. In fact, he hadn't realized a lot of things. Yet the minister's sermon had seemed so immediate, so much what his congregation needed to hear. It was like they were getting healed.

So why did they skip around the Bible? he wondered. Didn't they somehow need to know the whole story? And what was it about the minister's words that seemed to coat their grief? No longer wanting to feel locked out of the world, Ivan stared at the words. *In the beginning.* It was the perfect opening, after all, he realized. He didn't get far before he reached man's first lament. Well before Job. He read until his head began to nod toward the open pages. Then he crawled into bed and reached his arm across Janet's body. He could tell she was still awake. For the first time in years, she gripped his hand and drew him to her. He had left the Bible open on the kitchen table. When he went to bed, Adam was alone—and was just about to ask God to cure that for him.

CHAPTER TWENTY-NINE

TWO WEEKS AFTER DALLAS WAS BURIED, James rose from his bed early one morning and pulled on a green shirt and a pair of shorts. The end of summer was drawing near. James had only recently stopped crying every time he awakened, or went to sleep, or took a shower.

There was nothing special about this day, except that he awakened with the birds, and had been stirred by a dream, and couldn't go back to sleep. He tried to close his eyes, but the light from the eastern window, though dim, still buzzed beyond his lids, and he popped up from the bed. His feet found the floor, and he climbed the stairs to the kitchen. His mother and father were sitting there as usual, drinking coffee. Ivan was alert, but was surprised to see his son up so early. James stood in the doorway and stared at his parents. Ivan pulled the chair out beside him and patted the seat for James. Then he poured a half cup of coffee into a mug, filled it with milk and sugar, and slid it over to him.

"This'll give you a pickup," he said.

Janet, who ordinarily would have been lecturing Ivan, allowed this with a smile. James saw his mother's approval and took a sip from his first cup of coffee. It tasted like dirt, and he wasn't sure if he'd take another sip. Things were much quieter, James thought, ever since his father woke up the day after the funeral, gathered all his whiskey bottles from his horse barn, and poured them all down the kitchen sink in front of everyone. He had left one of the empty bottles of Fleishmann's up on the kitchen windowsill as a reminder.

"Before you go back to school, I'd like to teach you how to ride a horse," Ivan said to his son, rubbing the back of his shoulders. Janet stood up and went to the sink to rinse out her coffee cup.

"I want to go back in the woods," James said softly.

Janet looked at her son. "Please don't go far away from here," she pleaded.

James turned to his father, who shrugged and sipped his coffee.

"I'm not ready for you to go back in the woods, I'm sorry," Janet said.

"Okay, Mom," James replied, though inside, he'd made up his mind. He finished his coffee, got up from the table, and went downstairs.

In the kitchen, Janet and Ivan sat at the table. Ivan reached across and pulled the Bible over to him. He flipped it open and looked up at his wife.

"Maybe we should let James get back into his routine if he wants. I think the woods would be good for him. Therapeutic, don't you think?"

"I don't want him back where those sons a bitches can get him," she said emphatically.

Ivan knew not to press. He nodded slightly and watched the sun settle on her face. Ivan was startled at how young she looked in the light, the same as when she'd insisted on an official first date and he'd brought her to the beach. He watched her look out the kitchen window. He could tell she was conflicted. She knew she should let James go into the woods, but she couldn't find the strength to say so. She stood up and went to the windowsill, taking down the empty whiskey bottle. She caressed the clear neck of the bottle with her fingertips, down to the letters written on the cheap label. All the bad memories that bottle had caused. She stared at it in silence.

"If I knew that was going to be my last drink," said Ivan, breaking the tense silence, "I'd have picked a better brand than that stuff."

Janet looked over at him and saw that he was smiling. She returned the bottle to the windowsill.

Just after lunch, James headed out the front door and wandered down the street toward Floyd's River. He kept glancing behind him, nervous that his mother would catch him at any second. When he wasn't looking back, his eyes burned ahead for the mark. His mind raced with fear and anxiety, but his legs kept moving toward the patch of woods where Dallas had fought one of his last battles. The kids from down the street were probably finished with their fort by now, and he searched the tree branches above for the structure hanging in midair.

The dream that had startled James awake had been awful. He was sitting in a tree fort with Felix, and they were both laughing, rolling on their backs. Dallas climbed up the ladder that led to the middle of the floor, and poked his head through to look at them. His eyes were bloodshot, and his temples throbbed like a bullfrog's neck. He was angry at them, and told them this was their fault. Just as he was about to climb inside, he fell back down through the hole. When Felix and James leaned forward and looked down, they only saw the empty rungs of the ladder nailed to the tree trunk their fort was built upon. Dallas had fallen into nowhere, and when James turned to Felix, he saw that his friend's face was the devil's, and he had six rows of metal teeth when he smiled. When James woke up, he realized what Dallas was likely calling for, even from the grave.

Alone, his eyes now fell upon the skeletal structure of the fort, no different than when they had left it. He looked further into the woods for a sign of the kids. He kept glancing back, and occasionally stopped to listen for his mother. A few feet from the shoulder of the road, he saw the pile of wood they had made. The kids had not been back since the fight. Like a swarm of bees after the hive has been disturbed, they must have moved on to a different place, and left everything behind. It was just the sort of luck James was hoping for. He stopped again and listened, but his mother still hadn't called.

James grabbed the piece of plywood that he and Dallas had been carrying when they were chased. The board felt alive in his tender hands—a looking glass to things past. He shut his eyes. Pictured Dallas's face illuminated with mischief. He flipped the plywood over so it lay on top of two support beams they had carried off. He piled all the shorter pieces on top of the plywood, and stepped further into the woods, approaching the sagging structure. His temples throbbed. He could hear his heart. He saw the hammers lying on the ground and picked one up, then took a huge swing and knocked the rest of the beams loose from the tree trunks.

Frantically, he kept looking around as he stuffed the hammer into his shorts, grabbed the pieces of wood by their ends, and ran backward with them. He was desperate to get to the other pile. Every so often, the long nail sticking out of the other end of the board would snag a root, and send James reeling. He'd turn around, shake the board until it was loose, and then keep running backward.

When he reached the first pile, he tripped over it. The

sticks and pine needles jabbed his back. The boards he carried dug nails into his side, but James hardly felt it. He picked up the two support beams he'd used as runners for his sled, and began pulling the whole pile through shrubs, leaves, and between trees. He heaved with every last breath, pulling the sled down River Drive.

Panting, he looked through the woods once more, but saw no sign of the kids. He knew it would only be a matter of minutes before his mother called out. He wished he had Felix with him for help, but ever since the thing happened, his friend had been acting weird.

Halfway down the street, his legs gave out, and he fell flat on his stomach. Rolling over, he sat up and caught his breath. He took the end of his T-shirt and wiped his face dry. He could feel his cheeks burning red in the August heat. Then he stood to his feet, grabbed the two handles of the sled, and continued to run with the wood, until he fell again at the edge of his front yard.

Janet had just opened the door, and was about to call out for her son when she saw him lying flat on the lawn with a pile of wood at his feet. Her heart stopped at first, until he began to slowly sit up. She stood on the porch, her hands on her large hips. James looked over at her, breathless.

"What's all this?" she asked, pointing to the pile of wood.

"Building a fort," he confessed, still panting.

Janet closed her eyes. It was too soon, but somehow the world had begun to rotate again. She'd need Ivan to indulge her when she went back inside.

"Be careful," she finally said in a defeated tone. "I'm going to call for you in a minute." She stepped into the house and closed the door.

James sighed, and looked at the pile. He couldn't bear to

drag it another step, he thought, as he stood to his feet, picked up the handles, and kept pulling.

James dragged the pile deep into the woods, huffing, and searching for the three trees that had appeared in his dream—the trees upon which Dallas wanted the fort built. He could see, through the dense leaves, the faint lines of the Darwins' backyard fence. It was chain link, and ran along the back of the property to the western corner where a larger picket fence started up. Behind the picket fence was Felix's backyard.

Over at Felix's, James heard a crack. After a long pause, he heard it again. James wiped the sweat from his face using his shirt.

Another crack rang out, and something cut across the tops of the trees, spitting through the leaves until it landed some twenty yards away. James eyed the triangle of trees that lined the sides of the trail, and reached for the first piece of wood to build his foundation. He slid a beam out from under the pile. It took a considerable amount of yanks, and when it was free, it sent James flying backward into the brush that marked the edge of the trail. The sticks dug into his back.

Rising slowly, he grabbed the edge of the plank and dragged it over to one of the trees. He took the hammer and some nails, and placed the board flat to the trunk. It took several swings.

His hammer falls echoed in the silent neighborhood, but his mother still hadn't called. Suddenly Felix's fence rattled violently. James peered through the trees. A small head rose from the top of the fence; Felix pulled himself above the pointed tops. The boy stared at him, and looked at the wood. James could see that the deep bruise near his hairline had now faded. His lip was healing as well. James smiled tightly.

"I'm building the fort," he said, as if expecting Felix to hop the fence and join him.

Felix shook his head. "You just can't help but make a ton of noise, can you?"

"What are you doing over there?" James asked. But Felix shook his head once more, and jumped down. James watched the fence rattle where Felix had been hanging. He was confused. When he heard another crack, it occurred to him that Felix was not going to join him. He stomped over to the other tree, turned his ear to the air, and heard a faint voice calling his name. He dropped his hammer and ran out of the woods, sprinting for his front yard.

Moments later, he was back at the fort, and climbing awkwardly to the top of the support beam. Once he was up there, he was able to see into Felix's backyard. Felix wasn't there anymore. The noises had stopped. He turned his face down in despair.

Soon he was nailing down the plywood, for James had created a flat stage some nine feet in the air. When James heard his mother call out, he hung down and dropped. He could only half jog back to his house.

After his mother acknowledged his return, James went around to his backyard, turned on the hose, and drank greedily from the spout. The water made a large fountain as it gushed from the hose and flowed over his teeth. He gulped with wide eyes. He guzzled the water down as if it were his last drink. Then he poured the water over his head. But as soon as he shut the hose off, the sun started cooking him again, and the relief he had felt from the water was gone. Ill-refreshed, he headed back to the woods to see the work he'd done.

The next morning, James got to his feet and stretched slowly, putting on the same clothes as the day before and painfully climbing the stairs to his kitchen. Ivan was already up to the

Book of Leviticus, having read the whole previous day and into the late evening. James ate a bit of toast, gulped down a large glass of orange juice, and headed back out the door.

At the site, he once again heard yesterday's noise from Felix's backyard. He decided to ignore it, the way Felix had been ignoring him. James looked at the platform of his fort and knew it needed walls. The debris of plywood and scrap two-by-fours lay scattered at his feet. He didn't know where to begin, and the wood felt heavier than it had the day before.

A few scraps of fence slats made fine ladder rungs, and James took them to the tree. He nailed them into the trunk and used the ladder to help drop some of his wood onto the stage. His arms felt as if they'd been coated with lead sleeves. He pulled himself onto the platform awkwardly, flopping onto his back. The corner of a two-by-four dug into his spine.

He sat up, near tears. His face was sweating, and he felt a headache coming on. He had no help. He was all alone. His knees were bruised, and he'd smacked his thumb twice with the hammer. His thumb was white with dead and chafed skin, but under his nail the blood had formed a black pool. He was getting dizzy, and his temples throbbed. He could hardly move. He knew he needed water, and he regretted that he wasn't doing this with Felix's help, and that Felix was just over the other side of the fence, but didn't seem to care.

The stage had been built; wasn't that enough? But he knew that it wasn't enough—that a good fort needs walls, and a window to see approaching enemies. It needed a strong roof to shelter from rain and snow. It needed to hide him in plain sight.

A piece of plywood that was balancing on the edge of the stage teetered. It rose upward and began its cruel descent back to the ground below.

It was Ivan who caught the end of it, and used his other hand to catch the loose two-by-four falling along with it. James saw the wood slide down and had lunged forward when he noticed his father standing there, glancing up at him.

"Could hear you from all the way home," Ivan said. "Looks like you're having some trouble here."

James almost started crying, but suddenly everything seemed possible.

Ivan told James to stand back. He did so, and with one hand, Ivan shoved the wood back onto the stage. James pulled it the rest of the way up while his father tried to retrace his youthful steps. He took hold of the stage's support beam and heaved himself onto the second rung James had nailed to the trunk. Ivan noted that the beam held his weight.

"Built this thing pretty sturdy, son," he said.

"I don't know how to build the rest," James said. His voice cracked and some tears followed. It bothered him that his weeping couldn't be helped. He had no energy left to fight it.

"We'll get this built in a couple hours," Ivan responded, looking at his watch. "Plenty of daytime left." The words caused more tears. Ivan grew nervous. He glanced around at the pile of wood and stomped on the stage. It didn't budge. His back was turned. James was still crying, wiping his face with his shirt, and Ivan wanted a drink. It was not a feeling he had planned, and he'd not felt the urge in his mind this strongly in weeks. "If the foundation is strong, which it is," Ivan said, to distract himself, "then we're cooking with grease."

As Ivan pulled the plywood out from under the two-by-four, it made a great deal of noise, which Ivan had hoped for. He only heard a last sniffle before James rose to his feet beside him to help. The boy picked up a two-by-four. The tightness in Ivan's mind, the urges that made his hands shake so often before, faded.

"This'll be our corner," Ivan said. "Now ordinarily you need three studs, but one'll do just fine." He set the board in place. "Now nail her home, son."

James swung the hammer with both hands and soon had the bottom nailed in place.

"Now we've got the beginning of a solid corner," Ivan said. "We'll join the other piece of plywood to this and we'll have the walls up in no time."

His excitement renewed, James scrambled back to the ground and raised the second piece of plywood up to his father.

"Get those shorter scraps of two-by-fours, James," Ivan shouted from above, "we'll make the window with that!"

James obeyed, and the two of them built the window frame on the east side of the fort, just like he'd seen in the dream.

Ivan climbed down and gathered up the rest of the planks and two-by-fours. "The key to a solid wall, James, is plenty of support studs along the plywood. We'll nail these planks every two feet or so, and pretty soon this fort will withstand the surge of Achilles." Ivan laughed and wiped sweat from his forehead, leaving behind a dark trail of dirt. It was a different kind of sweat than he was used to.

James hammered away at the studs as Ivan stood them up.

"Now, you don't want the window too big," Ivan warned. "Otherwise the archers can get their flame-tipped arrows into your fort and capture your king."

James laughed. "Who's my king?"

"For the moment, you're your own king . . . Here. Same principle. When our corners are solid, our roof will never fall on us."

Ivan noticed their wood supply was running low. The dropping sun cast a cool shadow across the trees and for the first time, they worked without wiping their faces.

"The western wall will have to be where our day ends, son. Not enough wood to finish our roof."

James nodded. "It was all I could get," he said.

Ivan put his hand around the back of his son's neck. "King John's Castle took years to build, James, you've done fine. Let's get this wall up and box ourselves in."

James built the western wall alone, while his father coached him. When he finished Ivan took a deep breath. "I haven't been this tired in a long time," he said, climbing down.

James heard a loud pop coming from outside the east wall, where the small window had been framed. Then another noise echoed, and something soared through the trees. It was a rock, James could tell by its sound.

He went to the window and saw Felix standing a few feet from his house. He was serving himself rocks, lobbing them into the air and smacking them with a stick. One after another, he did this, serving himself from a pile at his feet. Expressionless. Blankly focused on his hands. James watched him swing away, until he heard his mother call out for him.

"Jeez, is that what she sounds like?" Ivan asked from below.

Felix also heard Mrs. Illworth cry out, and he stopped swinging. He locked eyes with James. The stick was propped at his side. The two boys stared at each other until Janet cried out again, and Felix held his arms out.

"Come on, James, before she loses a lung," Ivan said. James frowned and headed down the ladder.

James waited until evening. When he stopped hearing the crack of wood and the rocks tearing through the leaves, he went back. He didn't have enough lumber to complete the roof, but he had those two beams. He stood at the base of his fort and closed his eyes. Felt his mind drifting to sleep. He stood there for a moment, as if napping. There was no wind. The katydids were only just beginning to rub their wings. He opened his eyes, climbed the ladder, and pulled himself to the deck.

Felix's backyard was empty. James could see the stick leaning against the side of the house; a pile of rocks was stacked a few feet away. James kept looking into their kitchen window. He watched the soft yellow light shudder when someone passed the window, like old home movie frames. Mrs. Cassidy.

Then he saw Bob. *He's fuckin' dead*, James thought, suddenly. At the hospital. When everyone was standing in the hallway, just outside his room, and he heard the name David. It was David something—the kid that did this to Dallas. And James remembered every vile thing that spewed from Bob's mouth. "He's fuckin' dead!" he remembered hearing, and James feeling like he needed to lie still again and not move. There were some pounding noises on the wall. He could hear Bob's mother trying to soothe him quiet. Even when he saw Bob pass the window again in the dim evening light, he thought that all he'd ever think of when he saw Bob from now on would be his voice barking just outside the hospital room: "He's fuckin' dead!" *Fuckin' dead*. It echoed.

James climbed the eastern wall. Through the bright kitchen window, he saw Mr. Cassidy at the sink. He wasn't speaking, but it didn't look like he was listening either. Bob came into view to reach for paper towels, which hung just above Mr. Cassidy's bald head. James grabbed a nail and drove it into one end of a plank.

When he looked through the trees he saw Mr. Darwin

standing near his fence. He was wearing a thin pink robe with white trimming, presumably his wife's. It was untied at the front. Underneath he wore boxer shorts with black socks and a soiled white T-shirt. He held a drink in his left hand, which he swirled around so the ice cubes clinked against the glass like dull wind chimes. To James it looked like iced tea.

"It's you," Mr. Darwin said, resting both forearms atop his fence. James said nothing. Michael observed the structure. "Good-looking fort."

"I'm building it," said James. He stopped short of saying more.

Mr. Darwin nodded and took a sip. He lowered the glass and the ice swished back into the liquid. His eyes rose up to the treetops and he nodded again. James nervously looked up as well, as if down here they were missing out on a conversation. Michael gestured to James's chest. "That's Dallas's shirt," he said.

James looked down. It was. Dallas had given it to him when they went to raid the neighbor's fort. It was green, and Dallas wanted all of them to blend in with the leaves. James couldn't speak.

"You were wearing it yesterday too," Mr. Darwin said.

James clutched at the tail of the shirt, smoothing it out with both hands. He'd never looked at Mr. Darwin all that much. Never realized how closely his eyebrows matched the light color of his hair, or the boniness of his sharp nose. Mr. Darwin had a look in his eyes since he'd noticed the shirt—like he was about to toss his drink, hop the fence, and wrestle it off him. James was tired. He didn't want to think about how to escape, or worry over whether or not the man could reach him. He glimpsed the roof peak of his own house, just beyond the Darwins'. He wished Felix was with him. Anyone.

Mr. Darwin wasn't blinking. His glassy eyes, like a crocodile's eyes, were perfectly still.

"You don't say much," the man finally said.

James didn't know what to say. He feared that anything he said would be the wrong answer. The crocodile would snap. It was enough to just keep Mr. Darwin in front of him, glaring up at him. It looked to James like the man was now staring at nothing. Past, or through, James's stomach. He started to make a strange whirling sound with his mouth. Then he clucked his tongue a few times. It was as if his brain had climbed down to the hand that swirled his drink. Left the eyes fixed where they had last consciously looked.

Then, just as abruptly, Michael Darwin came alive again. Sipped his drink. He tapped the top of his fence hard enough to make the links rattle.

"Probably a good thing," he said.

James had already forgotten what Mr. Darwin was responding to.

Michael ran his hand gently across the fence top and started to back away. He looked up at James once more. "Putting a roof on it?" he asked. When he got no response, he nodded. He'd almost smiled. Then he focused on James's shirt again and the grin faded. He raised the glass to his mouth and drained it. The ice cubes crashed against his lips. He swallowed and lowered the glass to his waist.

"I wish you wouldn't wear that shirt anymore," he said to James. "I keep thinking it's him." Michael turned his glass upside down. Watched the ice cubes slide out and spatter in the leaves at his feet.

James noticed he was wearing slippers. And when Mr. Darwin tucked one hand into the pocket of his wife's robe and wandered to the front of his house, out of sight, James felt his lungs exhale. It seemed to him like the first time he'd breathed all day.

C HAPTER THIRTY

"GOT A LETTER FROM THE SCHOOL YESTERDAY. Says due to the outpouring of support from the community—no, the *overwhelming* outpouring of support—they're looking forward to me returning next year." Rebecca Darwin laughed bitterly as she rubbed a bowl over her towel-draped hand. "They called it a difficult summer and would like to see the new school year as a fresh start."

A sink full of dishes floated in bright suds. She placed the dried bowl to her left and stared down at the water, bit her bottom lip, and held a palm to her head. "Apparently, my job was under more of a threat than I thought. So they're doing me the favor of holding open a job they had no right to threaten to take away in the first place—isn't that nice of them?"

She always had headaches now. Dull ones. And sharp ones that poked just behind an ear, or an eye. She steadied herself at the sink. This was a dull one.

"They're going to pity me? Welcome me back and then pass me those looks?"

Rebecca reached into the sink as though it was a magic hat and pulled out a glass. She could count the seconds between any household chore and her next thought of Dallas. The boy emerged from the darkening sink water. He formed in the dust on the end tables. He wafted from the heat of the oven. His

voice rattled in baritone thuds with the submerged dishes, settling down after she removed the glass.

"There was this time when . . . this one time Dallas wanted
to go see a movie that was coming out and he was begging me
and begging me, and I said I couldn't let him because I hadn't
passed it by you or Minister Roberts yet. I told him I didn't
even know where it was playing. So he sulked into his room
and he must have seen the ad for the movie, because he came
running out all excited and he said, *It's coming to a theater
near us, Mom! It's at a theater near us!* Never made me laugh
so hard before then. He was full of all those little lines that
he thought were serious. But that's what made it funnier. And
I want to tell that story. I never thought to tell it before, and
now I want to."

Reaching blindly into the sink, she drew out a plate.

"But I can't because the moment I tell it, I'm going to get
that pitiful look and it's going to ruin the whole point. I want
to tell it, but I can't, and it pisses me off that I can't tell it . . .
Michael, are you listening?"

"You're telling it now, Rebecca," Michael said absently.
He'd been sitting at the dining room table ever since he'd drifted
in through the front door wearing Rebecca's robe and carrying
an empty glass.

"Yeah. Maybe." She turned back to her dishes. *But who's
listening?* she thought. He'd not been making much sense
lately. He'd developed a habit of sitting up all night in the
living room. The past three or four days had been the worst;
as soon as he stopped vomiting every morning he'd start to
mix his drinks. Then he'd scrutinize the wallpaper in the living
room and take out sheets of paper and draw a new pattern. He
kept insisting it was their ticket out.

Rebecca remembered Michael's boss telling him to take

all the time he needed before returning to work. But that was awhile ago. Now Michael's boss would call and she'd hear Michael repeating *Yes* continuously. Capitulating. A lot of *Yes, I know*s and *Yes, we'll see*s. Meanwhile, the checks had stopped arriving in the mail, but every time she'd try to rouse him to action, he'd say something meaningless and gloomy and it would infuriate her. Even news of David Westwood's trial wouldn't stir him to get dressed, or raise his voice.

He'd been so right about so much in their marriage. And trouble had its way of shaking out with the passage of time.

That's what he'd said about the whole incident with the hallway fight. Her mind, so vividly filled with violence now, cast back effortlessly to the boy walking out of the nurse's office with his parents. The hem of his skirt sweeping the dusty floor. Had she judged him? She had. She'd judged his parents. But when it came time to cover for Mr. Ragone's son, she couldn't do it.

The day she had resolved to lie for the bully, she'd seen the fragile boy coming down the hall. Odin. Strange name for a strange boy with a strange look, but when she saw him that day he looked nothing like the boy she'd rescued.

His black skirt was replaced with brand-new jeans. His hair was shorter, and his nails were washed clean. If not for the fading cut beneath his right eye, and the scab formed at his bottom lip, she may have never recognized him. And when he saw her, when he looked up from watching the floor, he stopped in his tracks. He stared at her a good while, and she gave him a familiar smile and waved. But he didn't return the gesture. In fact, he turned around and retreated back down the hallway in the other direction. Her gaze remained fixed on the empty space he'd once filled in the hallway and somehow she sensed that it was not the bruises that had made him feel ashamed to face her.

In that instant, she resolved to push forward and tell the truth. The sight of Odin disappearing around the corner steeled her nerves. It would all have to lead wherever it led. *Man plans. God laughs.*

Michael hadn't even questioned why she changed her mind and she loved that about him. Not everything had to be said. He just promised that in the spiritual timeline of an ordered universe, all paths lead to justice.

Now was just a matter of waiting. Waiting for him. Waiting for his eyes to blink on. Was the way to rescue him to not come to his rescue? That kind of rationalization was just convenient. The truth: she was exhausted.

The phone rang. Rebecca watched it while she dried a glass. Finally it stopped. She looked through the kitchen doorway at her husband. He'd gone to pour himself another drink, but she noticed that he turned the glass upside down and covered the mouth of the bottle. She looked away. She'd become more self-conscious about watching him.

"The phone rings all the time," Rebecca said. "If it's not that reporter from the *Turnbull Times*, it's someone from work. I have nothing to say. There are no words to make them understand, but I can't say that, because then they say, *I know, I know.*

"*Is there anything I can do?* That one's the worst. What do they think they can do? And it will only get worse when I go back to work in September, that's for sure. I'll get into the building and the lounge will be filled with baskets and flowers from people I don't know, and every person I see will drop their eyes and mumble something. And to see all those kids passing by and goofing off, and kissing in the hallways? Some of them were probably friends with those animals.

"And the worst part of it will be watching them all slowly

forget. Watching every one around me start to laugh again, and tell their Easter stories, and forget to hide pictures of their grandchildren. Not that hiding them would be any less painful. They'll all start to move away from it and forget about it. People have short attention spans for other people's suffering, they'll move on."

Reaching into the warm water seemed to soothe her. She pulled out another dish and heard her utensils settle to the bottom of the sink.

"I called my boss after I got the letter, and I told him I wasn't coming back. He got real silent on the phone and then he did just as I thought. He told me the job would always be open for me in the future. He had that tone of voice on the other end and I could feel his discomfort. I can't bear to go through that—I'll climb down into my own grave before I have to endure that.

"I know this puts more pressure on you. It's the last thing you need, Michael, I know that, but I can't do it. I have to stay away from that place." Rebecca looked over at her husband. He'd risen from his chair and gone to the window.

Lately he hadn't been listening. Not really. Just her general tone. Apologetic but angry. Restless and annoyed. Her tone seemed to always be reaching for some purpose, but the words it carried landed just inches before the feet of purpose. He knew this, now, that he hadn't been listening, and felt in some way that turning over his glass on top of the open neck of the bottle was the first thing he'd been aware of consciously doing since . . .

And yet, even his distraction from what she was saying to him just moments before felt different than the way he'd been tuning her out in the past few weeks. She couldn't know that, but it was true. Another conscious thing. He felt a tingling sensation behind his ears.

The young Illworth boy preoccupied him. Seeing him piece all his materials together to build that tree house had somehow cast Michael back to his own youth. He didn't build tree houses; they didn't interest him. He dove for clams in South Bay with his uncle. A smile nearly reached his face as he watched the trees in his backyard form a wall of shadows from the world.

He wouldn't tell Rebecca just then. It wouldn't make sense to her. But he told himself about the clams. How his uncle showed him the way to dig with his toes. How to decide by feel, what is a stone; what is the elongated black shell of a mussel. What is a baby horseshoe crab. What is a colony of snails clinging to sea sponge. What is the broken tooth of an old anchor. And, at last, what is a clam. The surf clam snuggled in the arch, the quahog was a golf ball wedged under the toes.

Then how to hold his breath. Dive down into the murky brine and reach blindly into the mud beneath his foot. Grab the clam and firmly pull it from the bed. How his uncle always told him the best part of clamming was that if you missed it the first time, you could always dive back down to get it. The same way he'd learned to stay afloat when the waves surged and lifted him from his feet, by keeping his face turned toward the sun. By taking deeper breaths.

"Otter," he muttered, his voice broken. The nickname his uncle had assigned to him for all the many times he had to dive back down into the now-disturbed water to redeem himself. He grinned inside the memory. Pressed his forehead to the window pane. The rush of cold from the glass felt good against his brows, which ached every day.

What sounded like a squeak escaped from Rebecca's voice and Michael rolled his head to look at her.

What is this—thing—they had? What word or phrase existed that could describe how they'd been avoiding each other while they still slept in the same bed, ate at the same table, held hands to the silence of the ticking clock on the living room wall? How many times this week did they hug each other, how often did one dry the other's tears with their own sleeve, or their hair, or pressed their faces tight against one another. And yet they'd divorced each other, somehow. They'd clung to small facts that were meaningless. She had said to him a few weeks ago, "You were going to beat him." He had pointed out how she always fought him on getting to the church early, and if they had gone early on that day . . .

And yet, it wasn't divorce. It was the furthest thing from it. Michael watched her as she methodically dried her dishes and he allowed himself to see her standing before him on their wedding night. How she had dropped her paper-thin nightgown onto the floor with a flirtatious finger and bit her bottom lip. It was all he could do to stay a gentleman.

They'd known without speaking when it was time for Dallas. They'd collapsed into each other that night, and the night after, and the night after, until she finally emerged one night from the bathroom, crying.

She was standing in the kitchen drying dishes and yet she was that woman; she was all of those women—a culmination of a life lived, and even though everything had changed, none of it could change. If anything could be said of his faith in God, it was that, though boiled away and maybe gone forever, he could not deny that the past would often circle back and become the present. And here was his proof, he thought, as he watched Rebecca in the dimming light from the kitchen become that woman who stood before him at the foundation of his world. Flesh of my flesh, he thought. And he knew what he meant.

Michael went up behind Rebecca at the sink and wrapped his arms around her waist.

"I'm sorry," he said, and kissed her squarely between the shoulder blades. Tomorrow, he told himself, he'd pull his tie on with his face turned toward the sun. He'd step into his old shoes, which were now his new shoes. For nothing would ever feel comfortably nostalgic again, and he knew he still had miles of regrets ahead of him. He felt Rebecca's hands grip his arms, which were now cinched around her waist. He was no longer a little boy. But in that warm instant he could hear something like a voice singing from his heart: *Dive back down. Dive back down.*

C HAPTER THIRTY-ONE

FELIX CASSIDY WAS STANDING JUST A FEW FEET AWAY from his back porch. Inside his house, his mother watched him from the kitchen window. His father was at work. Felix sent a rock over the treetops and watched it disappear. He picked up another one, and when his eyes fell upon the fort James had built, he twisted his body slightly and aimed for the structure. He hit a line drive and banked the rock off the side of the fort's wall. Then he went back to hitting them in no particular direction. James had been watching him, but was gone now.

When he saw James, everything that had happened weeks ago suddenly seemed to have happened five minutes ago. He remembered the fight in the yard, being beaten. His mind couldn't shake the demonic laughter—the two boys beating him up. He remembered James breaking the twig just before they were caught. And now the fort mocked him, hanging just above the fence line. He could have done a better job, he thought. He could have built it higher in the trees. He could have built it stronger. Felix took another serve and lifted the rock over the fence. It dropped just short of the fort. He tried again. That one banked off its hollow side loudly, ringing out into the air.

From the kitchen window, Anne Cassidy watched and unconsciously shook her head. Her son had been at this business for a few days now, and she was beginning to worry. She noticed he was getting more accurate with each swing, striking the small rocks and knocking them against the trees. But she wished that he would go back out and play with his friend again. Every time she tried to speak to him about all that had happened, he'd shrug and stare up at the ceiling. Occasionally he would even tear away from her violently, and move into the backyard. She worried even more because there would be a trial soon, and everyone's interest would intensify. She knew she couldn't protect him from people. But they couldn't get him to speak about it, and a grief counselor had told them to give him time. So time it was.

That evening, after Felix had fallen asleep, Simon and Anne Cassidy sat down with Bob to talk. Simon had gotten home from work that day and watched Felix hit rocks for the fourth or fifth day in a row. He hardly spoke at the dinner table, and he was all too eager to go to bed.

Simon was a large man, bald on top of his head, with fingers like rolled-out tubes of clay. He rested his hands on top of his belly like a shelf, and sat back in his chair. Anne sat across from him rubbing Bob's back with her right hand. Her feet were tucked under her on the couch. Simon rocked back and forth.

"I have no idea how long we should keep letting him do this . . . thing he's doing," Simon declared, looking toward the windows which were now black pools with funhouse reflections of their living room lights. Bob looked at the floor quietly.

"The grief counselor says we should wait . . ." Anne offered.

"Grief counselor doesn't know anything," her husband snapped. "They're not the ones watching this every day."

The family sat quietly again. Simon looked at his son, who

was staring at the ground. "What do you think, Bobby?" he asked.

Bob looked up at him and held out his open palms. Then he dropped his eyes again to the ground.

"I mean, have you ever in your life seen anything like this?" Simon whispered, shaking his head and tapping his hands on the arms of his chair. His knees jutted straight out in front of him, and he was slightly slumped in his small chair. He sighed loudly.

"What do you suggest we do?" Anne asked.

"Can't let this thing go on indefinitely. What does he say to you when I'm not here?"

Anne shook her head, staring out into space. "Nothing. He says yes, if he wants lunch, no if he doesn't. Shrugs a lot. He hardly says anything," she said, choking on suppressed tears.

"Well, what's he planning to do, hit rocks his whole life?" Then, as if feeling guilty that he'd lost his patience, Simon leaned back in his chair and bit his thumb nail. Bob stared at his father for a moment. A slight smile stretched across his face, but vanished.

Simon looked at him curiously. "What?" Bob shook his head and looked away, but his father pressed: "What is it? What's funny?"

"I was just going to say that he's doing wonders for the lawn. All those rocks aren't good for the grass," Bob said with a slight laugh.

Simon looked away as if he regretted even asking. His wife gave Bob a slightly amused slap on the arm.

Bob laughed through his nose. "Seriously," he said, "at the end of the day, he's at least doing something productive."

Anne shook her head and smiled softly.

Bob watched his father. He was sitting in his chair, hands

resting on the arms, staring back. Bob could tell he was trying to conceal a smile, which encouraged him.

"I got a friend in college," Bob continued, "his brother's got epilepsy. Pretty bad too, every so many hours he goes into a seizure. So they hand him the iced tea mix, or the chocolate milk. He makes a great blender for the family." He laughed, but tried to be quiet for Felix's sake.

"Bob," scolded his father, though even he succumbed to the joke, and his belly shook with laughter. Anne followed suit. Bob covered his mouth, and leaned back on the couch. But soon his laughter sobered, and he was suddenly sobbing into his hands. Anne stopped laughing and held her son.

Bob was not one to discuss things with them. But he'd spent the weeks following David Westwood's arrest thinking that had he not humiliated him that night, and had he not told Felix to stay with his friends when he saw him only moments before, his brother would be his usual self, and not half crazy, and his friend would be alive, and the whole world would not have changed.

Simon stared at his boy in wonder. Bob had only been joking, but somehow the joke had stumbled on what was now so obvious to him. What was clearly needed to connect Felix's grief to something he could use—something tangible. Something productive. He rose from his chair. Anne was still consoling Bob.

"I want to get my hands on him and kill him myself," Bob said, pulling on his own hair.

"But you wouldn't, Bobby, you're not violent like him . . ." Anne said.

Her son gave her a strange look that she did not recognize.

Simon heard his wife's words trailing off as he drifted down the hall to the basement door. He quietly pulled the door open and then closed it behind him.

The basement was where he went to take in the reflections of his life gone by. It was where he'd collected all of Bob's football trophies. His team picture. A framed jersey from his first varsity game. Felix's accomplishments were beginning to accumulate too—his citizen's badge, his physical fitness completion, the tin star he'd earned in first grade for Safety Patrol.

Simon had a metal shelf unit bracketed to the wall. The bottom shelf held Bobby's things, the middle shelf was for Felix, and the top one held all the trinkets and memorabilia from his and Anne's life. His high school yearbook, her wedding gown, folded and compressed in a lined box. Cookie cans of film chronicling their honeymoon, their first camping trip, the day he first taught her how to fire a rifle—when she swung the barrel of the gun around to face him, everybody dove for cover.

Then there were trophies from his own varsity years, pitching for the Baystone High School Arrowheads. A printed certificate recording his fourteen strikeouts in one game against Saybrook Central—the most in the school's history. For the first few years after he'd graduated—he didn't know why—he'd swing by Coach Ladski's office under the pretense of saying hello until the man would finally tell him his record was still intact. Eventually he stopped visiting.

He grabbed his old glove and flexed it open like a book. Hyperextended the thumb far enough to see the Spalding insignia—black ink in the dim light. He slid his hand into the glove and it came to life. He brought it to his nose, smelled the palm, and began to laugh at himself. Stupid nostalgia.

Simon tucked the glove under his arm. The bat wasn't far away and he slid it to the side the way a jeweler handles a diamond necklace. Observed the once-white smudges of his line drives, now darkened from age. He vaguely remembered his swing. The ball giving way to the lumber, moist in his hands.

"You poor old man," he said aloud. "You poor, rich old man," he cried, swinging the bat in sharp, expert strokes toward the outfields of ancient history.

The next afternoon, home from work, Simon took awhile to get out of the car. He was hauling a large plastic bag from a nearby sporting goods store. He looked into the backyard and watched Felix take a violent swing.

"Hey, kiddo, what're you doing?"

Felix took another swing, sent a rock straight up into the air. Simon tracked its flight, and when it dropped a few feet in front of them, he bent down to one knee and held up his gift.

"Why don't you try this?" he said to his son, holding up his old Louisville Slugger.

Felix stopped swinging and looked at it. It was a rosewood bat, with a black-taped handle. He eyed it up and down almost suspiciously, and then looked at his father, who nodded.

"Here, I'll take that stick, and you try this." Simon reached for the stick in Felix's hand. The boy tugged a little before giving it up and taking hold of the bat. He bent down to pick up a rock, but his father stopped him.

"Let's try something else," he said, and reached for the large bag.

Felix watched curiously. It was filled with baseballs. Felix's eyes grew wide at the sight of them—their perfect round shape, the red stitches. His father took a ball out and rubbed it with both hands like he used to. Then he scooped the bag up by the handles and walked about thirty feet away from his son.

"What are you doing?" Felix asked.

"Okay, I'll serve 'em to you, let's see what you got." Simon took a pitcher's stance. The old feeling was returning to him.

Felix began to smile slightly. He stepped with his left foot, dug in, and cocked the bat behind his shoulder. Simon went into a windup, and fired the ball, aiming for an imaginary catcher's glove. Felix swung and missed, spinning around awkwardly with the heavy bat. Simon glanced over and saw his wife and other son watching him from the kitchen window.

"Sorry, kid, I'll slow 'em down for you." Simon grimaced at the two in the window.

"Don't," said Felix, and after throwing the ball back to his dad, he dug in again.

Simon went into his old, exaggerated windup and delivered another fastball at knee height. Felix swung and connected with an echoing thunk. The ball leaped from Felix's bat, and Simon could only spin around quickly to get a glimpse of its flight. It cleared the treetops. Simon lumbered up to the fence, putting one foot on the lower strut and hoisting himself to see over it. Through the trees, he watched the ball bouncing in the middle of the street. Good Lord, he thought, this kid can hit! He jumped down and grabbed another ball from the bag.

"Nice shot!" he yelled. "There's home runs still in that old lady!"

Felix had dug in already. "Throw harder," he said.

His father wound up and delivered, using all his strength and weight. The ball sailed upward, speeding right toward his head. Felix dove back from the pitch, and the ball crashed into the side of the house behind him. He looked back and saw a piece of their asbestos siding fall to the ground. He stared at his father, mouth open.

Anne and Bob craned their necks to assess the damage from their position at the window. Simon covered his face with both hands and began to laugh. When Felix saw this, he laughed as well. He picked up the ball where it had bounced off the house, and tossed it back.

"Throw it like that again," he said, and got into his stance.

His father wound up and fired another fastball. This time the pitch curved in toward Felix's midsection, but Felix went inside and drove it the opposite way, over the fence. The ball clanked off the side of James's fort. Simon stared at his son and grabbed another ball. He whipped a pitch up high, and watched Felix follow the ball into the barrel of his old bat, driving it straight up, over the trees behind him, and it landed in the woods with a soft, leafy crash. The next pitch was low and fast. Felix adjusted, and golfed the ball deep into the woods again.

Simon smiled. He had given everything he could throw at his son, and the kid caught up to every pitch. At nine years old, he thought. What will he do when he's a grown man!

Simon called in sick to work the next day, and spent the afternoon at the high school baseball field with Felix, pitching him fastballs, curveballs, sinkers, every trick pitch he ever used on a batter, and watching each ball get clobbered by the Louisville Slugger. It had come back to life. He beamed, not only for his son, but himself, for having at least temporarily gotten Felix to shake loose the hypnotic trance that seemed to have held him in its demonic grip. He was hitting baseballs instead of rocks, just like his old man, and Simon had taken him to the field because he wanted to see just how far his son could tattoo the ball. On a varsity field, the balls were landing softly in shallow center, but in Little League, what things he could do, he thought. He's hitting everything. Everything! And Simon watched another fly ball sail into the bright August sky. Taking deep breaths of air, soaking in the lush green of the field, as if he could hear ghosts of the future cheering on his son for all the things he had yet to accomplish in his young life.

C HAPTER THIRTY-TWO

A MURDERED FACE MAKES FOR A POOR COMPANION. The look of disbelief in the petrified murdered eyes. The stiffening veins pulsing purple like earthworms retreating to the surface from the doomed soil. Hands clawing at the neck as though strip-mining for the obstruction stuck in the throat. A dying face is always a pleading one. It seems to always ask why. That question history can never agree on. That question sat beside David Westwood on the stainless-steel benches of his new life. A boy's pleading face just before dying is a terrible roommate.

It was mid-September. The school year had started without him. David was in his plain clothes. Not having been convicted yet, he didn't have to wear the issued uniform of the county jail. Other than that, there was little for David to be grateful for, and it was in his solitude, in his holding cell, that he realized something awful about himself. When he was free, on the outside, he'd spent a good deal of time thinking about the things he *would* do, and the things he *would* become. The future was always a horizon he chased, and it dawned on him, when his movement was confined with the slam of the bars, that he no longer had a future, and therefore could only think of his one, definable act. Not only would he be spending his life in prison, as the cops had told him when they brought him in, but the repetitive image of Dallas's desperate face emerging from the darkness of his cell seemed to be the only thing that occupied his mind.

The brightness of the boy's eyes had dimmed when David suffered the blow to his head, he remembered. He shuddered. Those eyes fell into a blank nowhere and his jaw fell loose, like a sack of marbles in David's hand. Why hadn't that stopped him? If anything, he remembered feeling even angrier. Like the boy was judging him. Not participating. Not giving him the satisfaction. He remembered feeling humiliated again. The rocks that struck him, like hot holes on his flesh. With each rock he shoved into the boy's mouth, he'd hoped to wake the boy's defenses. But the kid wouldn't get angry; he would only stare back coldly. Disciplining David through silence. Another judgmental face in a crowd of plenty.

Then the moment fell away and the boy was gulping at the air like a goldfish. Eyes wide. His body wriggling to free itself from suffocation.

David thought first aid was stupid, when they tried to teach him about it in health class. Thought the Boy Scouts and those outdoor survival classes were dumb when his father tried to sign him up. But as he squatted in front of the dying boy, he'd never felt so helpless.

Alone in his cell, the feeling returned. In fact, every time he closed his eyes he was back in Zambrini's Brick and Masonry Yard, kneeling in front of Dallas, imagining the disbelief, the panic, the sadness he must have felt. In that regard, he shared some of his grief. They both wished they could have left the lot in peace. That they could rewind the earth and begin anew . . . That just a few moments would have delayed their meeting. An untied shoe, a lingering minute at the bathroom sink at home. Incorrect change at Nino's register. So the two might have never crossed paths.

In David's calmer daydreams, the boy sits up in the morgue. The rocks fly outward from his throat. He takes a deep drink of air and his lungs inflate, as he jumps from the table to find his friends. The guard clangs on his bars and says, "Your lucky day, kid, the boy will be fine." They both collapse into their respective beds that night, and exhale in relief.

But the steel toilet and the thin mattress pressed against the wall were persistent, and after the dreams and the fantasies faded away, David was left only with a recent history as concrete as the walls that surrounded him. His emotions had taken what was a sporting prank on some neighborhood brats and turned it into a continuous cycle of night terrors. Clanking bars. Labored sleep.

Only his lawyer had seen him in his worst state, when the public defender met him at the jail and told him he was going to save his life. He had grabbed hold of the lawyer by the sleeves of his blue suit jacket and wept on his chest. The man was a total stranger, but David saw the life-giver in him. He read a sincerity he hadn't read in a person in his whole life, and now any chance of redemption, of happiness, hung on this man. His parents had only been to see him twice, and both times they said nothing important. His mother told him she was tired of going to bed every night petrified of what was going on inside the jail. His father bit at his lip as if he wanted to say something but couldn't find the moment. His lawyer did neither. He just wanted to know facts. For that, David opened his soul like black storm clouds and cried until the lawyer lightly wrapped his arms around him.

That was in the early going, and he wept quietly for a few more days after that, before his grief subsided to a colder feeling of hopelessness and wonder. The only thing that still nagged and bled into his mind was the memory of running from that little boy who squirmed and gagged silently on the ground, clutching at his throat. He had plenty of time to sit and recount that day.

He'd run for Nick's car shortly after the others took off, but when he got there, Nick looked back at him, shook his head, and jumped in. He reached for the passenger door, but Krystal had locked it. He went around the back of the car to get in behind Nick, but the car lurched forward and leaped off the shoulder, knocking him aside. Nick left rubber behind as he cut a fast left down Turnbull Road. David stumbled backward, looked down the empty street behind him, and jogged that way, passing the entrance to the side trail where the boys were still lying on the ground. His mind was frantic, but he rehearsed a short map of the back roads to his house, and began to follow them.

He figured the more back roads he took, and the more side streets he used, the further from his crime he would get, and perhaps no one would find out. When he thought about what he was doing, and what he had done, he became nauseated and had to step into the woods twice to vomit.

He wandered the streets for what seemed like hours, though when he decided against making a right, and went left down Cypress Avenue, he got no farther than ten yards before a police cruiser whipped behind him and opened both its doors. David turned away. His first impulse was to run, but both officers had drawn their guns and were shouting, so he dropped to his knees with his hands up. He called out that he had a gun but it wasn't real. One cop ordered him on his face, slowly approached him, grabbed the weapon and threw it away from him. He cuffed David behind his back, while his partner grabbed the gun with a plastic bag and sealed it.

Inside the car, the two hefty policemen told him that he

wasn't in a lot of trouble, and that they would take care of him. They told him it wasn't a big deal so long as he cooperated. Then when he got to the station for booking, he was approached by two other detectives who told him he was headed to prison for the rest of his life. They told him that his friends were the ones who called them, the ones who tipped them off about where he would be wandering. They had already confessed and were willing to testify, willing to put him in jail. Then another detective walked in and told him that he believed the victim was a relative of a powerful Mafia don, and that even if he beat the rap, he'd surely be killed out on the street, so he might as well confess and let them protect him. David was dizzy with fright, and the detectives wouldn't let him sleep. Yet their persistence was the very thing that kept David quiet, and he began to get the sense that it was all a lie. He kept recounting what he'd done in his head, and as the detectives leaned over him and filled the blanks, barking their own versions under the buzzing lights, he got more confused and argumentative. The detectives pounded, they shouted, and sometimes they even appeared to be his friend, pulling up a chair next to him and putting a large hand around the back of his neck.

"Son, it's okay. All you have to do is let it out. You were angry, those boys practically got what they deserved, I know," said one of the younger detectives. "I see these punk kids running around in this godforsaken town, sometimes I want run 'em over myself. Just tell us what happened, and if you're honest with us, we can't do anything to you."

They made him answer the same questions repeatedly. He was so numb with fear that he couldn't even cry out, and partly he didn't want to. He got the feeling that he was being broken, and he got it into his imagination that whenever the

detectives walked out of the room together, they were outside
the door placing bets on who could make him cry first. This
fantasy made him angry. The detectives picked up on his anger.
They responded with their own, promising to get the judge
to throw away the key. So long as they were alive, they were
going to make sure he never again saw the light of day. They
harped on his tone of voice. Every time he whispered, they
yelled at him to speak up. Every time he spoke up, they barked
at him not to get tough. When he leaned forward in his chair,
they told him to sit back. When he leaned back, they ordered
him to sit up straight. They told him their patience was wearing thin, and that they were sending someone in shortly to
smack him around a little. He lurched forward in his chair
and vomited. The detectives laughed. They threatened to give
him a "tour" of the jail, where he'd make lots of friends. David
didn't believe it. But then he would believe it entirely, and then
he'd only half-believe. Then he'd go back to being angry and
not believing any of it.

Then his lawyer showed up. His lawyer was a tall, wiry
man in a blue pin-striped suit. He had thick, curly black hair on
the sides with a bald strip up the middle of his head. He stood
in the doorway, his briefcase in one hand, his other jammed
into his pocket. He looked David up and down and said his
name was Barry Levin, and that he was there to defend him.

CHAPTER THIRTY-THREE

AT DAVID'S INDICTMENT, the prosecutor wandered around the courtroom and addressed the grand jury using exaggerated words and legal speak that David couldn't possibly follow. Only occasionally, during the boy's fixation with the prosecutor's mannerisms, did he understand what the man was driving at. Those rare moments when he used words like *depraved, animalistic, dangerous,* and *big shot.*

"He thought he was a big shot," the prosecutor said, pointing over to David sitting in his defendant's chair wearing a suit two sizes too big, because it was on loan from Barry. "So do you know what the big shot decided to do? He decided to take a couple little boys, bash one of them over the face with a heavy pellet gun, and then choke the other little boy and watch him die."

David trembled in his seat, even when Barry took the floor in his defense, illustrating that David had tried to help the victim, and only ran because of panic when he saw the kid couldn't be saved without professional help. He also pointed out that David himself was just a "little boy," scared out of his wits and coerced into telling police officers whatever they wanted to hear. David perked up at this notion. He hadn't considered himself a little boy in a long while, and didn't consider himself one now. Not with the way his life had changed.

Not after what he'd done. What do little boys have to worry about? He tried to recall his last true memory, but his mind snapped back to the present when Barry pointed a finger at him and asked something of the grand jury.

In the end, the jury indicted David on the charge of second-degree murder. The prosecutor indicated that he would be trying all four defendants separately. Barry was frank with him after the meeting, and told David that he was facing the most severe of the charges. While they waited for transport in the back room of the courthouse, Barry wrinkled his brow and looked down at David.

"Do you understand what we're up against?" he asked. David looked up at him and rubbed his right eye, the sleeve of the large suit hanging over his fist. "If you're found guilty of what they're charging you with . . . you may never get out of jail."

David felt a throb in his chest, and the sensation in his knees disappeared for a brief moment. He put his hand on the wall to steady himself. "I didn't mean to kill that kid," he whispered, on the verge of tears.

Barry breathed heavy through his nostrils and looked away from his client. "Then what did you mean to do?"

David was struck dumb by the question. In his cell he had wept over how angry he'd felt in that moment, but never examined why. As if emotions happened for no reason, like an itch or a muscle cramp, David believed his anger had somehow erupted from an unknown place inside him, uninvited. But saying that to another person had broken the illusion.

"I couldn't take being rescued by a girl anymore," David blurted.

The words awakened Barry's eyes. He lifted his head and looked at his client. David was drawing an imaginary square on the table, the shape of his jail cell. He shook his head in thought.

"You know, the first bet I ever lost was in gym class," the boy said. Quietly. Backing into the memory, his eyes locked on his hands.

Barry leaned forward in his chair. "When was this?"

"I was in third grade," David replied abruptly, as though it didn't need to be asked. "The teacher was showing us how to ride scooters. Mr. Platz. There were only three scooters in the school, so we had to go one at a time, and Mr. Platz put a single orange rubber cone on the far end of the gym, in the middle of the floor. And he told all of us that we had to ride the scooter down the gym, around the cone, and go back to where we started.

"Vinny DeFeo was standing in line behind me, and he poked me hard in the back, and said loud enough so everyone could hear that he bet me fifty cents I would crash right into the cone. I didn't want to take the bet, but he kept poking me and calling me chicken, and the other kids started poking me too. So I took the bet.

"I figured I would win it. I mean, how hard is it to ride a scooter around a cone when you have thirty feet of room on either side? I didn't have fifty cents. Vinny DeFeo didn't either—we were all on the free lunch program. I took the bet, because even if I won, I didn't care about the fifty cents.

"When it came my turn, I got on the scooter and Vinny told me I was going to hit the cone, so I kept my eyes fixed on it. Mr. Platz blew his whistle and I took off. I kept looking at the cone to make sure I didn't hit it, and I was pushing to get past it faster, but the closer I got to it and the more I looked, the more I started drifting right for it.

"My front wheel was wobbling and I could hear all the

kids screaming behind me, and I just kept staring at it, and it was like I couldn't control anything anymore. The more I told myself not to hit the cone, the more I seemed to be heading straight for it. I ran my wheel right into it and went over the handlebars and landed on my back. Everyone laughed and clapped.

"Mr. Platz stood over me. He was angry, and he asked me if I wanted to go down to the principal's office for fooling around. There was more laughter . . ."

Barry reached into his inside pocket for a pack of tissues and put them on the table. David ignored them.

"After that, Vinny kept hounding me for his fifty cents. Kept yelling for it whenever he saw me in the hallways, and pretty soon all the other kids started calling out, *Fifty cents!*"

"Why didn't you ask your parents for the money and be done with it?" Barry asked.

"I went to my dad, and he told me that at my age all bets should be friendly. But you know how bets are in elementary school, they're everything but friendly. Vinny said he wanted me to meet him in the trails across the street, but I wouldn't go. I should have gone."

"Self-preservation," Barry said, pushing the tissues closer to David, though he wasn't crying now. "No shame in that."

David laughed through his nose and stared up at the ceiling, swallowing hard. "Eventually it was Mrs. Ramiro, my art teacher, who gave me the fifty cents to pay Vinny."

"David, what are you telling me?"

"I didn't mean to hurt him," the boy said quietly, the words barely escaping through his tightening throat. "The night before, I watched Julia try to talk me out of my fight with that guy Bob, and then on that day I saw Krystal tackle the little kid and something went wrong inside of me. It was like I couldn't fight my own battles, and another girl had to come along and rescue me again."

A few weeks after the indictment, David started getting the newspaper regularly, and just as quickly as it became a new privilege, it proved an agonizing burden. He got the *Turnbull Times*, which seemed to report every detail of his hearings. Headlines like *Trial Set for Young Turnbull Killer* and *The Monster Faces the Music*. Articles about him picked apart everything his parents did through the course of a day. One issue spread out the chronology of his life, from his birth, to elementary school, to personal accounts from neighbors. The op-ed pages were filled with presumptions. Theories on David's behavior, from people he'd never met before. Barry was always in a bad mood about it.

One piece was headlined, *The Kids Are NOT All Right,* and the writer "trembled" for the future of America, with kids like David Westwood roaming the streets. David read the numerous letters to the editor, where some people in neighboring towns were calling for the reinstatement of the death penalty, while others wrote in to say they were praying for the victim's family. Such devotion to faith and prayer used to always annoy him, but now he began to know where they came from.

Moreover, he read all the articles about the Darwin family, and their dedication to their church. He read that some in their congregation held all-night vigils outside the jail, though he hadn't seen the outside since they brought him in.

It wasn't long before the papers started reporting on the prosecution's case, and the character profile it was building against David. Schoolmates, who were already almost two months into the school year, were interviewed. David could imagine the rumor mill, the wild stories circulating through the hallways.

A local writer named Elijah Fennecker started writing a series called "The Life and Practices of David Westwood." The series interviewed his neighbors and classmates. Very quickly, Fennecker stumbled on the nickname Red. The whole town was gripped by the life of David Westwood.

"Paper says you write diaries about all the things you hate? That you hate America; that you're a communist?" said Barry Levin during one of their meetings.

David sat across from him at the stainless-steel table and rubbed his arms for warmth. He had stopped eating the jail food, was getting sick to his stomach from it, but he didn't want to tell anybody. His eyes were heavy and dark. Barry was holding the latest issue of the *Turnbull Times* with Fennecker's article folded open. He spun it around. David dropped his eyes to the pages, leaned forward to take the paper by the corners, and shook his head.

"Any more surprises for me, David?" Barry leaned back and put his hands behind his head. He exhaled loudly through his nose.

"What does this have to do with anything?" David asked.

Barry smiled in disbelief. "It means nothing. You're just a stupid kid, but they're going to use this information to paint you as a danger to this town, to society, to this country. To national security, if they have to. This doesn't help them with the bare facts of the case, but it goes a long way in the court of public opinion."

"What does that mean?" David asked, the phrase burning in his mind like a branding iron. He had an idea what it meant, and he didn't like it.

"It means if the town thinks you're a rotten apple, they'll

be all the more anxious to toss you onto the compost."

"I never told anybody I hated America. I don't, really," protested David. "They were calling me a communist."

"Yeah, well, your classmates are having long conversations with this writer, and they're saying you used to go on about how bad America is."

"They hated me," David said, his head shaking.

"Who's *they?*"

"They, them! All those . . . I don't know, any damn one of those jerks in that school."

Barry kept silent. He spun the paper back around and continued reading the article. He picked at his bottom lip. Then he dropped a finger onto one of Fennecker's lines and looked up at David. "Says here you checked out a copy of *The Communist Manifesto* from the library?"

David shrugged.

"Now? In the midst of all that's going on with Beirut and the Olympics, you're going to choose to walk around with that stuff?" Exasperated, Barry slid the paper away and rubbed his eyes. He'd been working for hours on David's case, hanging up the phone in his office every three minutes after a reporter got hold of his number. Wrangling with the prosecutor since David's indictment. "I think we should start to seriously consider a plea arrangement," he added.

But David wasn't paying attention. He was reading frantically. His lips moved softly to the words and his ears grew hot and red at the horrors the article was saying about him.

Two days later, while David was reading the new edition of Fennecker's series, a guard stormed up to his holding cell.

"Visitor!" he shouted.

An electronic buzzer went off, and the cell door slid to the

side. David stepped out gingerly. The guard guided him down
the corridors of sliding bars, grabbing his shoulder every so
many feet.

"Wait!" he'd bark, until the bars behind them slammed
shut. New bars opened, and they could move ahead. David
could see a large room at the end of the corridor.

"Wait!" the guard ordered, and pulled on his arm. David stopped. Bars slammed shut. Bars slid open. "Move!" He
stepped forward obediently. His mind was beginning to race
ahead of him. Who could it possibly be? He thought it might
be someone from class.

"Wait!"

He stopped. It might be his mother. It had been awhile
since she'd visited. He feared it could be the victim's parents.

"Move!"

Could it be Elijah Fennecker? He began to sweat a little.
What if it was Julia? Oh God, what if it's her?

"Wait!"

He stopped. What would he say to her? What was he supposed to tell her—that he'd murdered that little kid?

"Move!"

That he'd been angry? He'd lost control and took another
person's life? I wouldn't know what to tell her, if it's her, he
thought.

And yet. Deep in that place where a person would rather
have knowledge than bliss, he wished it was Julia, and the
closer he got to the end of the corridor, the more he hoped
to see her eyes blinking from behind the thick glass dividing
them.

"Wait!" he heard for the last time. A buzz went off and the
door in front of him was pulled open. The guard led him to
a small stool and shoved him down onto it. David craned his

neck to see who was coming, and his eyes filled immediately when they fell on his father.

Mr. Westwood looked at his son as if for the first time. He gazed over his clothing, bit his bottom lip before he sat, and picked up the phone. Although they each held the phones in their hands, neither said a word.

His father finally broke the silence: "Are you being treated fairly in here?"

David nodded. The weight in his chest subsided, though he didn't know what to say.

"I just got out of a meeting with Barry. Says he's going to try to get you a plea bargain deal, you know, so you do less time." On the word "time" Mr. Westwood choked up and the word only made its presence in vowel form—a squeak that came from somewhere deep in his throat. He wiped his eyes and lowered his chin, burying his face into the mouthpiece of the phone. David looked with pity at the top of his head. A bald patch revealed itself under the jail lights.

"I'll be all right," David said. "How's Mom?"

His father sniffed. "She's hanging in there. Started a fan club for one of those soaps she watches."

David laughed uncomfortably. "Yeah, I remember her saying something about that. Sounds like something that's right up—"

"Did you do it, David?" The question exploded—as if it were the one and only question he'd come to ask. He didn't make eye contact with his son when he asked it; his eyes remained fixed on the steel desk while he waited for the answer. Like waiting for the punch he knew would knock him down.

On David's side of the glass, the question hit him like a rush of frigid air. This was the one person David didn't want to have ask that question. The cops, Barry, the prosecutors—he could answer them. But his mind was swimming for a suitable answer to give his father, who breathed heavily and repeated the question, softer this time: "Did you do it?"

"Why?" asked David, as if stalling for time.

"I need to know, from you, if you killed that boy. Did you do it, or was it one of the other kids and they're blaming it on you?"

There was a long pause, and David got that feeling in his stomach, the feeling he got back when he was younger and his father would ask him if he took out the trash, or did his homework. He decided to gamble on that old feeling, and answer him honestly.

"Yes," he finally responded. He watched his father close his eyes tightly as tears squirted out and ran down the lines of his cheeks. His hands started to shake. Then suddenly, as if a fever had just broken, he composed himself, sniffed, and cleared his throat. He looked at David.

"Then I have to walk away. You did a horrible thing, and you should be punished, and your mother and I have to walk away now." He quickly hung up the phone and stood up.

"Dad!" David yelled, and leaned forward to bang on the glass. His father had already turned away and was leaving. "Listen to me, Dad, come back!"

A loud crack rang out over the loudspeakers and a bored voice said, "*Prisoner Westwood for transfer.*"

David stood up and craned his neck as his father disappeared from view. In desperation he yelled out once more: "Dad!" Then a heavy hand clamped down on his shoulder and shoved him back down onto the metal stool.

"Wait!" the guard barked. A buzzer went off. "Move!" David heard, and he was pulled to his feet.

CHAPTER THIRTY-FOUR

To look at David Westwood's sketchbook is to gaze down the barrel of a mind poised on the edge of destruction. A disturbing journey through an emotional volcano of what would spill over on that sweltering day in July. It is also a rare glimpse of what we are about to encounter in our new generation—the angry teenager. The murderous youth.

DAVID SAT UP IN HIS JAIL CELL and read Fennecker's most recent essay in horror. He wasn't feeling well. His head swirled, and he felt constantly rushed, though there was nowhere to go. How did he get my sketchbook? he wondered, before he remembered he'd left his knapsack behind when he ran from Darryl Knight's party. The night he'd punched Phil Massa and was chased by his friends. That was the night before everything else. His sketchbook, of all the private things in his possession, was riddled with every bad, rebellious, perverse, cruel, and primitive thought he'd ever had. Every interesting turn of phrase he heard. He had wanted it that way. Wanted to pour himself out uncensored, both with the brush and the pen. He'd never dreamed it would be read, especially not under these circumstances. Barry would lose his mind, this was certain.

"One day we'll pay for how we treat the weak," he

writes in one entry. "And America will choke on its own capitalist gluttony." "Do everything your impulses tell you to do, you'll regret the things you didn't do when you get older," he states in another.

David scanned the middle paragraphs frantically.

Can a boy this young still have years left for redemption? . . . David Westwood isolated himself from his peers—and then he set to the task of isolating himself from God.

David recoiled from the words. He didn't consider himself a godly person—that was true. But had he cast God away? Did he really make a conscious decision to force God out of his life? That line about American gluttony? A publicity stunt in waiting. He remembered writing that down hoping one day it would cause a media stir when he was famous. The way John Lennon said the Beatles were more popular than Jesus. It was a plant, but it made David suddenly wonder if he hadn't written it with more seriousness than intended. Is it possible to be sincere even while being insincere? He didn't know anymore. That's how it is with these people, these writers, he thought, they start making you think that they know you better than you know yourself.

The article went on. A cold sensation flooded David's mind, like an ice cube inserted at the base of his skull, dripping slowly. He was a cautionary tale, it said. He was unwholesome, adhering to destructive philosophies. He didn't look a person in the eyes. He didn't hold his hand over his heart and recite the Pledge. He had no base in religious faith, and was in the "fringe minority."

David tugged at his hair. All these conclusions from a sketchbook, he thought. The smarmy enthusiasm of classmates. He glanced back at the final paragraph.

When I see him in the courtroom, I don't know how I'll fight the urge to yell across to him: "It didn't have to be this way for you!" But I know he'll probably not hear me. By his writing and behavior—his poor attempt at art excluded—he seems beyond reason. He seems to resent all that is fine. He is angry at times, brutally sarcastic at others. Antisocial. And he's a sober warning to us all. Don't let his legacy reproduce in our town.

David let the paper drop from his hands. He felt like he couldn't swallow. It was as if he'd been sleepwalking for fifteen years, and then awakened to all the horrible things he'd done, said, written, and believed. He wanted to reject all of what Fennecker wrote. He was not that person. But all of this was out there, outside the walls of his cell. Guards were reading it. His classmates were reading it. His parents and neighbors. Julia too. Beads of sweat formed on his brow. He hadn't eaten a solid meal in weeks. His head throbbed, and he suddenly couldn't breathe. Dragging himself up from the bed, he pressed his face against the cold bars. They felt good on his hot face and he leaned there for a few minutes. He still couldn't catch his breath.

"Help," he moaned weakly. "Someone help!" His eyes turned toward the back of his head, and now his body pulled away from his control. He seized, dropped to the floor with a thud, and let out a guttural noise. It was another call for help, but he knew his mouth couldn't form the word correctly. The throbbing in his temples grew louder. He heard a loud buzz and then his cell door sliding open. Boots clapped on the floor around him. A hand grasped his arm.

"Pick him up, we'll take him to the infirmary," one of the guards said.

"No," said the other, "bring the doc here. He could be faking this whole thing . . . Lay still, Westwood!"

CHAPTER THIRTY-FIVE

AFTER HE RECOVERED FROM HIS FEVER, David began eating the jail food again, by order of the doctor and his lawyer. The guards stood over him while he ate to make sure he cleaned his plate. They seemed to take some pleasure in watching him. David would pinch his nose and force the spoonfuls into his mouth. A few days earlier, he'd explained to one of the guards standing over him that the food gave him a stomachache.

"That's what the latrine is for," the guard replied flatly. He had his arms folded across his chest, and stood up on his toes from time to time as he looked around the mess hall. "You're not allowed to have any more fevers from malnutrition, so it'll have to be a stomachache, I guess," the guard said. "Eat."

David shoved a spoonful into his mouth and grimaced. "Disgusting," he mumbled.

"You'll get used to it," the guard said, his arms still crossed. For some reason, the remark almost made David cry.

Once he was feeling strong again, David sat down with Barry to discuss the possible plea arrangement. David had somehow become convinced that he could take a shot at pleading not guilty. The facts of the case had faded from his mind. A trial would be about clearing his character. He wanted the court to see who he was, and to expose all the lies and assumptions swirling outside like plastic bags in the empty parking lots of Turnbull. His guilt had subsided to sadness, which in turn subsided to desperation, as he spent his days reading about himself and waiting for the grown-ups to decide his fate. Barry said it would be stupid to try the case.

"The prosecution has so much wrapped up on you, I'd be lucky to get them to agree to any plea deal. Are you kidding, David?" he asked, leaning forward in his chair.

"But . . . Okay, so I'm guilty of this thing, but I'm not guilty of all these other things . . . all this stuff about me being a communist, and that I hate everybody. I'm a monster. I'm not guilty of that stuff."

"Look, the only time we should take this thing to trial is if the prosecutor wants to get you for first or second degree murder. If he takes a manslaughter plea, without question we should jump on it."

David picked at his lip as his lawyer spoke. He was shaking his head. "Why would he want to get me for that?"

"First degree?" Barry raised his eyebrows. "Easy: they want to get a serious conviction. And those people out there with picket signs wouldn't mind sending you upstate for the rest of your life."

"There's people picketing outside?"

Barry Levin turned his face down into a solemn frown. "And I have to convince the DA to ignore them and not go after you for premeditated murder."

"They can't prove it was premeditated," David said, frowning in disbelief.

"Sure they can. You had a run-in with these kids before, chasing them through the woods. You had a fight with one of the victim's brothers the night before. So you decide to get your revenge on the older brother by waiting for the younger one to come through the woods—"

"That's not what happened," David interrupted.

"Forget what happened, this is what they'll try to prove. You took out your revenge on the older kid's little brother, because he humiliated you in front of a crowd of people."

David felt the hairs on his neck sizzle. His temples pounded as he watched the lawyer shake his head in exasperation and fan out a short pile of crime-scene photographs.

Barry was focusing on the space around the small yellow markers, as if the story written in the sands of the victim's last few moments would reveal something he'd overlooked. But even as he placed them side by side, they were still empty photos of pine needles. The ghosts of sneakers.

David's eyes scanned the photos too. Laid out like poker cards, a royal flush of chaos. Each corner of one photo overlaid another. Leaning forward, he examined the one nearest him—a shot of the ground. Sand mixed with the tips of pine needles. A fury of footprints had overturned the earth. Small divots from the little boys—monstrous ones gashed deep behind from David and his friends. David wondered which were his. There were so many ruts it was impossible to tell. He could just make out the spot where James had fallen face-first. Where his hands must have clutched at the sand. A deep rut, from when David had dragged James to his feet, stretched across the composition and disappeared off the edge of the photo.

He looked over at another photo—a vertical shot just to the left of the fence opening. He focused on a small paper bag lying in the sand. Candy wrappers were strewn just inches from it.

David hadn't remembered such a detail for the cops, but his mind drew a fresh replay of that day. Yes, James had tossed a brown bag to the side before he ran. Naturally it was still there, captured in the photo, the candy bars melted in their packages, nestled in the sand.

David took the photo by the corner. He could make out the distinct wrapper of a Charleston Chew. He couldn't possibly know, yet he sensed that the Charleston Chew was intended for Dallas. The feeling hit him like a slow wave, starting at the downward corners of his mouth and moving to his throat to the point that he had to bury his chin into his chest to keep breathing. His bottom lip trembled and he hoped Barry wouldn't notice. He himself had been eight years old not that long ago. He could still know the mounting anticipation, the joy, of holding something like a candy bar until you were ready to rip it open. He had taken that away. He had stolen those joys that people like himself and Dallas, and his parents, and all of Turnbull, even, had come to believe were pure and attainable.

He nearly dropped the photo. He shut his eyes and drew the image of his father coming home from work, always carrying a bag of groceries, courtesy of the night shift at the supermarket where he worked.

Sitting in his dad's worn-out La-Z-Boy, David would crane his neck as his father made his way down the hall to the living room. His father would sometimes yawn and just wave to David. But always, he would reach into a bag and pull out a frozen Milky Way. Toss it to his son, who would be squirming his way off the La-Z-Boy. He'd suffer at the side of his dad's chair through the news, or sometimes, when he could tell there was nothing to talk about during commercials, David would retreat to his bedroom with his Milky Way. It prolonged his bedtime, David remembered, defrosting the chocolate bar in his mouth. They were the most spectacular candy bars he'd eaten in his entire life.

Then one day his father stopped bringing them home. He'd said something about a new boss coming in and making them pay for everything. Or was it just that his dad grew tired of bringing home bags all the time? It didn't matter then; it mattered now. An uneaten candy bar, an empty seat at graduation, the absence of laughter in the Darwins' home, an unfinished college degree, a canceled wedding, an empty crib. He hadn't just robbed the child of the pleasure of eating a candy bar; he had murdered joy itself. David turned the photo over and pushed it away.

"They probably won't get premeditated, but they're definitely going to want you for second degree," Barry said, as he gathered the photos together.

Barry's words pulled David from his thoughts. "I can't have my day in court? I want to have my say," he mumbled shakily.

"No way in hell," Barry said. "Defendants don't say anything. You show up, you wear a suit; you listen to the judge when he tells you to do something and you keep your trap shut. Don't make faces, and you don't make eye contact with the jury."

"But I want to clear up all this stuff, this crap in the newspaper about me," David said.

"Right now you don't even have that option. I have to see if the DA will even consider a plea bargain, so knock on wood, you're in for a bumpy ride, pal." Barry gathered his papers into his briefcase while David seemed to crumple in on himself on the opposite side of the table. Barry latched his briefcase shut and rubbed his eyes in tired circles.

"It should only be oak," David said, as Barry stopped rubbing and stared back at him. "In Native American culture the oak stood for strength and power, and children who played tree tag would only be safe if they touched an oak tree. So in America, when you knock on wood for good luck, it should only be oak."

Barry nodded and tried to smile but his face was tight. In the buzzing lights, David looked like a little boy waiting in the principal's office. The way he held his arms and leaned back in his chair. The immediate trouble likely foremost on his mind, but lurking just behind the frown, a deeper misery seemed to gnaw at the corner of his thoughts. The look reminded Barry to explain about his birthday.

"I can't get you anything for your sixteenth," he said. "They won't let me pass anything to you. But for what it's worth, happy birthday."

David hadn't forgotten his birthday, but he'd lost track of the usual buildup. Those few days beforehand that inch closer with anticipation. Without those days, his birthday had suddenly arrived without warning. It was just a day. Sixteen, David thought. And only a year away from driving. He wished Barry hadn't said anything.

The days were only short gaps between sleep, and before he knew it, he was tightening the knot of his tie for his court appearance. It was the first time since his father had visited him that he'd be seeing people from his community, civilians on the outside. He could only imagine the protestors and shouts, and all the angry faces in the crowd. What was that line in that book? he thought to himself, trying to remember his ninth grade English class when he'd read about some guy who'd shot a Hindu or something. On a beach. Before his execution the man thought, I hope they meet me with "howling wails of hate," or something like that. Only David didn't hope that at all.

He pulled on Barry's suit jacket. The lawyer had explained the whole proceeding to David. Gave him a whole list of do's and don'ts, but David had already forgotten them. His hands shook. He paced about his jail cell for a few minutes before a buzz rang out and a voice echoed: "Prisoner Westwood, for transfer!"

When David was escorted into the courtroom in cuffs, he immediately looked up at the crowd that had packed themselves on the prosecution's side of the room. He glanced at his side. Mostly empty seats. A few faces and some reporters.

He saw Mr. Hopkins. He was sitting there, straight-backed and proper, his fingers joined in his lap, as though he were waiting for his soup to come. David wished he could go to him. Tell him something interesting he'd remembered while sitting in jail. The month of May had begun on a Sunday. Any month that begins that way will always have a Friday the thirteenth. But he couldn't even whisper it to him. He was seated about a dozen rows away. Another thing incarceration had changed for David: space was extreme. A cell, when the door slammed, felt like a coffin, and the mere twenty feet between himself and Mr. Hopkins was like a day's journey.

He couldn't see it in that moment, but the rows of benches bolted across the expanse were like ripples of time flowing outward into the future. Mr. Hopkins would come to visit him in prison. He would read him sections of *David Copperfield, The Count of Monte Cristo*. The Arts & Leisure section of the *New York Times*. David would ask him if these new artists were any good. He'd make Mr. Hopkins promise to go to the museums and report back. Never much of a sports fan before, he would later close his eyes and listen to every word ever written on Bill Buckner and the '86 Red Sox. He would shake his head about the death threats. Other inmates would get to know the old man and look upon David with envious eyes, and catcall Mr. Hopkins, calling him "Hop." He would wave back at them and shake his head. He would have a habit of calling everything he laid eyes on, including David, a "shame." In short, he would close the distance. Make those twenty feet of benches seem like a laughable crack on time's roadway.

But for now, they were bolted, and David could only return the tacit nod Mr. Hopkins had given him from his quiet seat in the back of the courtroom. He scanned the benches for his parents. They were not there. A lump rose in his throat. His spine tingled, and his joints ached at the prickly realization that all eyes were on him.

The bailiff escorted him to his seat behind a table and pushed him down into the chair. Barry took a seat next to him. David looked back over his right shoulder to scan the crowd. His heart jumped. Behind the prosecutor's desk sat a row of parents, and the two little boys who were with Dallas that day. He suddenly remembered the gun he'd held on the smaller one, James. He noticed how much cleaner the kid looked since the last time he'd seen him, caked with blood and dirt. How small he is, David thought. The other boy, Felix, appeared huskier and stared straight ahead, scowling. David's eyes wandered along to Bob Cassidy. He felt a pulse of fear in his chest. Bob stared at him as though he were wishing to be locked in a room with David, just the two of them—one-on-one. David turned away. Barry noticed.

"What did I tell you?" he whispered. "Concentrate on your own side."

David glanced over his left shoulder. His eyes fell on Darryl Knight, who had his arm draped across the back of the bench and was slouched down, as if visiting the ducks at the park. He grinned and nodded to David. One kid's on my side and it's him, David thought, remembering the night of the party. Had David been any judge of character at all? He couldn't help but cast his mind back to all the terrible things he'd thought about Darryl, and yet, seeing him sitting leisurely on the bench while droves of people walked into the courtroom scowling, David realized this bravery of Darryl's completely betrayed the narrative David had given him. Another miscalculation. Darryl was running toward the fire, while most in David's life had fled. The moment was too immense and he felt ashamed. His eyes filled with tears and he looked away.

Suddenly a loud, rakish laugh rang out on the other side of the courtroom. David watched an old man with brown tufts of hair sticking up on each side of an otherwise bald head, maneuvering his way toward the first few benches. He was carrying a pad, and he seemed to know everybody in the room. He wore a tweed suit jacket over a brown pin-striped shirt. Loose flesh gathered in rolls at his fat yellow necktie. He sat down between two officers of the court. They shook hands, and shared something. Another loud laugh rang out. The big laugh didn't match the man's stout body, David thought. The man acted like he was settling in at the drive-in, with popcorn on the way—chatting away with the people around him; occasionally jotting something down on his pad. He licked his pencil tip before he wrote. A person would whisper something to him, and he'd throw his head back with another booming laugh. Some people were still filing in.

"Well, there's your man," whispered Barry, nudging David on the arm. "That's Elijah Fennecker."

A tall man came up behind Fennecker and tapped him on the shoulder. The journalist leaned back, took the man's hand, and laughed. His eyes finally fell on David, and when he noticed the boy staring, his smile dropped.

The judge entered and everybody stood. He was a nerdy-looking man with brown hair and thick-rimmed glasses. He shuffled some papers and spoke to a woman from behind the bench.

David listened to the charges against him, read out by the prosecutor in quick, violent barks. He stared at the prosecutor, sizing him up. David figured he must have seen a hundred murder cases, and here he was facing the judge and ringing off these charges as if for the first time in his career. Exaggerating his outrage, David thought. As if he needed to exaggerate. It made him sick to his stomach. The prosecutor went into some details of the murder and a whimper came from the other side of the room. The judge warned against emotional outbursts. The prosecutor replayed the animosity between the defendant and Bob Cassidy, one of those listed on the prosecutor's witness list. David scanned the courtroom again. Some gave him hateful glares; Fennecker's articles had done their damage. He wanted his sketchbook back.

David's mind raced. He wanted to have his say. Pleading guilty was equal to admitting the town had defeated him. He knew they hated him, but he wanted them to at least hear his voice.

The prosecutor read the exhibits. David's own statements while in custody. Then he itemized the witness list.

"Matthew Milton was present at the scene and will testify that he told the defendant to let the Darwin boy go free."

Before or after he beat the other kid to a pulp? David thought, and shook his head. Barry leaned over and told him not to make faces.

"Nick Darcy and Krystal Richards were also present and will verify the statements of Matthew Milton. Mr. Robert Cassidy," the prosecutor continued, "will testify to his confrontation with the defendant the night before the murder took place. Mr. Philip Massa was present on the night of this altercation and will testify that the defendant lashed out violently at him, to seek revenge on Mr. Cassidy for the incident."

David heard the judge mumble something to the prosecutor. "Yes your honor," he answered. "Character witnesses will testify to the violent and antisocial nature of the defendant. Mr. James Levgrin, a classmate of the defendant."

"Who?" asked David in a whisper that reached across the courtroom. Some people turned. Barry put a finger to his lips to shush him.

"Mr. Arnold Polinski, another classmate of the defendant."

David looked around the room almost frantically. "I never even heard of these goddamn people, Barry," he whispered.

"It's okay, just shhhh," Barry said.

"Mr. Albert Sigorsky is a classmate of the defendant who was present the night of the altercation with Mr. Cassidy." Finally, a name David was familiar with. He remembered Albert at Darryl's party. Both his hands up a freshman's skirt.

"Ms. Hanna D'Amico witnessed the altercation as well, and was in one of David's classes this past school year." David remembered the whole argument he'd had with her about Russia and the coming nuclear war. He turned around and saw Hanna sitting a few rows behind Bob Cassidy.

"Mr. Nunzio Bartalemeo owns a local delicatessen the defendant often frequented, and in fact the murder took place just behind his establishment. He saw the defendant only moments before the crime.

"Ms. Julia Dawson," the prosecutor announced, and took off his glasses to clean them. David's heart stopped. "She is the ex-girlfriend of the defendant. She will testify to the defendant's erratic behavior, his mood swings, his violent temper . . ."

David wheeled around to look for her and caught a shimmer of her hair in the far back corner of the courtroom. She was there beside her father, who sat with his arm around her and glanced at David with a slight scowl. Mr. Dawson looked as if he didn't understand how this had all transpired right under his nose. He stared up at the judge, back at his daughter, and held her tightly against his side. His knee was bouncing up and down. David hoped for Julia to make some sort of eye contact, but she didn't.

His breathing became labored again. His eyes blurred with tears. The prosecutor moved on to the next name on the list. But David stopped listening. He tugged on Barry Levin's arm until he got his attention.

"I want to change my plea to guilty," he said. "If you can get it for me."

CHAPTER THIRTY-SIX

BARRY VISITED DAVID THE NIGHT BEFORE his sentencing, to once again review the plea deal he'd reached with the DA. David sat in cold silence. Eight years minimum, and he'd be transferred after his eighteenth birthday to an upstate facility. He asked Barry if his parents had been told. Barry said he'd sent notice.

"Did my father say if he'd come to the sentencing?" David asked.

Barry took a deep breath. "The important thing for you to understand, David, is that you've been given a second chance to do something positive with your life. Don't focus on all these details. Stay out of trouble when you get inside, and keep going with your education. Finish high school. Get a college degree while you're in, so you can get a jump start on your life after prison."

The word "prison" sent a chill through David's body. Barry took silent note of this, and continued: "Use these years to find yourself. Prove to the world that you're not the person they think you are. Through your actions, not by getting on a stand and telling them. They've arranged for you to receive counseling while you're in there. Take advantage of it and listen to what they have to say. This doesn't have to be the end of your life." The lawyer leaned back in his chair.

David nodded solemnly. "You got the paper today?" he asked.

"Don't . . . It's not good to read that stuff, David."

"I want to read the paper, did you bring it?"

Barry took the paper out of his briefcase and slid it across to him. Then he stood up from his chair and banged on the door for the guards to lead him out. He turned when David called his name.

"In the 1300s, a pig in France was publicly hanged for the murder of a child."

"You are a fount of useless information," Barry said and smiled at him. "Look sharp for the judge. Don't say anything. Let him speak his mind. Do this thing with dignity. I'll be right next to you the whole time."

The guards opened the door and Barry was gone.

What is this about? wrote Elijah Fennecker, after spelling out the details of what would happen in the courtroom, now just a few hours away. David sat on his low bed and read the next few sentences, licking his lips.

> *This is about teenagers engaging in destructive behavior without any emotional attachment. Our young are being led to the slaughter in this country, because fear is no longer in them. The fear of consequences, the fear of God, even the fear of prison no longer keeps them pointed in the right direction.*

More conclusions, David thought, looking over the stacked inches of sentences, all conclusions about his emotional state. Led to the slaughter, yes, but who holds the bolt gun? Wasn't it fear that caused all this in the first place?

More and more in our society they become desensi-
tized to violence. They see the wily coyote get up time
after time after being dropped, shot, burned to a crisp.
They see the evening news. Violence wraps them like a
blanket.

David could hardly read through it all. Fennecker's lecture
to parents. His pleas for them to teach kids nonviolence. The
violence he'd committed made it impossible for him to imagine his parents could have stopped it, and he died a little each
time he thought about it.

When I look at David Westwood, I don't see fear in
his eyes. I see rage. A symbol of what some teenagers
have come to represent. An angry generation. Raised
by parents of that selfish ilk that led to defeat in Viet-
nam. This is the inheritance of parents who, when
they were younger, decided to skip out on their patri-
otic chores.

But he wasn't a generation, David thought. If he was, he
would have blended in. He would have done the things that
generations do. Not something that caused everyone to flee
from him, like a monster. He wasn't a symbol. A symbol stood
in for others, but David never met any others. He thought he
had, with Julia, but he was wrong. He read the closing words
with a tight throat.

By the time David Westwood leaves prison he will be
a man. Hopefully he will emerge into a peaceful world.
And given his violent tendencies, hopefully he won't

*feel like the world has outgrown him, or rejects him
the way they must for committing this crime.*

David was led out in leg irons and handcuffs and placed in his
seat by an expressionless bailiff who towered over him and
clasped his hands in front to show his biceps. Barry was at the
prosecutor's table going over some papers. The judge had not
yet arrived, but the courtroom was completely packed. David
turned around and looked at the people sitting behind him.
His eyes rested on Mr. Hopkins when a grown man's voice
boomed from the back row.

"Turn around, son. None of us want to see your murdering face!"

David obeyed quickly and stared at the table in front of
him. He heard a woman whisper, "Murdering bastard," and
he squeezed his eyes shut.

Moments later, a familiar laugh rang out from the back of
the room. David watched Elijah Fennecker take his usual seat
in the courtroom. David stared at him, and waited for the guy
to make eye contact. After he shook a few hands, he finally
gazed across the room. His face dropped; he sat down. David
smiled at him. It was forced, but he wanted to smile. Elijah
looked sideways at him. So much like a turtle. Recoiling into
the loose flesh of his neck. Unable to stare directly into the
horror of David's smile.

There was a strange buzz in the room, almost separate
from the business of the day. David could hear the people mur-
muring about something excitedly. The sound of newspapers
flipping wildly.

Barry had the day's *New York Times* on top of his briefcase. David imagined his lawyer would go out to the park afterward, have a sandwich, check out the paper. He read the

top of the paper and was surprised. He'd lost track of events outside. *October 26, 1983. 1,900 US Troops with Carribbean Allies Invade Grenada . . .*

David looked over his shoulder again at the packed benches behind him. The parents of Dallas, James, and Felix were all sitting in the row behind Elijah. David looked at James. A faint scar glistened on his forehead, the sight of which burned a pit in David's stomach. James's parents sat beside him, and on the other side of them sat Felix with his perpetual scowl. David took notice that James and Felix didn't seem to be speaking to each other.

Dallas's parents were sitting behind the Cassidys. David stared at Mr. Darwin. A stern expression made his pale face look like a mask, the muscles in his jaws clenched tightly. David couldn't peel his eyes away, not even when the man's wife glared back.

Something nudged David forward in his mind. This was important: the look on Mr. Darwin's face. It was the face of a father without answers. Seeing that look, David could only think of the horror movies—a man petrified at the sight of a monster. And in this case, David was the monster. He knew that now. It wasn't time, or coincidence. It wasn't rage, or humiliation. Neither was it absurdity—the incalculable cruelty of heaven's random summoning of souls. It had been his decision to choke the life out of a boy. To rob him of the luck of falling in love, because he himself had been turned away by it. He thought of those tragic candy bars lying melted in the sand, and it couldn't have been clearer to David. He was an executioner. He was a monster, just like they'd said. A monster now standing before his own wreckage and watching Mr. Darwin's face, scrubbed expressionless by a love he'd never get to feel again.

But he wouldn't stay a monster forever. They needed to know that. It suddenly occurred to David that these people would be gone from his life in a matter of moments, and it became important that they realize he saw what they saw. He knew Barry wanted his silence, but he was bursting with a desire to speak.

The judge entered the room, banged his gavel, and told David to rise. He obeyed, getting to his feet with Barry's help. His knees were shaking, and his head swirled as if he'd stood up too fast.

"Counsel, the people have understood that your client wishes to change his plea to guilty, is that correct?"

"Yes, Your Honor," Barry answered.

"Mr. Westwood, you are hereby entering your plea of guilty. Is this correct, young man?"

"Yes sir," answered David, shaking all over, body and voice. He turned his head to look at Michael Darwin again and heard the crowd collectively gasp.

"Turn around!" a man shouted from the back of the room.

"Counselor, please advise your client," the judge said as he smacked his gavel.

But David wouldn't turn around. He gazed upon Mr. Darwin as if he wanted to speak directly to him, and another shout erupted from the back of the courtroom. Barry yanked on his arm.

"Focus on the judge, David, I'm right here," he said.

David turned his attention back to the front of the room. "I won't stay a monster," he whispered to Barry.

"Shhh." Barry patted David on the shoulder.

"I'm a monster, but I won't be like this forever," David whispered.

The judge was rifling through a file, calmly licking his fingertips. "Counselor, your client is how old?"

"Sixteen, Your Honor," said Barry, clearing his throat. "He just turned sixteen a few weeks ago."

The judge crossed something out. Shook his head. "Very well," he said. "Mr. Westwood, under the terms of your plea to voluntary manslaughter, I hereby sentence you to serve no less than eight years, and no more than fifteen years in a juvenile penitentiary until your eighteenth birthday, whereby you shall be remitted to a maximum-security prison to complete the term of your sentence."

Eight years for a life, David thought. He turned to look at Mr. Darwin again. The man's face hadn't changed, and David wanted him to know that he could see himself now. Clearly. Mr. Darwin didn't need to be afraid of him.

"Knock it off and turn the hell around!" a woman screamed as the judge lifted his gavel.

"Counselor, is there some fascination your client has with these families?"

Barry pulled on David's arm again. "No, Your Honor, please proceed."

"I mean, is there something your client wishes to say?"

Barry leaned over to David's ear. "I'm right here. You're not alone," he whispered, and straightened. Then: "We'd like to proceed, Your Honor."

"Mr. Westwood," the judge glared at him from the desk, "I hope I'm only imagining it when I say that I have observed your behavior in this courtroom and can only characterize it as the same callous indifference you likely used during the commitment of your heinous crime. It is my sincere hope that in eight years, I won't just be unleashing another criminal out into the unsuspecting public. When I look in your eyes, and observe your demeanor, I am very skeptical. I'm not sure there's anything left redeemable in your body, but I do hope you prove me wrong.

"It deeply saddens me to see this today. At this very moment, young men only slightly older than you are landing on foreign shores to defend the very freedoms of this great nation that you seem to despise. It pains me to see you, and think what could have been a more heroic fate. I want to make something perfectly clear, Mr. Westwood: I do not want to see you back in my courtroom again. You, for that matter, do not want to see me ever again, for if you do, rest assured I will do whatever is in my legal capabilities to ensure you never return to society. God be with you. And may He provide the forgiveness that this court is not so anxious to provide. You'll be taken away to begin your sentence immediately. This court is adjourned."

With that he banged his gavel.

The bailiff grabbed David by his arm. David looked over at Barry. The finality of it glued his feet to the ground. He scanned the courtroom for his parents. People were crying and holding one another.

Suddenly a voice on the far end of the courtroom screamed: "Eight years is an outrage!" The judge banged his gavel again.

David was led to an open door beside the bench, Barry trailing behind him. David turned one last time to the restless audience. They were on their feet. He noticed a face, bloodred with anger, lean forward. It was an old man, pudgy, with a thin comb-over and a mustache. He pointed a finger at David.

"I hope they get you in there, scumbag!" he screamed. The judge demanded order. "Better watch it," the man continued. "I hope you get it right in the ass, you little punk." His finger was shaking.

The door closed behind David, as more people began to shout at him. He could only hear the muffled sounds of rage and hissing in the courtroom.

"Well, that didn't go exactly as I'd hoped," Barry said, exhaling.

But David's mind could only hold a picture of Mr. Darwin's face, sitting humbly in his seat. His grief, pointing the way to David's redemption. With Barry's hand resting on his back, so much like a father, David readied himself for the locked doors to open.

CHAPTER THIRTY-SEVEN

BENEATH A BLANKET OF BURNING STARS, James lay on his back and watched the faintest puff of steam rise from his exhale. Alone, but not lonely. Spybot's chin rested loyally upon the floor of their fort, his eyes turned up toward the opening in the roof, brow and forehead wrinkled. In rest he didn't look so worried. His body was warm under the soft pats of his new master. James made Leonardo's *Vitruvian Man* with his arms and legs. A steady breeze blew a handful of leaves from a tree. Some dropped noiselessly into the forest. Others, James imagined, must be settling on his newly constructed roof. It was October. The smell of cut grass and chlorine had gone, replaced by woodsmoke from the scattered chimneys around the neighborhood. He was still wearing his shorts, but he had on Kevin's jean jacket.

It was part boredom, part need to escape the heat in his living room, that had driven him out to the fort—with his father endlessly stoking the fireplace and stacking logs atop the flame like he was building a pyramid.

Sheltered from the October wind by the fort's walls, James could hear the structure groaning in the swaying trees. He wasn't afraid. His father had done a thorough inspection, pulling with all his weight on the support beams and driving in some fencing spikes to make sure it was stable. Instead of worry, James enjoyed the sensation of movement; it kept him from having to lie still and remember. He could stare up at the sky. Rub the silky underside of Spybot's ear. Watch the blinking strobes of red lights from airplanes without feeling sad.

His only melancholy came when he'd hear the report of Felix's bat hitting a baseball into the net Mr. Cassidy had tied into the canopy of trees above him. Moments before, the light in Felix's backyard had turned on and James lay perfectly still to listen, as Felix began to gather his baseballs strewn about the yard. The first crack had startled James; the ball ricocheted off Felix's fence, making it rattle. Spybot's ears flickered like raised thumbs. They were only yards apart, but James was determined not to sit up in the window and try to talk to him.

His school psychologist, Mrs. S, had told him that Felix was trying to get better on his own. And when James said that Felix wasn't cut when the fight happened, she told him he needed to heal in other ways.

James heard another crack of the bat and watched the shadow of a ball darken in and out of view, rolling along the net into the air and then back to earth.

Thinking of Mrs. S caused James to remember the itch he used to feel around his scar, and he reached up to touch it. He was well enough away from his mother to poke at it freely. At home, when he'd press on the purple tube of raw flesh that ran from his forehead down to his cheekbone, his mother would yank his hand away. Tell him it would never heal if he kept touching it.

But it was his wound. His head. His itching. Besides, his father had assured him it would heal. The day after they watched David Westwood get pulled across the courtroom to prison, his father had caught him pressing on it at the kitchen table. He'd asked him if it still hurt. James said no.

"It's just ugly now."

His father rubbed his shoulder and mussed his hair. "Don't worry," he said. "A thing doesn't stay ugly forever."

It would heal. Or it wouldn't. Either way, James felt a sense of satisfaction when he pressed on it. Then it just became a habit after the itching stopped. In the mirror he'd watch the deep purple turn white under his fingers, and when he let go, the color would flood back urgently. He'd play a game of "way back" from time to time, pressing down and saying: "Last year." Letting go and saying: "This year." Last year. This year. When I was seven. When I was eight. When I didn't grow nervous at the sound of curse words . . .

A dull thud resounded from Felix's backyard, and James could tell that Felix hadn't hit the ball squarely. He didn't need to watch for the flight of it through the opening he'd left in the roof, but he did anyway.

It's been said that openings—doors and windows—are opportunities to invite the spirits to enter. Beseech them to depart. Perhaps this was partly why James left the roof open. Having brought the piece of plywood up and dropped it into place—he had then looked at the sky and thought better of it. A hole in the roof would remain, and James would suffer the labor of sweeping out the snow that dropped inside.

He had done the hard things. He hadn't used any shortcuts. A beastly sort of courage was full-grown inside him and he could sense that others noticed. Kevin. His father, who would recite Bible stories to him with a fearful kind of reluctance, continually interrupting his own narration to remind him that men should be careful of their own strength. James didn't understand. Why his father suddenly believed these stories hadn't escaped him. It was probably how the Bible got written in the first place. Terrible things happened and then guys got together to try to explain it and to make a rule so it wouldn't happen again. A bunch of things written to fix things after the mistake was already made.

What James now possessed wasn't exactly fearlessness, for much of his calculations when building the fort were born out of fear. It was more genuine than bravery, which is what Kevin had called it once, on the car ride to the courts. It frightened his mother too, for lately she'd been telling him it was okay to feel like things were unfair. That he didn't deserve what happened to him. But fair's got nothing to do with it. *Deserve* is nothing more than whoever flips the coin.

James heard his father's sniffle well before he watched his head emerge through the hole in the floor. In the moonlight Ivan's white hair at the temples appeared to be forced outward from the weight of his tweed cap. Spybot rose to his feet, crossed the fort, and licked Ivan's hand.

"Why does he always have to lick everything?" Ivan asked as he hoisted himself into the fort and sat, Indian style, against the western wall. He pulled off his cap and James saw that he was staring up at the square hole in the roof. Ivan nodded. Told James he thought he could use some company. He slid down to his back and inched closer to his son. "I can see the draw of being able to stargaze," Ivan said. In the dark, James could only hear his voice, and make out the blackened outline of his nose.

Spybot came back to James's side and dropped down. James put his hand back on top of the dog's head, but kept his eyes focused on the sky.

It would take a long time, perfecting the fort. He would be working, fixing. Building something larger than himself. He was lucky. He'd figured out that the world was made of builders and wreckers, and Turnbull was full of wreckers. David Westwood and his friends were wreckers. Felix's brother wanted to be a wrecker. But builders made things possible.

He probably would never truly stop building the fort. He'd paint. He'd gather more wood, and start a second floor. This time with more windows, and places to hang bird feeders, a room for Spybot. Another floor for his parents and one for Kevin. The top floor would house the wire man that Dallas had twisted for him, and a bin for more collected friendship wire. A couch for Felix when he eventually came around.

Yes, he thought, reaching over to draw Spybot closer, he'd build and build and reach the top of Turnbull, where no one could touch him. He'd gaze out over the town and see over the rooftops, the smoke rising from the chimneys. The Long Island Sound stretched before him. The Atlantic Ocean, a blue carpet beyond.

His dream must have masked the sensation, for James suddenly realized his father had reached over and placed his hand on top of his sneaker. Then he felt the hand tighten its grip and soon his father was gently rocking the foot side to side. When he stopped, he left his hand there. James let it rest. The hand felt warm in the increasing chill.

Another thump, followed by the loud smack of the ball hitting the slats of Felix's fence. James heard someone clapping shortly after, and then Mrs. Cassidy called out something in her singsong voice. James wanted to know what she was telling her son, but she was speaking too softly.

The wind was beginning to pick up. Spybot swung his head over and rested his chin back on James's leg. The Big Dipper bowed to James from behind the opening curtain of clouds. He heard the bat again. The ball seemed to disappear into the swirling branches.

The wind was the only thing you could see, hear, smell,

taste, and touch, James thought as he inhaled and took in the faint scent of cinnamon and pumpkin pie. He remembered Dallas's father saying that this was why man never loses faith in basic things.

It was almost musical, the sound of the ball when Felix hit it on different sections of the bat. The latest report was a sharp high note, and the ball cut through the leaves on its upward streak into the darkness.

A D-flat followed and sailed atop the wind, which bent the branches backward. But the trees settled and straightened when the net caught the ball. No matter how many baseballs Felix drove, the trees danced back into place. James imagined Felix trying to flatten the world with his Louisville Slugger, ceaselessly enduring the leaves whistling back.

James stretched out his limbs to feel large again. He folded his hands together and listened for the next hit. The ball launched into the air and spat through the leaves, and the leaves made whirling circles before they settled back to touch hands again, like paper dolls.

Acknowledgments

Little Beasts was more than ten years in the making, so apologies if I miss anyone in these acknowledgments. First and foremost I'd like to acknowledge my mother, Jeanette McDermott McGevna, for tolerating the too-many years her poet-slacker son lived with her so he could pursue his artistic aims. I'll also thank my wife, Joanne, for her years of support and for believing in my abilities. My brother, Sean, for lending his freezing art studio one January so I could finish the first draft all those years ago. My sister, Colleen, for lending her ear to my complaints and fears. Thanks to Kaylie Jones for her faith in this project from the first paragraph she read in 2004. Thanks also to Trena Keating, my agent, for her work revising and coaching me through the publication process. My team of hero readers over the years: Danielle Zahm, Adam Penna, Douglas Howard, Elizabeth Cone, Sarah Kain Gutowski, Jack Best, Nina Solomon, Tim McLoughlin, Renette Zimmerly, Tom Borthwick, Robert Knightly, Theasa Tuohy, Annamaria Alfieri, and Laurie Loewenstein. The amazing staff at Mastics-Moriches-Shirley Community Library, where I wrote many pages and conducted almost all my research. I'm indebted to David Wynne and Jerry McGarty for their help with certain descriptions of the sheriff's eviction. Thanks also to my early influences at William Floyd High School: Bill Pike, Donna Gaspari, Judy Bauer, and Lisa Pantorno-Guzman, who handed me my first creative writing award. Of course, the Fasanello family who continuously lent me their word processor in high school and college, so I could . . . process words. A final thank you to the Poets House in New York City and every single bar, pub, diner, coffee shop, locking bathroom, commuter train, airplane, log cabin, back deck, pool deck, backseat, front seat, front porch, library, and bank vestibule that provided solid surfaces for me to jot down my notes during this amazing odyssey.